W9-CAL-489

FIERCE HOMECOMING

Deliberately I breathed him in, taking the scent of him deep inside of me with a fierce possessive joy. This was what I had been waiting over twenty long, parched years for. A messenger from my world, an initiator into my real life. This was what had been vitally missing in the few men that I had taken into my body. None that I had been intimate with was of my chemistry, my kind. I hadn't known what was wrong with them, with me, until that moment when I had sensed Gryphon with primitive recognition in that sterile emergency room. Mate. Now he was here . . .

My hot breath wafted over the pale sweep of his neck just above where that slow pulse pounded. "Don't you want me to be yours?"

He shuddered and closed his eyes. "More that I wish to live."

"Darkly erotic. Wickedly clever and very original."
— *New York Times* bestselling author Bertrice Small

"Sunny is a stay-at-home mother of two. But when she writes her alter ego takes over." —Channel 7 News, Boston, NBC

"Oh my! What a fabulous story! I absolutely adore this awesome book . . . I could not put this book down until I had finished reading it. Sunny has created a new and unique race of people that is sure to fascinate readers. I highly recommend this unusual and exhilarating story to anyone who enjoys tales of fantasy and the paranormal. I love this book so much that I am not above begging for more Children of the Moon, please!"

—Susan White,
reviewer for CoffeeTimeRomance.com, 5 cups (highest rating)

MONA LISA AWAKENING

SUNNY

NORTH SHORE PUBLIC LIBRARY
250 Route 25A
SHOREHAM, NEW YORK 11786-2190

BERKLEY BOOKS, NEW YORK

THE BERKLEY PUBLISHING GROUP
Published by the Penguin Group
Penguin Group (USA) Inc.
375 Hudson Street, New York, New York 10014, USA
Penguin Group (Canada), 90 Eglinton Avenue East, Suite 700, Toronto, Ontario M4P 2Y3, Canada
(a division of Pearson Penguin Canada Inc.)
Penguin Books Ltd., 80 Strand, London WC2R 0RL, England
Penguin Group Ireland, 25 St. Stephen's Green, Dublin 2, Ireland (a division of Penguin Books Ltd.)
Penguin Group (Australia), 250 Camberwell Road, Camberwell, Victoria 3124, Australia
(a division of Pearson Australia Group Pty. Ltd.)
Penguin Books India Pvt. Ltd., 11 Community Centre, Panchsheel Park, New Delhi—110 017, India
Penguin Group (NZ), Cnr. Airborne and Rosedale Roads, Albany, Auckland 1310, New Zealand
(a division of Pearson New Zealand Ltd.)
Penguin Books (South Africa) (Pty.) Ltd., 24 Sturdee Avenue, Rosebank, Johannesburg 2196,
South Africa

Penguin Books Ltd., Registered Offices: 80 Strand, London WC2R 0RL, England

This book is an original publication of The Berkley Publishing Group.

This is a work of fiction. Names, characters, places, and incidents either are the product of the author's imagination or are used fictitiously, and any resemblance to actual persons, living or dead, business establishments, events, or locales is entirely coincidental. The publisher does not have any control over and does not assume any responsibility for author or third-party websites or their content.

Copyright © 2006 by DS Studios, Inc.
Cover design by Brianna Lohr.
Text design by Kristin del Rosario

All rights reserved.
No part of this book may be reproduced, scanned, or distributed in any printed or electronic form without permission. Please do not participate in or encourage piracy of copyrighted materials in violation of the author's rights. Purchase only authorized editions.
BERKLEY is a registered trademark of Penguin Group (USA) Inc.
The "B" design is a trademark belonging to Penguin Group (USA) Inc.

FIRST EDITION: September 2006

Library of Congress Cataloging-in-Publication Data

Sunny.
    Mona Lisa awakening / Sunny. — 1st ed.
        p.   cm.
    ISBN 0-425-21160-6
    1. Nurses—Fiction. 2. Greenwich Village (New York, N.Y.)—Fiction. 3. Healers—Fiction. I. Title.

PS3619.U564M66   2006
813'.6—dc22

                                                                                        2006013922

PRINTED IN THE UNITED STATES OF AMERICA

10   9   8   7   6   5   4   3   2   1

To my extraordinary editor, Cindy Hwang, and my superagent,
Roberta Brown. And special thanks to Laurell K. Hamilton and
Anne Bishop, whose wonderful stories inspired my
Monère Children of the Moon series.

MONA LISA AWAKENING

ONE

SICKNESS AND DEATH was in the air—women crying, men cursing, unwashed bodies. The stink of suffering and anguish. It was a dwelling I'd deliberately chosen and placed myself within. A dwelling of desperate need that lured me to its bosom with the stench of fear and pain.

I was an ER nurse on the lonely island of Manhattan. Sickness called to me. Darkness and light lay within me. I'd always known it, sensed it . . . a dormant force that lay quiescent along with the latent ability to heal, untapped as yet—to my relief, to my despair. Waiting. Until then, sickness called to me and lured me with its invisible tendrils of aches and pain.

Around me in the emergency room of St. Vincent's Hospital, in the heart of Greenwich Village, the hustle and bustle had already begun. In bed one, a young woman's face was covered with blood, lacerated from temple to chin—a dear price for a fragile whore to pay walking the dark alleys of the street. Strapped down in bed two was a disheveled man stinking of alcohol, thrashing in delirium and withdrawal. In bed three, a child screeched with pain, tugging the tender cords of my heart. It was a cry I could not ignore.

I rushed over to bed three, to find Dr. Peter Thompson there. He was one of the good interns just starting his ER rotation, humble and grateful for help, unlike those jerk know-it-alls. Even better, he had a girlfriend and was faithful, not one of the grabbers.

"Oh, good. You're here, Lisa," Peter said, flashing me a smile of relief. "You're great with kids. Can you help me with this?"

"What have we here?" I asked.

A young boy of about six with soft brown hair and lots of freckles was curled up into a tight ball, his thin arms holding his belly, tears wetting his face and shirt as he wailed with pain. His mother, a young brunette, gripped the stretcher rails with white knuckles and chewed her lower lip helplessly.

"Kurt was fine until an hour ago when he said his stomach hurt," the mother said, sizing me up, uncertainty in her brown eyes.

I knew that look. *Why am I talking to you and not the doctor?* it said.

It was entirely my fault. I've always looked younger than my age of twenty-one. No complaint here, but this was the medical profession. Credentials on the wall and silver in your hair went a long way with patients. But one thing I've learned: Don't judge their judgment. Just do what you have to do.

"Kurt," I said, stroking the child's damp forehead. "Is that your name, honey?"

At my touch, Kurt opened his eyes. His big, brown, trusting eyes studied mine, unknowingly opening the window of his soul to me. Our souls bonded and he was mine. Calmness came over the boy's face and his crying stopped.

"Now can you show me where it hurts, Kurt?"

His eyes fixed on me with wonderment and curiosity, Kurt un-curled his arms and pointed to a spot above his belly button. "It hurts here," he said in a clear, high voice.

I touched the spot.

Kurt tensed, but didn't resist. "It hurts when you touch it," he said, tears spiking his long lashes.

"I'll be very gentle," I promised, and placed the heart of my palm over his abdomen.

The power in me stirred, coming to the fore from the depths within, taking me over entirely as if I were merely a vehicle through which it channeled itself into the world. When the boy opened the window of his soul, it was really the eye of my power that gazed through my lenses and reached out to the child. It came forward at the call of pain, not at the urging of my will—a cycle of energy that stirred from its root within me but could only be completed by the beckoning of another.

My hand tingled with warmth as I sensed the radiation of heat rising from my core.

Kurt's eyes widened. "Awesome. It doesn't hurt anymore, Mommy!"

"I'm going to leave you to Dr. Peter. He's a very good doctor and he'll make sure your tummyache doesn't come back again." I winked at Kurt and he winked back.

I made my way to the staff bathroom and locked myself inside, resting on the toilet lid. That power of mine was a curse and a blessing all in one. One would think that to be equipped with such a thing would double, if not triple, my own energy. But no, it always left me feeling drained and exhausted afterward. And I used it to merely diagnose ailments. The power to heal hadn't come to me yet. I wondered if it ever would.

Minutes later, recovered, my composure regained, I shuffled

back to the madhouse. Peter dropped down beside me as I made a pretense of charting down some notes. A fine tremor shook my hands. I set the pen down carefully.

"Thanks, Lisa," Peter said as he took off his glasses and cleaned them with a coat corner. "I couldn't have examined that kid without you. The mother was useless." He peered sharply at me. "What's with that touch of yours? That moment? I sensed something. Are you one of those?"

"Those what?" I gave him a look.

"Those secret healers?" he whispered.

"I wish. That moment that you sensed has a name."

"What is it?"

"It's called compassion, doctor."

Peter laughed. "Right. Well, I'm going to order a CBC, Chem-20, urinalysis, and a quick strep. What do you think?"

"Don't forget an abdominal X ray, flat and upright." That would pick up the stuck quarter that was troubling little Kurt.

"You know, you have incredible instincts. You picked up that appendicitis last week that I almost missed and there was that other thing you . . ."

"That also has a name. Experience."

He snorted. "Yeah, eleven long months of experience, you old hag, you."

At this point, a grabber would have reached out his paw, going for one of the usual localities, but not this one. "You'd make a great doctor, I bet."

"Are you trying to get rid of me?"

"Do I sound like it? You should think about going to medical school. Really." He walked away, flagging the orders in the chart.

He did have a nice butt, now that I was looking at it. Too bad there wasn't any desire in me to do more than appreciate the view.

Medical school. Ha! Not for me, not in this life. Couldn't afford it. The two years of nursing school had been a miracle already, the full scholarship and living stipend a true blessing. It had brought to fruition my childhood dream, a calling almost, to be near the sick and infirmed, the pained, the suffering.

The money also freed me from the confinement of my foster home, memories that I'd rather leave behind, buried and untouched. I still remember those first heady days of independence, free like a young bird just untangled from its nest, testing its wings, breathing fresh air. An exhale after a long, long inhale.

My thoughts of the past were suddenly disturbed by a tangible force. A force ringing in the air, penetrating through the throngs crowding the wards, through the chatter, the shouts, the din. Dense in the space, filtering past the generic furnishings, the white partitioning curtains. Reaching for me like an invisible arrow seeking its targeted prey.

I looked up into the path of that oncoming force and saw the air ripple like an invisible tidal wave rolling over all obstacles, big or small, pushing forward and burying me in its deluge.

I stood, stunned and dazzled by the invasion, trembling as I was hit by the seeking force. It was as if I had been electrocuted, my whole body tingling. The fine hair all over my body stood on end. I shivered, feeling weakened and dizzy, and leaned on my desk.

God! What the hell was that?

The invisible grip suddenly softened and my body relaxed as if a burden had lifted from my chest. But before I could breathe once more, the force turned naughty. It explored me, touched me like a lover's invisible fingers, caressing me, stirring foreign urges and feelings within me that I had never felt before. My body softened, grew moist and heated. I shivered. Then I smelled him. Blood.

My nostrils flared. I turned my head, tracking the scent, and saw him, the source. Bed eight.

He was sitting alone on the stretcher all the way across the room, his blue eyes gazing intently at me. His long hair, darker than midnight, fell in soft waves to brush his shoulders. He had skin the color of ivory, luminescent and pure like the full moon against the ink-black sky, and a face that had the power to make his maker weep with joy or jealousy. An angel fallen from the sky. *No*, I thought, looking into predatory eyes. *Not fallen . . . kicked out.*

The sight of him left me breathless. I watched as his nostrils flared, as he deliberately filled his lungs with air, and knew as surely as I had smelled his blood that he was taking in my scent, smelling my arousal. His lashes dipped down then fanned back up like the graceful sweep of a butterfly's wings. The power and heat that had come from his eyes intensified the caressing effects on me, penetrating through my outer self, pulling tautly at my core, calling up my own force to the fore in response. Our energies met and meshed. My nipples hardened to stone, my inner sheath quivered, and I wanted to go to him. Go to him and pull him to me.

The air crackled with such vibrancy that I was sure others had to see it. But the nurses were busy with their needles and notes, and the doctors were busily minding their patients.

The pull between us tightened like a rope. Desperately I fought that pull the only way I knew, wave against wave, tide against tide. I intensified my force, marshaling up my last ounce, countering it. The air between us practically sparked. Still, it took every ounce of my control to just sit there and not go to him. Perspiration sheened my skin and my trembling grew harsher.

I'd never felt anything like this before in my life. Was he like me? Was he one of my kind, whatever that might be? Or was he an enemy? One thing, though, I knew for certain. He was a bastard. My eyes narrowed in anger. How *dare* he try to use his powers on me.

I stalked over to where he sat on the stretcher, his legs dangling over the side, and stopped inches away from him. "Stop it!" I snarled.

His eyes widened. "It is not I who is doing it." His deep, melodic voice was as beautiful as the rest of him. Unfair.

"Don't lie to me!" I hissed.

"I would not dare."

"Just . . . just stop it!"

He gave a Gaelic shrug, a fluid ripple of shoulder and chest, a simple movement that was not simple at all, for it touched something inside me like a literal caress, causing me to shudder and drop down my gaze to take note of the bulge that had risen between his legs. His eyes closed and still I felt the pull, undiminished. Confused, I suddenly noticed the careful stiffness with which he held himself, the whiteness of his knuckles as he clenched the metal frame of the stretcher, the dampness of his brow. He seemed to be fighting the attraction as much as I.

"You feel it, too," I said, frowning.

"Yes." His blue eyes snapped open and speared mine with sudden intensity. "Where are your guards? I sense no one here other than you and I."

"Guards?"

He frowned. "Surely you are . . ." Carefully, slowly, he reached out one hand, stopping just short of touching me, and stroked above the bare skin of my forearm. His force, though invisible and without contact, was palpable just above my skin. I felt his stroke as surely as if he had caressed me.

"You feel like a Queen," he murmured.

I stepped back, wondering if he was one of those madmen who

frequently found their way to St. Vincent's dehydrated, famished, and highly delirious. And yet there was something very different about him.

"What are you talking about?" I demanded sharply.

A plump tech bustled up, a bright smile creasing her matronly face. It was Sally, the ward clerk who took the vital signs of all the new patients, helping lighten the nurses' loads. "My, my, aren't you the pretty boy," Sally murmured, glancing down at his data sheet. "David Michaels. Just what I needed to brighten my night."

He smiled, a lethal combination of teeth and dimples.

She smiled back. "I'll have his vitals for you in a sec, Lisa." In so saying, she reached out to take his pulse.

It registered then—what should have registered immediately had I not been so stunned by his beauty and my body's reaction to him. His heartbeat. His very, very slow heartbeat. Not more than thirty beats per minute. Far below the normal human rate of sixty and above. My own heart sped up from its usual sluggish fifty, hitting the sixty mark when Sally frowned and looked up.

He captured her gaze with his eyes and I felt then the gentle flow of his power. Shit. He really hadn't been using it before now. What then was this peculiar, strong attraction between us?

Sally's frown lines smoothed away like unrippled water. "A pulse of sixty and a blood pressure of one hundred and twenty over seventy." She jotted down the numbers on his sheet, not seeming to notice the blood pressure cuff that lay unused beside her. She hadn't touched it.

I swallowed. "Thank you, Sally."

"No problem. He's all yours." She winked and bustled off to the next patient.

After Sally left, I turned to David Michaels, or whatever his name really was, with a stern look on my face. "You took control of her mind just now, didn't you? She didn't even measure your blood pressure."

He leaned back on his pillow, his eyes closed, looking even more pale than before, if that was possible, and laughed feebly. "Goddess, I can't believe that so simple a task exhausted me. . . ."

"What *are* you?" I whispered and pulled the privacy curtains tightly closed around us.

His dark lashes fluttered up. "Never mind what I am, who are you?" he asked, shifting forward. The movement caused him to wince and his hand moved to cover his belly.

"You're injured." With only a slight tremor, I lifted his shirt. It was an inch-long gash. One drop of red blood gleamed like scarlet against the pearl white of his skin, alluring, irresistible. At the sight of his blood, something clicked open in me that I hadn't known existed. As if in a dream, I watched my finger dip down and scoop up that tempting crimson pearl onto my fingertip. Watched him shudder as I touched him. Watched him shudder again as I licked the blood off my fingertip and tasted him.

It was sweet, so sweet, though tainted by an odd metallic tang.

What was he, this creature before me? And what had injured him?

Gently, I covered his wound with my palm. The center of my hand tingled and strummed. My senses seeped deep down below his skin, revealing to me clearly the torn passage through his tissues.

"You were stabbed. With a stiletto. And I sense something more. There is a . . . poison within you."

"Poison." One corner of his lush mouth lifted in bitter wryness. "An accurate labeling. A blade dipped in liquid silver. Now that the liquid poison is within me, it will spread slowly. Already it weakens me greatly."

"Who stabbed you?"

"My Queen, Mona Sera."

"Of course, your Queen," I said, wondering once again if he was mad. "Is she visiting from a foreign country? And why did she stab you?"

"I was leaving her," he said simply, "and this was her parting gift. Usually a wound like this would heal within several hours, but she punished me by using a silver blade."

"Why is silver bad?"

"Because the inherent quality of silver runs afoul with our bodies, causing us to then heal like humans. Slowly."

Like humans.

"Sure. So you're not human."

He flashed me a curious look. "Of course not."

"Then what are you?"

"Do you truly not know?"

"Why should *I* know?"

"Because you are as I am."

I swallowed. "Which is . . ."

"Monère. The children of the moon."

"Of course," I soothed. "Children of the moon." This guy was a total wacko.

"I am not mad, as you think." Frowning, he looked deep into me, probing with the dagger of his power so that I sensed again that arcing heat from before.

"Ah, that explains it," he breathed, wonder in his eyes. "You are a Mixed Blood."

"Mixed Blood?"

"Yes. A small part of you is human."

"A small part?"

"A quarter, I believe."

"I'm totally human as far as I'm concerned—a head, four limbs, two eyes. . . ." I said, backing away.

"No, don't go," he said, reaching out his hand out to me. "There is even more. You are a Queen."

"A Queen! That's a crock. I'm not even a Beauty Queen in Queens. I'm just a nurse."

"No, you don't understand. You have *aphidy,* the unique halo of fragrance inherent only in a Queen. All Monère men are drawn to you because of this."

"Talk about natural chemistry. And here I thought it was my dripping charm and striking beauty that attracted men to me," I said sarcastically.

"All things you may doubt, but you must believe you are in danger now. I am being hunted by Mona Sera's men. They are tracking me by my blood scent. And if they find me, they will find you. Are you protected?"

"What do mean, 'protected'? I protect myself."

"No guards?"

I shook my head.

A genuinely pained expression swept across his face and I found my heart yielding to his deep concern. Although what he claimed was impossible, a part of me responded to his words. They resonated with rightness somewhere deep within me. And there was no denying his unusual power, so like mine. I started to believe him.

"Do you have anybody else like . . ." he waved his hand, searching for words, ". . . like you?"

"No," I whispered. "You're the first I've ever met."

"Sweet Mother Moon." His head sank down. His perfect shoulders slumped. He laughed without humor. "What am I going to do with you?" The last was whispered as if to himself. He sounded weak, defeated, and that bothered me. A lot.

"Will you recover with time?"

He shook his head. "Not without the antidote."

"What is the antidote?"

"I was hoping you could possibly tell me," he said with that bitter, wry smile. "But, of course, that would be too much to hope for. Some claim there is no antidote, but others whisper that only Queens have it. And so I am fleeing to the nearest Lady of Light, the nearest Queen, to beg mercy and seek aid."

"You have more than one Queen?"

"Each territory is ruled by a Queen," he answered. "And the land is divided into many territories."

He said that I was a Queen, but I couldn't be a true one or I would be able to help him.

"I'm sorry," I said, deep regret in my words. "I would give you the antidote if I had it."

"Would you really?" he asked with a little smile. "A rogue male injured by his own Queen's hand? How curious. And yet I believe you really would."

"Why did your Queen poison you? Why did you leave?"

He sighed. "Mona Sera is among one of our worst Queens. Those of us she takes in, no other Queen will have. Twenty years with her and I was sick to my very soul. But though she is a bad Queen, she is wise in matters of business and has accumulated vast wealth and power in her dealings with humans. She forces us to sleep with humans in return for concessions she desires in business. Humans are drawn to us by our uncommon beauty, even to the least of us. But we derive no pleasure in return. We are two different species. Our skin does not fill with light when we are with one of them."

"Fill with light?" What was this light thing, I wondered.

"Our hearts are left with emptiness," he continued. "Mona Sera created a caste of comfort women and men for these outside duties."

"Were you one of them?" I asked quietly.

"Yes," he said, shame lacing his voice. "I was one of her comfort men. This last time she sent out my half sister, Sonia, our beloved midwife, as punishment for her recent rebelliousness against this practice. These matings, though joyless and loveless, do bear fruit at times."

"Like me."

"Yes." He nodded. "And it is Sonia's duty to deal with such consequences. She delivers the babes and abandons them to the humans to keep the purity of our line. She has done so dutifully until her daughter's recent miscarriage from one of these unfortunate unions with humans. Since then, Sonia could no longer look upon the practice of abandonment with detachment and petitioned the Queen to resign from such a task. As punishment, Mona Sera sent Sonia out to sleep with a human male notorious for his twisted enjoyment of sex. Sonia returned with bloody lashes, cuts and bruises upon her. I hunted the bastard down and killed him. I couldn't stand for anyone to treat my sister so. The dead man was the son of a Louisiana billionaire senator, Mona Sera's man in the human capital of Washington, D.C. Instead of punishing me, Mona Sera had Sonia raped before my eyes by one of our most ferocious warriors, Amber. That broke me," he said. "The tyranny, the cruelty, the malice. I denounced Mona Sera in front of our people and severed all my allegiance to her. It was something that had never been done before. Mona Sera became enraged. She had her guards bind me to the whipping post. But instead of killing me quickly, she wanted me to suffer a lingering, painful death, so she plunged her silver-poisoned dagger into my belly. Just before dawn, one of the comfort women cut me loose and I fled."

"What is your real name?"

"My true name is Gryphon. What is your name?"

"Mona Lisa," I heard myself say, and the name felt strange. Without conscious thought, I had given him my full name, the name etched on the back of the cross that I had worn as an infant when they found me—my most cherished possession, the only tangible tie to my mother.

"It is my honor and pleasure to meet you." Gryphon bowed with a flourish, the gesture natural and graceful, until he winced.

"Stop that. You'll aggravate your wound."

"As you wish, Mona Lisa." He said my name like a caress and the lilting utterance of my birth name from his beautiful lips touched a part of me, an empty part of me that I had not known existed until now.

"You must seal this wound with something not permeable to air," Gryphon said, "or they shall continue to track me easily through my blood-spore scent."

"A doctor should see . . ."

"I cannot wait for a doctor. I must leave quickly. Help me, please."

How I wished I could heal him. Never before had I felt the lack of my untapped ability more keenly. "I'll get the liquid bandage," I said.

A swipe of liquid, a gust of paraffin spray, and the wound was sealed. After it dried, I applied Steri-Strips. Over it, I applied a clear plastic adhesive dressing. The sharp smell of his blood dissipated. Disappeared.

"My thanks, Lady," Gryphon said. For the first time, I felt him hesitate. "I know not if you would be better served with me, or alone here, unprotected. I am injured, weak, and hunted, and can only offer you poor protection. In truth, my chances of survival are quite dismal."

"Will the Queen you are fleeing to help you?"

"I do not know." Again that graceful shrug. "She is not so terrible as Mona Sera. I do not believe any of her men have ever fled her." He looked at me, tired, weak, clearly torn over what to do, and it gratified some tiny part of me that he could worry so about my safety when his own condition was so clearly desperate.

After a long, contemplative moment, he finally stood. He was a tall man, six feet. Four inches taller than me. "It will be in your best interest if I leave you now. The men hunting me perhaps may not come into this place of healing. It is their habit to avoid public domains such as this. But if they should come upon you, now or some day in the future, do not fight them, no matter what they do. They are full-blooded warriors, stronger and faster than you. Fear not, you will be drawn to them in the same manner as you are drawn to me," he said gently. "Afterward, claim the High Council's right of protection and demand that they take you to Bennington, Minnesota, where the Council's Court resides. The men shall have no other choice then but to take you there if they desire to live."

"Why could I not go to Mona Sera?" I asked.

"That you wish to avoid above all else," Gryphon said adamantly. "If Mona Sera detects the intimate scent of her men upon you, she will slay you all. She will kill you because she will see you as attempting to take her territory, her men. She will destroy the men who dare touch you because she will view it as betrayal against herself, a rejection. And as you can see," he grimaced and gestured to himself, "the lady does not take rejection well. If, in the unlikely event the men manage to constrain themselves, do what you can to seduce one or two—*all* would be best—and make them yours. Do not, at any cost, allow them to take you to Mona Sera. Competition or challenge by another Queen she will not tolerate."

Gryphon bowed in farewell and swept open the privacy curtain. He was going! In that short moment, I felt the room empty out, felt my heart sink with the rock of disappointment. My senses, my power, beyond my control, reached out for him. "Wait," I blurted out.

He stopped, obedience to a Queen deeply ingrained.

"It is imperative now for both our safety that I leave quickly," Gryphon said softly, regretfully.

It required no further thought. I was committed. A part of me that I could not deny knew what it wanted. I reached into my pocket and pressed my keys into his hand. "Go to my apartment. Wait for me there. I live two blocks away at 156 West Eleventh Street, apartment 7-B. I will be there in an hour when my shift ends."

He looked at me, uncomprehendingly, dazed by the all-too-brief, pleasurable touch of my hand against his.

"Do you know what you are offering me?" he asked.

"No. I do not know and I do not care. I only know I wish to help you."

"I cannot draw you into my plight. It is not safe. . . ."

"It is my wish," I interrupted, my voice firm. "And it is my command."

He struggled against the need to obey. "It is not wise. . . ."

"Please." I begged him with my eyes, with everything in me.

"Ah, little one." Gryphon sighed, his shoulders slumping in defeat, succumbing to my plea. He clutched the keys tightly in his fist. "You fight most unfairly with your eyes." He bowed in acquiescence, a wry smile curving those beautiful lips. "As my Queen commands."

Two

DARKNESS WELCOMED ME. Cold wind licked across my skin, soothing me. The stars winked and the waxing moon, three-quarters full, beamed benevolently down, its invigorating rays caressing my face. I walked quickly down the street, alert, watching, searching with that extra sense. There was no one. No one else out there like me. They had either come and gone, or they had not yet come.

With Gryphon's blood scent gone, there was no way to detect if he had passed this way. My heart clenched as I wondered if he had. Passed this way, that is. Perhaps he had changed his mind and fled. The thought of him weak and alone out there quickened my steps. I entered the apartment, a modest brick building, and passed by the elevator—it would be too slow. I walked to the stairwell and took the steps six at a time in that effortless strength that had always seemed a part of me, bounding up the seven flights of stairs in less than a minute. I stood before my door, hesitating. Then I heard it, that wonderfully slow heartbeat.

"It's me," I whispered and the door opened.

I slipped inside. The locks clicked loudly into place in the fluid silence and Gryphon stepped back quickly, careful not to touch me. The room was dark, no lights, but I saw him clearly. He was more beautiful than any man had a right to be. The alabaster white of his skin and deep red of those full lips were a siren's call that I had no desire to resist, and his sad blue eyes had a quiet allure I could not deny. He smelled like the night—a faint scent of trees, wind, and earth. He smelled like home.

Deliberately I breathed him in, taking the scent of him deep inside of me with a fierce, possessive joy. This was what I had been waiting over twenty long, parched years for. A messenger from my world, an initiator into my real life. This was what had been vitally missing in the few men that I had taken into my body. None that I had been intimate with was of my chemistry, my kind. I hadn't known what was wrong with them, with me, until that moment when I had sensed Gryphon with primitive recognition in that sterile emergency room. Mate. Now he was here, in my apartment, waiting for me in my home.

Some strange malady possessed me. A bold, aggressive spirit that I had not known was within me came to the fore and controlled my next actions, and I succumbed to it because my body wanted him, and my heart desired him, too.

Gryphon stepped back as I approached, a hand held up in strained beseechment. "No." He shook his head as I advanced, retreating until his back was pressed against the wall. "It would not be wise. Mona Sera . . ."

"You left her."

"But she still thinks of me as hers, to punish, to destroy."

"But you are not hers." I stopped, my body a mere whisper away from his. "Don't you want to be mine?" My hot breath wafted over the pale sweep of his neck just above where that slow pulse pounded. "Don't you want me to be yours?"

He shuddered and closed his eyes. "More than I wish to live."

My eyes glittered in triumph.

"But it would not serve you well."

I pushed away from him and he breathed deeply in relief until I pulled loose the elastic band, spilling my black hair to fall in an inky wash down my back, around my shoulders, the front strands teasing over the gentle rise of my breasts.

Gryphon froze in a stillness so deep he seemed like carved marble.

"You told me to seduce the men and make them mine." I kicked off my shoes.

He swallowed, his jaw clenched. "So that they would be bound to you and protect you."

I bent over. Watching him watch me, I pulled up one pant leg, smoothed down a sock. Both of us watched it fall to the ground.

"There is no need to seduce me." His voice was gratifyingly strained. "I would protect you to the best of my ability without claiming you."

"I know." I pushed down the other sock. He stared, seemingly fascinated at the simple sight of my bare feet.

"You already have the benefit without the risk." He breathed heavily as I untied my pants and let them pool around my feet.

"If you take me, Mona Sera's rage will be great," he said hoarsely, but there was a wild inconsistency between his spoken words and what his eyes bespoke. He wanted me.

"Rage great or little, she'll still want to kill us both, you said."
Slowly, oh so slowly, I lifted my top up. His eyes fastened on the
smoothness of my belly and his breathing grew harsher.

He tore his eyes away from the yearning indentation of my belly
and forced himself to look up into my eyes. "Your chance of surviving her will be greater if we restrain ourselves."

I ignored his noble plea and pulled off my top and dropped it to
the floor. No bra. Gryphon clenched his fists, his eyes falling irresistibly down to my small, high, firm breasts. The peaks stiffened
and pebbled beneath his gaze and I felt a wave of triumphant satisfaction wash over me at the knowledge that the sight of my body
could affect a man so powerfully, bringing a flush to his face and a
tremor to his hands. It was glorious.

"Our chances of survival with Mona Sera are small either way,"
I whispered. "Don't you want to live now, fully? I do. I want to
touch you. Have you touch me in return. I want to know what it's
like to take a man into my body and truly enjoy it." I closed my
eyes. "My body weeps for you. I want you so much. I've never felt
like this before, ever."

"You wear silver," Gryphon said with surprise.

It took me a moment to comprehend what he was saying, so
caught up was I in what I was feeling. My hand flew up to the
cross I wore always around my neck, covering it. "I'm sorry. Does
it hurt you?"

"Why would it hurt me? It lies against your skin, not mine."

"Does the holy cross bother you in any way?" I undid the clasp,
walked away from him, and dropped it into the drawer of a cre-
denza set against the wall. Then I turned back to face him. With the
distance of the room between us, I felt that peculiar possession
leave me and felt myself reverting back to my old self, filled with
trepidation and self-consciousness, remembering once again that

pain, not pleasure, was all that I usually harvested when I tangled men upon my bedding sheets.

"We can touch and look at the holy cross and enter churches without impunity. It is only the silver content that irritates us. Does not the feel of silver against your flesh disturb you in any manner?"

I shook my head in denial and crossed my arms over my bosom, coldly naked, coldly aware that I inhabited a body men would never consider voluptuous. That awareness prompted me to venture the conclusion: "Perhaps you are not pleased with my body."

"No," Gryphon said gravely. "Your body is most pleasing to me."

But in the sudden chaos of my emotions, I could not discern the truth of his words. I did not believe him. The pull between us was there and strong, but that seemed to be instinctive, something he couldn't control. His willful choice, however, was clear. He hadn't moved. He did not want me.

"I'm sorry." I laughed brittlely. "I don't seem to be too good of a seductress. Men are attracted to me at first but afterward they say I'm cold. And I am. Frozen inside."

"We are not attracted to humans," he explained again, quietly, patiently. "We do not feel with them what we would feel with another of our kind."

The irony was that I wasn't sure whether he included me in with those humans. "I see. You're right, of course, about us. We shouldn't . . ." I inched toward the haven of my bedroom. "I shouldn't have tried to force myself on you. I'm sorry."

Gryphon crossed the ten feet between us with one giant leap, moving so quickly, he wasn't even a blur. He was just suddenly standing there, an inch away from me. I gasped.

"I've changed my mind," he said softly, perverse man that he was.

Anger flared up, burning away my self-consciousness in a wonderful wash of cleansing heat. "I don't want your pity," I hissed, backing away from him, retreating into my bedroom, silently cursing the vagaries of all men, no matter what their kind.

"Good. Neither do I desire yours," he said shortly, pursuing me until the back of my knees bumped up against the mattress. My bedroom was so small there was no room for anything other than the bed and bureau and a few feet of walking space.

"The last emotion I feel for you is pity," Gryphon said, his eyes soft and luminous. Unbuttoning his top two buttons, he tore his shirt over his head and let it drop to the ground. The sound of a zipper rasped loudly in the tense silence. Gracefully, he stepped out of his pants and stood before me, baring even more of himself to me than I had to him. I still had on my underwear. All that adorned him now was the white bandage on his left side. It did nothing to hide his glory.

I sank down onto the bed, my knees suddenly weak, marveling at the revelation of how lovely the male form could be. Clothes had hid him, masking him in commonness. Unclothed, his full beauty was revealed. He was divine.

I let my eyes wander freely over him, to and fro, over the excessive loveliness of his form. Allowed my visual senses to gorge without restraint on the sensual feast that he was after a lifelong famine. His chest rippled, more muscular than I could have imagined, more than that brief, tantalizing glimpse of his abdomen had hinted of when I had tended to his wound.

He was sleek, powerful, dangerous. A graceful, deadly predator with wide shoulders that tapered down to slim hips, powerful thighs, and thick calves roped with muscle. The only soft thing about him was his swathe of dark hair that fell in thick waves to tease his shoulders. My hands itched with the need to bury themselves in the long strands, to discover if they would be as soft and silky to the touch as they promised to be. His chest was smooth perfection, needing no other adornment but the twin areolas that were the color of warm chestnuts and would no doubt be as tasty. Crisp strands of hair arrowed down his belly to bush in a dark frame around his stiff, rampant rod that rose up eagerly to meet me, an elegant melding of form with function. It brushed against the hard ridges of his abdomen, bobbing almost as if in greeting. A nervous giggle escaped me and I clamped a hand over my mouth.

"Do you not still want me, Mona Lisa?" he asked softly, his eyes glowing.

I licked my dry lips. His sizzling eyes followed the movement.

"I will always want you," was my simple, truthful reply.

His eyes squeezed shut, then opened, blazing like burning sapphire. "You are more than I ever hoped to find, a Queen I never dared to even dream of. Will you not lay your hands upon me? Grant me permission to lay my hands upon you?"

He crawled with sinuous grace onto the bed, his knees resting on either side of me, sinking down onto the mattress, moving carefully as if afraid of frightening me. He needn't have bothered. The extreme lust I was feeling for him, the desperate control I was exerting not to fall ravenously on him and devour him up was scaring me near to death as it was. I scooted back a few inches and fell onto my back as he straddled me and lowered himself down, his arms braced on either side of my head, stopping just short of contact.

"Do you not wish to touch me?" he asked.

"Yes." *Oh, sweet mother may I, yes!* Taking a deep breath, I reached out a trembling hand and laid my fingers upon his chest. His skin was cool and smooth, silk over living rock. It felt so good it edged toward pain. We both groaned with the thrill of contact. I snatched my hand back.

He rolled in a fluid motion onto his left side. I turned to face him. He reached out his right hand and I was comforted, reassured when I saw its fine trembling. He touched me lightly in the same spot that I had touched him, just above the heart. I gasped at the pleasure of it. Nothing more, just that light touch, and liquid desire trickled down my thigh. The scent of my arousal thickened and permeated the room. Gryphon's nostrils flared and he breathed harshly, deeply, but did nothing more. When I could stand it no longer, I reached out and placed my entire palm flat against his chest. He shuddered and grated, "Yes. More."

I stroked him, unable to stop myself, not wanting to, and his hand moved as mine did. A light stroke along the collarbones, a second hand to trace along the line of his shoulder, down the slope of his arm. I buried both hands in the cool falling silk of his hair that felt even better than I had imagined, and made a surprising discovery at his nape. "You have soft, downy . . . feathers?"

He hummed an acknowledgment, absorbed in the feel and play of my own hair.

Suddenly, I had to taste him. I whispered my need, "Gryphon," and rose up on my knees and lowered my lips to his. Satin smoothness. Sweet coolness. And soft. So soft. I brushed my lips against his, enjoying the smooth glide of skin against silken skin until he moaned his need for more and parted his lips. My tongue slipped into the shockingly warm cavern of his mouth and I lapped along his teeth, traced the wet lining of his cheeks, and brushed against the roughness of his tongue. Gryphon groaned again, slid my underwear down my legs, and pulled me to him. The pleasure-pain of flesh against flesh, the meeting of my peaked nipples against the smooth hardness of his chest, the brush of his warm, swollen member against my soft belly spurred him into action. He rolled, pinning me beneath him, his lips moving aggressively against my lips, his tongue entwining with mine in a rub-slide-enter-retreat plunging motion that had me parting my legs and arching my hips against his. I pulled him to me, wanting more of his delicious weight. I slid my hands with frantic greed down his back, over his slender waist, to the succulent round globes of his bottom, urging him to come into me.

His hot mouth moved down my cheek, onto my neck, and I gave a keening cry as I felt the bite of his teeth there where my pulse pounded. He filled his mouth with my flesh, pressed his teeth down with restrained ferocity, growling with his desire to pierce the flesh and taste the sweet blood. But instead of biting me, he sucked hard and released me, laving me with his rough tongue, and dipped down to taste the hollow at the base of my neck.

"Tell me you want me," he said roughly.

"Yes," I cried.

He took my nipple into his mouth, laving the sensitive tip again and again.

"Please, Gryphon," I gasped.

"Yes, say my name." His voice rumbled in a pleasant sensation against my breast. "Tell me you need me."

"I need you now. Please."

He bit down gently on my nipple and I reared up, crying out as he tugged and sucked with leashed savagery, his other hand molding, caressing, squeezing my other breast, his thumb rubbing over the tip, sending thrilling sensations spearing through me.

"Oh, God. Gryphon . . . Gryphon!"

"Yes, yes. Say my name," he said hoarsely, his other hand sliding down my stomach to brush through my curls. He parted my folds and slipped a finger into me and I stilled in shock at the wonderful, surprising sensation—such magnificent pleasure—not even daring to breathe as he stroked gently in and out.

"You're so tight. Relax, yes. Let me . . ." He slid a second finger into me and I quivered uncontrollably and whimpered, my lashes fluttering shut. He stroked and soothed me with his other hand as he pushed in past the second knuckle, then farther.

"Yes, that's it," he crooned. "How beautiful, how sweet you are. More than I ever dreamed." He stretched me wide with his fingers, then slid out. His weight lifted, and my eyes flew open with a cry of protest that stopped as he stood and pulled me forward until my hips hung over the edge of the bed, and he lifted my legs over his shoulders. His cheeks were slashed with color and his dark eyes glittered like blue diamonds. With his eyes locked on mine, he guided himself into me, filling me slowly as my eyes widened at the incredible feel of him, at the supreme agony of being stretched by him.

"Oh," I breathed at the breathtaking miracle of wet pleasure instead of dry pain.

"You're so hot. So hot," he panted. "Yes, like that. Take me. Am I hurting you?"

"No. Your wound . . ."

"I'm fine." He groaned and thrust in all the way. "Fine," and started to move.

"Yes." I moaned and held myself still for fear of aggravating his wound, of hurting him while he devastatingly destroyed me with his deep, measured strokes. I watched him, drank him in, the sight of him, the feel of him—the sweet agony of pleasure clenching his face, the rightness of his body sliding into mine, letting him control it all while I took him and held him tightly within.

He began to move faster, muscles rippling, straining, as he thrust deeper, more forcefully, destroying me, tearing me apart with such frightening pleasure. I felt myself tighten even more, moving toward something that grew and grew in power. And when I thought he could not be more savagely beautiful, he began to glow. *We* began to glow, a light that started at our joining and spread up our entire bodies, filling us with an incandescent glory that made his skin translucent and limed his mink-black hair with a halo of light, lighting him with a terrible beauty that brought tears of agony and joy to my eyes.

Yes, came the thought. *This is what we were meant to be,* and that power swept over me, flooded me, tore me apart, and rebuilt me even stronger. I convulsed, pulsing and pulsing and pulsing. Blindly above me, I heard Gryphon cry out, "Mona Lisa . . . mine!" and then he was pumping hotly inside me, groaning sorely, dearly, as he filled me with his seed.

THREE

THE GENTLE FINGERS of the moon caressed Gryphon with loving tenderness as he lay beside me, asleep, a creature so beautiful that he stopped my breath, his lovely perfection so unreal I
would have doubted its true existence were I not touching him, my
leg entwined with his. His arm was flung over me, chaining me to
him in sleep, desiring as I desired, that skin-to-skin contact.

He was cool to the touch, cooler than I, and I didn't know if
that was his normal condition or a result of the poison within
him. He had seemed better than in the hospital, more rested, his
strength quite evident in the soreness I now felt in my thighs, between my legs. But his trembling, in the end, had been equal parts
passion and exhaustion and he had fallen deeply asleep immediately afterward. I let him sleep, knowing it was the best therapy
for him, content to lie there beside him, secure in his arms, and
to listen to the soft soughing of his breath and the slow beating of
his heart.

It was frightening. No, terrifying, in truth, the fierce possessiveness I now felt for him. I needed this quiet period of companioned solitude to absorb the changes and revelations he had wrought with his entry into my life.

He stirred several hours later, making the transition from sleep to total awareness with one blink of his piercing eyes. His arm tightened around me, then relaxed. "I didn't dream you, did I?" he asked, pulling me closer.

"No." I breathed my soft confirmation against his shoulder where my head nestled, my heart settled and happy once more as I inhaled the essence of him. "You smell so good."

I felt him smile against me. "What do I smell like?"

"Like the night, the soaring wind, the verdant fields below . . . and of feathers." I lifted up to gaze down at him. "Why do you have soft down at the base of your neck?"

"My other form is a falcon."

"Your other form?" I tasted the strange phrase slowly, unable to prevent my voice from rising to a squeak. "You mean you can become a *bird*?"

Gryphon nodded, smiling as if I had amused him.

Gryphon. Gyrfalcon. A fierce bird of prey.

I could see it now in some of his features—his sharp, piercing eyes, the strong hooked blade of his nose, the wide shoulders, the long, slender fingers. *Would they become talons?* I wondered.

"What is your other form?" he asked.

I shook my head, dazed. Was that what it was, that wild thing caged within me that I suppressed? "I don't know."

"Do not worry. You are young. It will probably come to you later, although not all Monère possess the ability to transform into another creature." He frowned and reached up to smooth back my hair with a gentle touch. "Exactly how old are you?"

"Twenty-one years old. When did you attain your other form?"

"When I reached puberty at eighteen. But you are a Mixed Blood. Part human. It may come later for you."

"Do you know that for certain?"

He hesitated. "No. You are an entirely new entity."

"What other forms have Mixed Bloods attained?"

"None of them have had other forms, as far as I know."

"Bummer," I said with relief. I did not wish to have another form. Not if it meant unleashing that scary, restless force that had prowled within me since puberty.

"But you are an entirely new territory, to all of our kind."

"What do you mean?"

"That you are a Queen is a frank miracle in itself," Gryphon said with grave solemnity. "There has never been a Mixed Blood Queen before."

"Ever?"

"Never in our entire history since the Great Exodus from the moon."

"The moon?"

"Four millennia ago, a disaster befell our Mother Moon. The seas dried up and mountains crumbled. Monère desperately departed their dying planet. Many came to this world, carving out an existence here, all hoping that one day the moon would return to its former glory and we could return to our home."

"Where do others of your kind live?"

"We carved out colonies across the face of the earth, in the forests, amidst the deserts, on islands, along the high steppes. Most remain pure, though some have lived among the humans, but it is not easy to live in isolation among them, away from our kind."

"So just how old *are* you?" It had been a question that had bedeviled me since he first opened his mouth and those delightfully quaint words and phrases flowed from his lips.

Gryphon laughed, a rusty sound that twisted my heart. It made me want to entice it from him again and again until his laughter came freely with ease. "Not that old. I am only seventy-five years old."

"Seventy-five! But you don't look more than thirty."

"What are you doing?" he asked as I bent over him and combed my fingers through the long, thick strands.

"Checking for white hair," I muttered, then jerked and moaned as he nuzzled my breast and drew a nipple into the warm, wet cavern of his mouth. "Oh, no you don't. I want some answers first."

"I have no white hairs," he said, giving my pert tip one last luscious laving of his tongue before drawing away. "Seventy-five is considered young among our people. A warrior is considered mature at one hundred and seasoned at two."

"Two hundred?" I said, squeaking like a mouse again, which drew a smile from Gryphon. He watched me, pleasure alighting his eyes as I walked naked to my closet. Drawing on a robe, I returned to the bed to perch beside him.

"Our average life span is three hundred years."

"And Mixed Bloods?"

His smile faded, elusive once more. "They possess the lifespan of humans. One hundred years, mayhap."

Again I felt a mixture of emotions. Pleasure at hearing that I would likely live until a hundred—a lengthy age that few humans reached—and pain that I would not live to three hundred. I felt cheated somehow.

"Do not worry. 'Tis my belief you shall live longer than that. More Monère blood flows within you instead of human blood, and your heart beats slower than those of your human kind."

"Fifty beats per minute."

"The few Mixed Bloods I have encountered have rhythms of sixty and higher, like other humans."

"So?"

"So do you not see that the slower one's heart beats, the longer one lives? A hummingbird's heart beats more than three hundred times per minute and they live briefly, gloriously, for one year. A turtle, on the other hand, possesses a rhythm closer to mine. It is not unusual for them to see two hundred, sometimes even three hundred years of life."

"So you're saying I will live longer than most humans."

He nodded, his eyes a quicksilver flash of crystal blueness. "That is my belief."

I took his hand and laid it against my cheek, my smile bittersweet. It was all a moot point. Two hundred more years to live with him would be a lovely prospect, but a longer life would be pointless without him. An amorphous aloneness and gray solitude was all I had known up till now. I had not truly begun to live until my eyes first fastened upon him. I wondered if my new life, my life with him, would be even more fleeting than that of a hummingbird.

"How much time do you have before the poison kills you?" I asked.

"No longer than a full cycle of the moon."

Thirty days. Shit. "When did she . . ."

"Yesterday."

Just one day, and how weak it had made him in that short period of time.

"What is it?" he asked, his hand moving down to stroke my neck, his thumb brushing against my pulse.

"I was suddenly worried about the proper care and nourishment of my Moonie," I said, forcing a smile to my lips.

"I wonder who your parents are," Gryphon mused.

"The only thing I have from them is the silver cross you saw." Retrieving the cross, I showed him the engraving etched on the back.

"Mona Lisa," he read. "Your name."

"Yes."

I watched as his eyes narrowed. "May I?" At my consenting nod, he took it from me and held it by the chain. Very lightly, delicately, he grasped the cross and examined it more closely. There at the base was another word etched so tiny, so meticulously, that human eyes could not have detected it without the aid of a microscope.

"Monère," he read. Carefully, he released the cross and returned it to me, rubbing his fingers together absently where he had touched the silver.

"Where did you get this?" he asked.

"It hung upon my neck when they found me as a newborn, and the name engraved on the back was the name I was given at the orphanage."

He gazed at the cross I clutched tightly in my hand and stilled into that sudden immobility, a deep stillness that was beyond human. "Your hand," he said with odd carefulness. "May I see it?"

I set the cross down and gave him my right hand. He uncurled my fingers. With reverence, he touched the mole there in the center of my palm. It was just a slight roundness, like a pearl buried halfway in my flesh. He held out his other hand and I passed my left palm into his care. He looked down upon the slight rising there, also, then gazed from one hand to the other.

"What is it?" I asked.

He did not speak for a moment. When he finally did, it was with a question of his own. "What powers do you possess?"

I shrugged. "I can see through the darkness and hear for miles around me, if I wish. My sense of smell is acute. I am fast like a cat,

strong as a lion. With effort, I can control people's minds with my
gaze. With my hands, I can detect ailments within the body and, to
a small degree, ease some of the pain, but I have yet to obtain the
ability to heal."

I waited for Gryphon to speak but he just stared down at my
palms.

"Well?" I finally prompted.

He kissed each mole with careful deference and pulled me down
until I lay beside him once more. " 'Tis my belief that you bear the
mark of the Moon Goddess, her tears."

"The Moon Goddess?"

"Yes, a deity whom we worship. Our earliest ancestress, the
mother of us all."

"And why do you say you 'believe'? As if you're not sure," I
mumbled against the hollow of his neck.

"You are most uncommon, my young Queen. We have only
heard of the mark of the Goddess's tears through our lore and leg-
ends since the time of our Exodus. Those few Queens who were
blessed with such marks were extraordinary healers and great
warriors."

"So what happened to these blessed Queens?"

"Great gifts beget great peril. They were both blessed and
cursed by their gifts."

"Sounds like a mixed review to me."

My stomach suddenly growled and I jumped. Gryphon gave
that rusty laugh again and I rewarded him with a grin. "I'm starving. Do you eat? Or do you need to drink blood?"

His brows rose. "And would you offer me your lovely neck if
I did?"

"Sure, if you needed it."

"Ah." He sighed, his eyes growing soft. "You are like a fresh breath of wind. No, we do not drink blood. We partake of food as humans do. Did you think me *vampyre*?"

"Yes." I blushed. "I craved your crimson blood the first time I saw it. I was overwhelmed with a desire to taste it. And when I did, my heart melted. It was the first time I'd ever felt such an urge."

"That is because it was the first time you have been with one of your kind. The urge to taste each other only arises between Monère lovers, never with humans. The resulting bite mark is the highest form of honor, evidence of the deepest of passion."

"You didn't taste my blood." I touched the unbroken skin of my neck where he had pressed his teeth.

His blue eyes sparkled with simmering heat. "I restrained my-self because of those who hunt me. It would be my honor and even greater pleasure to taste you and leave my mark upon you when the time is right."

I blushed again. "So we're not vampires by nature. Are there such things as vampires, then?"

A bare hesitation, then, "No, there is no such creature. The vampire stories originated from those of us who can take on the form of a rat or a bat."

"How about werewolves? Are they real?"

"Again, that lore is based on those of us who can shift into wolf form. But as with the *vampyre,* there is a little truth and much mis-information that humans have concocted."

"Like holy objects causing you to burst into flames. What about wooden stakes through the heart and garlic cloves?"

"Myth only. Stakes through the heart . . . that would not kill us. Our healing body would eventually spit the wood out."

"So, what are our fatal vulnerabilities?"

"The usual ways. Cutting our hearts out. Severing our heads off.

But the most painful and lingering deaths are through silver or sun poisoning."

My eyes grew round at the gruesome methods he ticked off. "The sun can kill you?"

"Most definitely. Its hot rays burn us even at its weakest hours. Does it not burn you?"

"No, I have no such problems."

"Ah," he said, pleased, as if I had confirmed something he had already suspected. "The ability to withstand the sun is not unusual for Mixed Bloods."

I swallowed. "Do you have to sleep in a coffin or in the ground?"

He kissed me, a light peck of affection. "No, a soft bed will do very well. We are nocturnal. We sleep during the daytime hours. Humans are made for the heat of the sun. We are cold-blooded creatures. The night," he glanced longingly out the window, "is our domain. The darkness, the soothing air, when the world is shrouded in serenity, and our bodies, enlightened, are infused with energy from the moon. Don't you feel that, too, when night falls and your soul awakens to the calling from above?"

"Yes, I have felt that way since my childhood, only I didn't know then what it was, what made me so different from other children."

"That must have been hard for you, not knowing what made the days dreary, the sun glaring, and your body leaden with fatigue." He stroked my hair. "Tell me more about your childhood."

"I will, later. Your well-being is what concerns my heart now. We must act soon to find the cure to stop this poisoning. Thirty days is not a long time."

He smiled and whispered in a most gentle tone, "I care not that I live another moment. I care only that I am in your arms. I feel like a camel reaching an oasis after a long trek in the dry desert. I feel as if I have lived my life, that I could close my eyes and fall asleep and rest in your presence forever."

"Don't close your eyes now." I pressed a kiss to his brow. "You are too young to die."

He looked at me quietly for a moment. "I could just stay here and use the rest of my days, however short they may be, to pass you knowledge, teach you of our kind, acquaint you with people and names that may prove useful to you as a Queen," he said gently.

He lay there in my arms and my vision was suddenly keener, more perceptive, allowing me to glimpse deep into his weary, battered, undernourished soul and see with sharp clarity what he had chosen—death. He wanted to rest, to die here in the comfort of my presence instead of fight to live. And I saw clearly that neither soft kindness nor sweet pleading would sway him from his chosen path. He needed something harsh, something stinging to wake him up; I knew this, somehow, deep in my heart. A core of hidden knowledge within me seemed to have awakened with his entry into my life.

"You call me your Queen," I said, my voice cracking like a whip, "but in your heart you do not truly mean it."

"No—" He jerked back at my sudden attack and sat up.

I ruthlessly cut off his cry of bewildered protest and continued scornfully. "You have resigned yourself to death, even welcome that final rest, for you are tired of the pain and suffering of living. You lie when you call me your Queen, for you serve no one but yourself in giving in so easily to the death waiting to claim you."

Gryphon tensed wildly beneath the lash of my words, unable to deny the sting of their truth.

"You appease yourself by offering to pass me a pittance of knowledge before you die in return for the comfort and ease I give you." I smiled contemptuously. "You treat me no better than a whore if you believe I am willing and desperate enough to settle for so little in return."

"No," he choked in agonized denial, shaking his head furiously. "No, my Queen."

"I will not settle for thirty days of your half-hearted service and then allow you to leave me alone and unprotected while you go to your rest," I said harshly. "If I am truly your Queen, then I require and demand from you *all* that is due me from a male in my service."

I glided to him and he watched me as if mesmerized, with something new in his eyes—a touch of fear and caution.

"You are mine. Every part of you belongs to me," I said, caressing his chest just above that slow, steady beating, feeling him tremble and smiling because of it. "Your brave warrior heart, your poisoned body, your weary soul." I breathed the words against his lips as I buried my hand in his hair and gripped his scalp hard. "Your brilliant mind," I whispered and brought my lips against his in a chaste kiss. "By my *right*, I claim every part of you in my service, and demand and require that you desire to live with your entire breath and being, with your very heart and soul. I hold you to your duty to seek a cure for yourself and not to abandon me. You owe me two hundred and twenty-five more years of service and I will not be cheated with a paltry thirty days, do you understand?"

Gryphon sank to his knees before me, silent tears of shame coursing down his cheeks. "Yes, my Queen," he said, yielding all because I demanded it.

"Your oath on it."

"I swear it," he said harshly.

"Swear it by that which you hold most dear."

He lifted his eyes to me. "I swear it on milady's heart," he said, bowing his head.

I tenderly stroked Gryphon's hair, a bittersweet smile twisting my lips. I had won. For now, I had won. I had seen what weapon to use and had used it ruthlessly to achieve my own end because I did not want to be alone, because I had only just begun to truly live and did not want to see that life die in its mere infancy. I smiled bittersweetly because I did not know that I was any better than that other terrible Queen, Mona Sera, in her calculated cruelty and, even more frightening, I did not care.

"I will not make it so easy for you to leave me." It was a soft promise, a gentle threat.

Gryphon drew in a deep gulping breath. "No, my Queen," he whispered.

FOUR

Taking a leave of absence from work, I set my heart in pursuit of the antidote. I felt a keener sense of myself, like a fresh young blossom of spring sensing the world for the first time, my tattered old self diminishing with every new breath I took in.

The idea of searching out the other Queen, Mona Genesa, was soon abandoned. Gryphon had only a poor idea of where she was and an even poorer expectation of how he would be received, being the runaway slave of another Queen, the most despised of his kind. Had we been able to find her, she would likely turn us away like hunted dogs, chasing us far from her. Helping unwanted fugitives was an unspoken taboo among the Queens.

So, what to do then? There was only one choice, I told Gryphon. Face his enemy, and I would help him conquer the unconquerable. Reluctantly, Gryphon agreed.

Where did a Monère Queen live? In Queens, of course. Oh, the ego Mona Sera had. Thus we found ourselves the following night, shortly before midnight, outside a desolate warehouse in Flushing, the most easterly outpost of Queens, near an old railway depot. Rusty tracks lay abandoned and unused under the gleaming moon. Surrounding us on both sides were empty railway box carts, the kind once used for shipping before highways and trucks made many of them obsolete. They were stacked one atop another in a colorful array of dulled orange and grey, to tower over the undistinguished warehouse.

The full moon hovered above us in perfect round glory. Why were we here? To search Mona Sera's chambers for the antidote while everyone gathered for Basking.

Gryphon had said to me the previous night, "A sad pity we could not search for the antidote during the full moon tomorrow while everyone is gathered for Basking, but we shall have to stay here and Bask ourselves."

"Bask?" I had returned. "What's that?"

He had looked at me, stunned. "Basking is when we stand beneath the full moon and the Queen opens herself and the moon showers down upon us her rays of light, renewing us all."

And so I came to learn a bit more about the children of the moon. Queens were precious, indeed, because only they had the ability to pull down the moon's rays and allow others to Bask in its energy. Without Basking, the Monère aged more quickly, like humans. Queens held the ultimate power: They prolonged life. I, unfortunately, did not know how to Bask. Oh well. But at least we now had the perfect moment for entering the premises with the least chance of detection.

A cool wind swept the tree branches, causing a flurry of red and gold leaves to dance and flutter to the ground. An owl hooted as we swiftly crossed and blended into the shadows of the building's northern wall. Gryphon entered through a second-story window like a shadowy ghost. A moment later, he opened the front door, letting me in.

All the lights were off, but darkness was no obstacle to our kind. Our eyes were equipped to see things as if night were day. It was deserted inside. That was no surprise. The surprise was how richly furnished—opulent, really—the interior was, with veined marble flooring, finely woven Persian carpets, and a magnificent crystal chandelier. I followed Gryphon up the grand, winding staircase in silent wonderment and down a hallway that held nothing but a single door at the end.

My skin prickled as an acute fragrance rushed toward me from that door. A fragrance feminine and jarring, giving me a sense of being in a place where I ought not to be, as if I was impinging upon another's realm. It had to be Mona Sera's chamber.

Gryphon opened the door and disappeared inside. Taking a deep breath, I followed him and entered into the spacious living quarters of the master bedroom. It was lavishly furnished with plush carpeting and heavy, gilded frames of art. One I recognized as a Renoir, another a Rubens. A huge, draped four-poster bed dominated the room. It was twice the size of a king bed, enshrouded by curtain wisps that framed it in sheer decadent glory.

Gryphon's touch broke my spell and I blinked at him. He gestured me toward the adjacent dressing area while he went to the bed and began searching it. The dressing area was a room as big as my living room and decorated much, much nicer, with framed prints, carpeting, draperies even, and a comfortable chaise. I opened the closets. Mona Sera's gowns and apparel lined the racks with her shoes in the space below, numbering well into the hundreds. I shook my head in bemusement. What do you know? Mona Sera had a thing for shoes.

I looked carefully on the shelves and through the custom-fitted

drawers, ran my hands down the clothes, peered in the shoes, prod-
ded the little toes within, but found nothing. I even ran my hands
along the walls and floor but could sense no hidden seams or com-
partments. I returned to the boudoir and looked at Gryphon. He
gestured to some vials on the mirrored bureau top. I came to his
side, lifted the lids, smelled nothing but perfume fragrance, and
shook my head. We searched the rest of room, even peering under
the mattress of the huge bed but found nothing except a simple vial
hidden in a bedside drawer.

Before I could lift the stopper of the vial, Gryphon was at my
side, his hand over mine, shaking his head furiously. Carefully, gingerly, controlling my movements with dreadful care, he put the vial
back and pulled me into the bathroom where he had me wash my
hands three times before continuing our search. It was fruitless.

Disappointment weighed heavily in my heart as we slipped back
out into the hallway and made our way back down. We had agreed
beforehand to search only the Queen's private quarters where the
antidote would most likely be hidden. Gryphon waited for me down
by the front door, but before I reached him, I stopped and turned.
Something drew me, some amorphous thing coming from the east
wing. Instead of leaving, I veered right, following the irresistible
pull down an empty corridor.

Gryphon stopped me, a hand gripping me urgently, shaking
his head and urging me back toward the entrance. But I shook him
off, called onward by something I could not deny, some force that
pulled me forward until I stumbled into a grand hall. Only then
did I recognize it. The feel of power, old power. It hit me with a
spine-tingling rush.

The great chamber was exposed to the full moon through an
open skylight. A score of men and a handful of women faced away
from me, their faces lifted to the streaming rays bathing them in

pale light. On the center platform, a woman lifted her arms in joyous welcome to the round, luminous planet that had once been their home, her hair streaming down her back, hair so black that it shone blue in the silvery light. She was naked, unrestricted by clothing, her flesh pure and unblemished, her breasts jutting out full and proud. From the waist down, her body was a serpentine flow of smooth, rippling muscles covered by glistening scales. She had no legs, just the body of a snake. I looked at her with wonder and thought *lamia,* what the ancient Greeks had called the snakelike creature they had believed to be vampire, a creature of legend and lore that I would have claimed only a moment before did not exist.

A moonbeam fell on the snakewoman and the power that filled the room grew. With a burst of brightness, little butterflies of light showered down from the heavens, darting into her and entering into all the men and women around her, making them gasp, bowing their backs as the light streamed into them until they glowed with blinding brilliance.

And still the power did not abate but continued to grow, tightening more and more within me until I felt as if I would surely burst. And then it seemed as if I did. With another flash of light, moonlight darted to the back of the hall, to me, finding me and touching me with cold light, showering me with flittering energy and sharing that invigorating power with Gryphon, making us gasp and glow with radiance. Only then did the power fade with one last loving caress, leaving us behind in the quiet afterglow with all eyes turned upon us and the cold discovery that several men had moved behind us and now held us captive.

Basking, as far as I was concerned, hadn't been worth it.

"Well, well, well. What have we here?" Mona Sera purred. A forked tongue flitted out in the air, tasting us. I felt a surge of energy. Before my eyes, the lamia's vertically slitted pupils rounded out and her scales melted away into legs that flowed with sinuous grace toward us.

A woman brought a robe to Mona Sera and she slipped her arms into the garment and belted it, to my immense relief. The fact that a naked woman coming at me was scarier than the warrior behind me, holding me captive in an iron grip, said a lot about my priorities. Homophobic, me? Nah. I just felt more comfortable fighting. Street fighting and a hodgepodge of other disciplines thrown in.

With a twist I broke free, my arm slipping out at my opponent's weakest point where his thumb and fingers met. I grabbed my captor's arm. Another twist, a grunt from me as I bent and lifted, and the man went sailing over my head to land with a nice thud on the ground, surprise darkening his eyes.

Geez, he was a massive brute, at least six-four and close to three hundred pounds I'd bet, with a barrel-like chest and arms and thighs as wide as my head. I was surprised I'd been able to throw him, and surprised even more at what he wore at his waist—a genuine sword sheathed in its very own scabbard, like what they used back during the Crusades.

One of the two men holding Gryphon lunged at me and I ducked back. Let's see, two opponents in front, twenty behind me. Forward, definitely forward, was the way to go. Knives suddenly in hand, I leaped and slashed a white-haired warrior in my way, slicing his chest and drawing blood, then darted past him as Gryphon plunged an elbow into his opponent and dropped him with a kick. The stench of Gryphon's blood filled the air. Damn, his belly wound had broken open again.

We dashed down the corridor, out the front entrance, and came to an abrupt halt. Ten men formed a half circle in front of us outside; they must have come through the skylight. I wondered briefly if they could fly, and that reminded me of something.

"Gryphon, fly," I said. "Fly away from here, now. Do it."

His eyes burning, he obeyed me. His clothes ripped away and he transformed with a brief surge of power, his face changing, his mouth lengthening into a sharp beak, snowy white feathers flowing on his arms, all over, as he became a huge bird of prey. But his eyes, his beautiful intelligent eyes were still the same, fixed on me as he spread his wings in flight. Fixed on me as he swung his powerful feet to grip me, his razor-sharp talons carefully wrapping around and not into my waist. We were three feet into the air when the realization that he was trying to fly us both out hit me, the same time a heavy rope net was thrown over us.

The falcon gave a piercing shriek of rage as he slashed some of the rope with his beak. He might have broken free had he used his talons, but he could not employ them without dropping me. And he did not release me. Inevitably, the net tangled with his wings and we dropped back to the ground. Another surge and Gryphon was back in his normal form, a sprawl of arms and legs, naked, panting with exertion, weakened by the poison, drops of blood glistening on his pale skin as the net was lifted off us. My knives were snatched away and powerful hands that I was quickly coming to recognize gripped my arms once again, bringing them together behind me, manacling them both with huge iron fists that allowed me no room to maneuver.

"Quick learner. Too bad," I muttered, and arched back my head in a sudden move, landing a solid blow to the giant's nose. Good thing I was tall for a woman. He bellowed with pain but still held me secure. He drew me back firmly against his massive chest and tilted his head out of reach. That awareness, that sharp attraction of like to like, of Queen to male that had been present all along, burst into full awareness and I felt something rise behind me to prod at me from down below. Could have been the sword, but I doubted it.

I struggled fiercely, energized by something that tasted like fear. My feet slammed into the giant's shins. He grunted but didn't move; his pain tolerance was impressive but not to my advantage. Only when I lashed back and up, trying to kick between his legs did he lift me easily and take me down to the ground, sweeping my legs out from under me quickly and efficiently, with no wasted effort or emotion. He followed me down, his great weight trapping me and immobilizing my legs, damn near squashing me. Good thing I didn't need to breathe as much as a normal human or I would have suffocated.

The other men, including the white-haired man I had cut earlier, gazed down at us from a distance, making no move to come closer, which I didn't mind in the least. Nor had they made a move to help at any time. Of course, it looked as if the giant hadn't needed their help, the big brute.

They had shackled Gryphon not with iron but with silver manacles, hands and feet, and left him on the ground. He struggled, straining against the restraints until his wrists and ankles were raw and abraded. I felt a shimmer of energy from him but he couldn't transform. We lay several yards from each other, helpless.

"She gave you a bit of trouble for such a small thing, Amber," hissed a sibilant voice to my right. I craned my head and saw her. Yup, Mona Sera, the snake bitch. And it was Amber, of the raping Sonia fame, on top of me.

Mona Sera came closer and I felt her definitive presence like an irritating buzzing against my senses that annoyed the heck out of me, and I wondered if this was what silver felt like against the skin of a Monère. If so, I could understand their aversion to the metal.

I felt the cold touch of manacles clamp around my wrists and wondered if they were silver also. They didn't bother me, nor would they be able to hold me, though they evidently thought that they would, for some reason. Interesting. I looked at Gryphon. I'd thought his inability to break free was due to his weakened condition, but perhaps touching silver weakened Monère in some way. Perhaps it weakened me the same way. Mentally I shrugged. We'd see soon enough. But now was not the time to test the restraints, with us surrounded, outnumbered, and outstrengthed, and with Gryphon trussed up and laid out beside me like a plucked turkey. I'd wait for a better time and opportunity, like when the sun was hot and high in the sky. While they slept, maybe.

I was flipped onto my back and saw for the first time the face of my opponent, Amber, close up. He was beautiful in a brutish manner, the way a towering oak tree was, built for power and endurance, his face roughly hewn, with big features—a prominent forehead and brow, a bold nose, a jutting jaw that fit the massive body, and straight nut-brown hair. His dark blue eyes were large and deep-set. There was an odd emptiness of emotion in their depths. Not anger or irritation or lust, just a cool control that had not changed in any way while we had fought. Not one single emotion but for that brief glimmer of surprise when I had thrown him.

"Amber, rape her," Mona Sera commanded.

Perhaps waiting for the right time was not an option after all. Both Amber and I tensed, but Amber made no other move, just stayed straddled over my thighs. I had wondered why they hadn't chained my legs, and now I knew. It was so he could rape me. I'd just as soon have not known, actually.

We stared at each other, both of us still, the tension stretching taut between us. Neither one of us made the first move to break it. Something flickered in those turquoise depths. His pupils constricted, his heartrate went up, and his nostrils flared as his breathing quickened. I braced myself for his attack but all he did was turn his head to Mona Sera.

"Milady . . . she is a Queen. I can sense it," Amber said.

"Yes, then you are not so dumb after all. Obey my order. *Rape her!*" Mona Sera's voice cracked like a whip and Amber flinched. His hands lifted, reached for me, then dropped helplessly. He looked at me and I realized what I was seeing. Fear. Not lust. Fear. It writhed like a trapped animal in his eyes.

"Please, milady . . ." Amber beseeched his Queen.

"So shy?" Mona Sera purred. "You were most eager with the others. Indeed, there seems to be no problem with the amber stone." Her gaze dropped down to his bulging crotch. "Why so hesitant?"

"Milady, it is forbidden to rape Queens," Amber said desperately, sweat wetting his brow.

"And yet so many of you men have done so throughout our history," Mona Sera said, her voice as cold as ice as she delivered the death blow. "Like your father. Did he not rape, then kill, his Queen, breaking the ultimate law?"

I looked at Mona Sera then, really looked at her, and with that new sharpened vision, I sensed it, her secret, her fear. A little kernel within her that had blossomed and grown. And I realized this wasn't about me at all. This was to test and punish Amber, whose father had committed the ultimate taboo, not only raping but killing a Queen. Large, strong, massive Amber, whom Mona Sera secretly feared and hated in the way only a woman, weaker and smaller, could fear a man, even a Queen. Perhaps especially a Queen.

"Does not the desire run in your blood?" Mona Sera asked, her voice dripping with sweetness. "Come, come. We can all see that you want to take the little Queen. You cannot fool us."

He quivered, a mass of great strength and masculine control reduced to no better than that of a helpless trapped animal. Poor brute.

Satisfaction glinted hard like a diamond in Mona Sera's eyes. With my deeper vision, I could almost read her thoughts. If he

raped me, a Queen, it would confirm all that Mona Sera had secretly feared all along, and it would be his own death sentence. If he
didn't, he was refusing his Queen's direct orders. Amber was
screwed either way and the realization of it was evident in the sea-
blue turmoil of his eyes.

I wondered how many years Mona Sera had made Amber pay
and pay for the sins of his father. How many times she had ordered
him to rape someone before her and watch her worst fear reenacted
over and over again, prodding at it like one would a sore tooth.
How sick and twisted Mona Sera must be to test both of them so.

Gryphon had said that those here had nowhere else to go. Perhaps if Amber had been less tall, less strong—just less. But with his
massive strength and height, no Queen would ever feel completely
safe around him with the insanity of his father's history, and it was
insane to kill off your life source, condemning not just you but all
others to a shorter life.

"Amber, I ordered you to rape her. Didn't you hear me?" Mona
Sera's voice grew shriller, louder.

Amber slid off me. Crawling on his hands and knees, he pros-
trated himself before Mona Sera. "Please, my Queen. I beg of
you . . . I do not wish to."

"You lie," she said, her voice pure melodic poison. "One clearly
sees that you do wish to."

He shook his head, his face in the dirt.

"You dare disobey me?" Her voice was a deadly hiss of warning.

His hands stretched beseechingly up to her, then dropped, not
daring to touch her.

"Well I, for one, would be most happy to carry out my
Queen's command," said the man I had cut, youthful despite the
whiteness of his hair, his cheerful voice breaking the spell and

drawing all attention back to me as I was inching my way closer to Gryphon. Great. Just frigging great.

I started to struggle to my feet and the white-haired warrior did that fast-action, leap-and-bound thing, his body on me in an instant, pinning me down before I even had a chance to rise. With calculated deliberation, he tore open the front of my shirt, revealing my cross and laying bare more cleavage than I was comfortable with flashing.

Yup, no more waiting. I flexed, broke the short silver chain easily, slammed a manacle-clad wrist into the handsome, winsome face above me—rapists came in all kinds, I guess—and watched with satisfaction as he flew off me.

I *tsked-tsked*. "No one teaches you boys manners anymore."

Gasps of surprise flew around me. I ignored them and scrambled to Gryphon, ripping off his manacles quickly and easily, and pulling him to his feet as men ran toward us.

"Wait," came a woman's voice, clear and loud, not Mona Sera's. And for some reason, perhaps from nothing more than mere surprise, everyone halted, including Gryphon.

"Why do you interfere, Sonia?" Mona Sera snapped. Sonia—Gryphon's half sister.

"My Queen," Sonia said, her voice ringing with desperate certainty, "she is your daughter."

FIVE

THE PRONOUNCEMENT STOPPED me short. *My mother?*

I stopped yanking Gryphon and swung back to stare at Mona Sera. Focusing my vision, I searched her face. Her eyes were cold and her lips were thin, cruel. But those cheekbones, the strong line of her jaw, that black hair . . .

Oh my God, there *was* a resemblance.

"Do not be ridiculous," Mona Sera said sharply, with what almost sounded like pain.

"Milady. She wears a silver cross against her skin and it does not weaken her," Sonia said. She was a gentle woman, with kind eyes and light brown hair the color of autumn leaves after they had fallen from the trees. "She is a Mixed Blood."

"She cannot be a Mixed Blood. She has our strength and speed, and she is a Queen," Mona Sera said. But she narrowed her eyes and looked with that extra sense beyond the five that humans possessed. "How interesting," she murmured. "When were you born?"

I arched my brow. "The day I was found in the orphanage was October 31, twenty-one years ago."

"Is that the date?" Mona Sera queried Sonia. The other woman nodded.

My eyes narrowed. "You have to ask someone else when your daughter was born?"

"Why should I remember it?" was her arrogant reply.

"Bitch," was mine.

Gryphon squeezed my shoulder in warning as I processed the information that the cross I had cherished and worn against my heart all my life had not been given to me by my mother as I had thought. Mona Sera had not recognized the cross in any way.

With slow certainty I turned my eyes to the woman who must have given it to me, who must have named me. The woman who had remembered the day and year I had been born. Who had recognized that cross.

"Her palms," Sonia said quietly. "She should have the marks."

"Show us your palms, girl," Mona Sera commanded.

I curled my hands into fists, bristling against the order. Gryphon squeezed my shoulder gently, persuasively. But it was the quiet plea in Sonia's compassionate eyes that I could not resist.

Goddammit, why couldn't you have been my mother instead? I wailed inside as I uncurled my fists and held out my palms. Everyone gasped again. I was beginning to feel like a circus monkey, performing trick after trick.

"The Goddess's tears," Mona Sera said, looking at my pearly moles. "I remember thinking it such a waste on a Mixed Blood child."

I'd always wondered who my mother was. Looking at Mona Sera's proud icy face that reflected not one ounce of maternal warmth, I felt the truth of that old adage: Be careful what you wish for.

Then my eyes fell to Amber's quivering prostrate form and things shifted into better perspective.

Okay, so my mother was a sick, murdering bitch. At least she was sane.

∿

I FOUND MYSELF locked in the dungeon for the rest of the day. A real honest-to-god dungeon. What else did one expect in the basement of a beautiful manor house masquerading as an ugly warehouse? The stone walls were damp and there was no light, but I didn't need any to see. If this was how she treated a daughter, I wondered how she treated an enemy.

The door was made out of silver, and no, that didn't stop me. The slow beating heart armed with my own knives behind the door did, however. That, and the fact that Mona Sera was taking and presenting me to the High Queens' Council the very next night. It was what Gryphon and I had wanted, after all.

I sank down onto the stone floor and felt the sun rise and worried about Gryphon. He had been taken away and I had forborne asking Mona Sera about him, instinctively knowing that any concern evidenced for him on my part would be seen as a weakness to be used and exploited by her. I wasn't a daughter to her. I was just an interesting tool, like a hammer she could swing, a novelty she could present to the court and claim credit for. None of it mattered, as long as she took us there.

I must have dozed. The sound of a key turning and door opening awakened me. The light from the stairwell fell on my guard's hair showing its true color, a blond so light it appeared white at first glance, but upon closer look revealed that faint touch of yellow. His eyes were a striking green, not that brownish mix of green more commonly seen, but pure emerald green that made one think of the rich verdant jungles of the Amazon. He had the same cheerful smile that he had worn when hc was about to rape me.

"Allow me to introduce myself. Beldar, at your service." He bowed with a courtly flourish, and held out a package to me, his eyes fixed politely on my face and not on my exposed cleavage, smart man. A cleavage that he himself had exposed, allowing all eyes to see. "My Queen invites you to break fast with her and bids you wear this gown."

I took the package from him and opened it. It was a long dress. Black silk.

"Step outside and close the door while I change," I said.

"You wound me with your mistrust," Beldar replied. "Surely you don't hold our little skirmish against me. I was the one wounded."

I sniffed and didn't smell blood. "Your wound seems to have closed."

He flashed me a charming smile, arrogant devil. "We heal fast. Say you forgive me."

"When you return my knives."

"Not until we reach the court," returned Beldar regretfully. "By my Queen's command."

"The door," I said.

With a sigh, he closed it and I quickly changed. The dress fell about my feet in a full, rich swirl. A near-perfect fit at the waist but a bit loose at the chest, confirming my suspicion that the dress was Mona Sera's. Pity I hadn't inherited her full bosom. Not what I would have chosen to wear, but it was better than going around in a torn shirt with my breasts half hanging out.

"I'm done," I said, not bothering to speak loudly, knowing he would hear me.

The door swung open and Beldar's eyes widened in appreciation. He gestured up the stairs and inclined his head. "Ladies first."

"No, you first. I insist."

"Don't trust me at your back?"

"Nope. Not someone who would have raped me with a smile on his face."

"I would have thanked you afterward," he said winsomely, and I couldn't hold back a small smile. He might have been an opportunistic bastard, but there was no denying he was a charming one.

He grinned back at me. "Very well."

I followed Beldar up the stairs and he led the way to the dining room. It was furnished with austere simplicity, with elegant black chairs set against neutral walls and natural wood floors. Everyone was already there, seated around a long formal table set with fine china, polished silverware, crystal candelabras, and gleaming candlelight. Mona Sera sat at the head of the table. Only the men were present. No other women. Nor were Gryphon or Amber present, I noted unhappily.

Beldar seated me at the foot of the table, a position of honor, perhaps, or maybe because it was the farthest seat away from Mona Sera. Far enough so that the irritating, abrasive presence of another Queen was hardly felt. The presence of over twenty men in close proximity, on the other hand, was like a fresh punch to my senses. I didn't fight the awareness, just let it flow over me, grateful to be sitting down. The trick, I learned, was to absorb it, then tune it down like unwanted noise. The men closest to me held themselves stiffly and looked at me warily, and I wondered sardonically if it was because they were afraid of jumping me or afraid that I might jump them.

Mona Sera inclined her head, the gracious host. "I am so pleased you could join us, Mona Lisa." She'd had to ask my name last night. Nope, my cross had definitely not come from her.

"My pleasure," I said dryly, knowing she would have ensured I joined them whether I had desired it or not.

The food was brought out and I found out where the women were—serving us, silly me. From the corner of my eye, I watched Sonia serve Queen Mona Sera first. A quiet, subdued woman—all the women seemed quiet and subdued, for that matter—laid a plate before me. I glanced down. The steak was bloodier than I was used to but I forced myself to eat a few bites. A girl had to keep up her strength, especially in this crowd.

"We have a surprise treat for dessert," Mona Sera said, evil satisfaction lacing her voice. It had been surprisingly quiet and civilized up until then. I'd known it couldn't last.

The door opened and the smell hit me first: heated raw flesh. Gryphon stumbled in, supporting a barely conscious man. Both wore only pants, their tops naked. Gryphon's chest and face were reddened as if he'd gotten a light sunburn, but the other taller, bigger man was a mass of fiery, lobster-red flesh covered by not just blisters, but boils—huge half-dollar size boils that had broken open and oozed a pink-tinged exudate. His eyes were so swollen and puffed with fluid that he couldn't open his eyelids, and his lips were thickened and covered with open sores. His face was distorted beyond the point of recognition. Only the man's size and chestnut hair let me know that it was Amber I was seeing.

Gryphon guided Amber to kneel before Mona Sera. A thick peel of skin sloughed off from beneath Amber's arm and side as Gryphon removed his supporting arm and fell to his knees as well.

"Amber, you seem to be a little tired after your day in the sun, your punishment for disobeying me," Mona Sera said with a chuckle. The laughter stopped abruptly. "But you, my dear Gryphon, seemed to have acquired nothing more than a light tan."

She swung her narrowed eyes my way. "Let me guess, dear daughter. The sun's rays do not burn you."

"No more than it does most humans," I acknowledged.

"Dear, dear. You seem to have passed your gift to our sweet Gryphon," Mona Sera said. "And after only one night together. How interesting."

I was beginning to hate it when she said that. It meant that she was thinking, and nothing good could come of that.

"Fortunate for me that Gryphon was hardly damaged by the ordeal. I'd like him to be of *some* use to me at court," I responded coolly.

Mona Sera looked at me thoughtfully. "You speak as if Gryphon is yours."

I shrugged. "I thought you had thrown him away. I find myself having to take what I can find. Your damaged goods . . . unless you care to gift me with some of your healthy, strong men. Like your lovely Beldar, perhaps."

I smiled at Beldar and he froze into stillness, the look in his eye not thanking me at all for drawing him into this. *My pleasure,* my eyes conveyed back to him.

Mona Sera bared her teeth in a chilly smile. "No, daughter, I think not, although it is true. You must have some protection at court."

"Then I must make do with your castoffs—Gryphon . . . and Amber."

"You would take Amber as well?" Mona Sera lifted a brow at my presumptuousness. "I doubt he will live in any case."

"Better for me if he does. Would it not be an impressive statement to the High Council to have him seen under your daughter's leash?"

"An impressive statement, indeed. I like how your mind thinks."

Mona Sera smiled thinly but her eyes were cold. "But why should I be so generous?"

I leaned back in my chair. "It was my birthday last week. I'll take them as a birthday present."

Mona Sera looked at me for a long moment in utter silence. Then she threw her head back and laughed and laughed until tears of mirth flowed down her chiseled cheeks. And all the men laughed with her. Not because they found it funny but because they were afraid not to laugh.

"A birthday present!" Mona Sera wiped away her tears, chuckling. "Very well. My gift to you." The laughter ceased abruptly. "Be ready. We leave in an hour."

❧

WE WERE DOWN in the dungeon once again. Even with Gryphon's substantial helping hand, it had taken a monumental effort on Amber's part, using up the last reserves of his strength to make it down the stairs without falling.

"There's no place to lay him down," I said, wanting to help but unable to hold Amber any place without sloughing off more of his burned skin.

"The ground," Gryphon grunted.

"It's dirty."

"We do not get infections."

I laughed humorlessly. "Just sun and silver poisoning." I spread my old pants and shirt on the floor and Gryphon gently lowered Amber down to the ground. The wounded giant let out a harsh groan of pain as his raw, ravaged back touched the floor.

"God," I breathed, looking at the horrible mess he was. "Can his body heal this?"

Gryphon looked at me and shook his head. He glanced at Beldar, who was supposed to be guarding us but instead hovered by the door. "Beldar, could you bring us some water, clean cloth, and some salve?"

Beldar hesitated, clearly torn over whether or not to leave us unattended. His gaze drew almost compulsively back to Amber. Or rather, to what used to be Amber. Nodding jerkily, his face wiped clean of humor, Beldar left, leaving me troubled.

In that brief unguarded moment, I had caught a glimpse of the man beneath Beldar's carefree façade and I realized that I had underestimated him. I would not do so again.

"What can we do?" I asked Gryphon.

"You passed your ability to withstand the sun's rays to me," Gryphon said. "Perhaps you can do so as well with him."

I looked at him blankly. "You want me to *fuck* him?"

Gryphon spread his hands. "As you see, males may gain power from joining with a Queen."

"Gryphon," I said carefully. "Even if I wanted to, I don't think he's in any condition right now for sex."

"I can think of nothing else that might save him, milady."

"Queens don't fuck all their men. Even I know that," I said harshly.

"You are correct," Gryphon said, his own voice edging with hardness. "But it is a Queen's duty and responsibility to care for her men in the same manner that those men care for and protect their Queen."

"Perhaps you should tell Mona Sera that instead of me."

Gryphon sighed, a weary sound from deep within his soul. "As I have stated before, Mona Sera ranks among one of our worst Queens."

"Always nice to hear that about one's mother."

Gryphon pressed a comforting hand to my shoulder. I brought his hand to my cheek and went into his arms, seeking comfort in his embrace. "Thank God you're alive. I'm sorry, so sorry. It's my fault we were caught."

He shushed me. "I should have realized the pull the moon, the ceremony, would have over you."

"How could you when I'd never felt it before, not that strongly?" I sniffed and pushed away from him. "Mona Sera claims she does not have the cure for silver poisoning." In truth, she had told me that there was no cure.

He dredged up a smile. "It was a poor hope to begin with."

"But we're going to the High Court. We'll ask the other Queens there. Seek out healers."

Gryphon smiled, raised my hand to his lips and placed a tender kiss there. "My heart," he murmured. "But if I am to die, all the more reason to try to save Amber. Though his spirit has been damaged by his years under Mona Sera's rule, he is still a great warrior and will serve you well if you can but save him."

I gazed at him with stricken eyes. "How can you want me to sleep with him?"

"Only a small part of you is human," Gryphon said gently. "The greater part of you is of the moon. We are not like humans. It is natural for Queens to be drawn to more than one man, to take many of them as lovers, as is it natural for men to desire to join with a Queen. It is a survival instinct deeply inbred to increase the chances of a fertile union."

"It might not even help," I said. "He's already burned."

"But it cannot hurt him," Gryphon returned with infallible logic. "And I sense a strong healing power hidden deep inside you. Perchance you may pass that to him. If you truly wish to claim him as you said, then be his Queen. Be our Queen."

I gazed down at Amber. His swollen eyes were closed so he could not see us. I didn't even know if he could talk. But he could still hear us.

"Do you wish this, Amber?" I asked.

Amber lay there unmoving for so long that I thought for a fleeting moment he had lost consciousness. Then his breath wheezed out of his swollen passages and his cracked, blistered lips moved, straining to speak. But his tongue was so thickened and his mouth was so dry, only a garbled sound emerged. He swallowed painfully and tried again. Once more, mutilated sound came out, not words.

"I can't understand you, Amber," I said. "Just nod or shake your head."

Amber's tense mouth and neck relaxed. He nodded.

I took a deep breath and bent down to him, the decision made. I would try to save him. He was under my care now. I just hadn't known what it would mean when I'd bargained for him.

Gryphon carefully removed Amber's pants. Untouched by the sun, Amber's skin below the waist was smooth, marble white. Unblemished. His long shaft was soft, too wracked by pain to be aroused.

I couldn't do it. It seemed wrong to touch him like this while he was in agony.

"Close your eyes," Gryphon whispered, kissing my lids closed. "Just touch him like this." He guided my hand to Amber's thigh. With my eyes shut, I did my best to block out the smell and just concentrate on the pleasure of touching him. He was hairier than Gryphon, with long cinnamon hair dusting his thighs and legs. They were silkier than they looked. I smoothed my hand down his leg and felt the tingle of desire strengthen and spark between us.

"Your skin is so soft," I murmured in surprise and appreciation, flowing with the natural attraction, bringing my other hand up to stroke around the bones of Amber's knee and down the hard swell of his calf, to trace the graceful lines of tendons and muscles. I rubbed my cheek against his hairy shin and caught the faint scent of his skin.

"You smell of musk. Like fur." And I liked it. The smell called to something within me. I kissed my way up a few inches then nuzzled him behind his knee, licking him in that soft, vulnerable spot. His leg twitched in my grasp.

"You taste of salt and sweat," I said, and did not protest when Gryphon unzipped my gown, lifted it off me, unhooked my bra, and slid my underwear down. I slid my body around that strong leg, rubbed my breasts against him and felt his hair tickle my sensitive nipples. I opened my mouth and sank my teeth into his sinewy thigh, stroking the firm muscles with my tongue, making my way up in leisurely manner, stopping here and there to take a mouthful of that brawny flesh, to test its suppleness between my teeth, to lave and lick him until I reached the hollow of his groin. I opened my eyes then, careful to look at just his lower body.

"Ah. You're happy to see me," I murmured. "And very, very big, like the rest of you." I took him into my mouth, my hair spilling over him like a flowing silk curtain. I had to stretch my mouth open to its widest so I could take him in. It was an unusual sensation, having him within my mouth, and not an unpleasant one. I swirled my tongue over the ridged head, and felt his thighs tense beneath me as I licked the sensitive rim around his cap.

"So thick." A tiny pearl of pre-come fluid oozed responsively out like a sweet tear. I put my mouth back over his tip, lapped him there, and sucked hard. Drawing out every last bit of the fluid, I swallowed and rumbled my appreciation. "You taste even better than a lollipop. Salty and sweet." The scent of our arousal lay heavy in the air as I nuzzled him.

Closing my eyes, I straddled him, guided him to me, and felt his thick shaft probe my entrance. But he didn't go in. I groaned with pleasure and frustration. Circling against him, lubricating him with my moisture while pleasing myself, I sank down onto him once more.

"Oh, God," I breathed. "You're so big." I took him in, centimeter by delicious centimeter, feeling his broad head stretch me more and more. And he was still only a couple of inches within me. I lifted up, felt his cry of protest and drove myself back down onto him, deeper. I groaned with the luxurious feel of him within me and circled my hips, taking him increment by tiny, torturous increment into me. Then lifted up and sank down again and again, until he glided more smoothly, more easily within me.

"I want all of you." I panted, lifting up and thrusting down with more force. Still, it was not enough.

His hands suddenly gripped my hips, holding me down, as he speared up into me, making me cry out. He withdrew and plunged again, and light shimmered beyond my closed lids and I knew we were glowing. I felt the wave of power grow and grow with each stroke that I met and matched with my own rhythm and force. He tilted me abruptly forward so that his shaft rubbed against my wet, swollen clitoris and thrust into me with a strength that made me gasp, burying himself to the hilt. And I thought desperately, *Heal* . . . *Heal* . . . as the wave broke and my climax burst within me.

Amber withdrew and drove within me two more times. Then he cried out and grew rigid, spurting deep within me, filling me with his warm essence.

"Your hands are hot," growled a deep voice.

It took me a moment to realize that it was Amber who had spoken, and to register the significance of it. I opened my eyes and found my hands resting on his chest and saw with shock and wonder that his flesh was whole. Amazingly whole. Free of boils and sores. All that lingered from his ordeal was darkened skin like Gryphon's, faintly reddened. His lips were no longer swollen and his blue eyes had changed to startling amber flames, like his name. They blazed up at me with golden crystal clarity.

The world suddenly reversed and I found myself on my back, Amber looming above me, his brawny arms braced on either side of my head. I gasped as he moved, as I felt him lengthen and harden within me in the space of one slow heartbeat. He moved again, the slightest caress, growing even bigger, and a moan slid out of me and my lids fluttered shut. But some other sound, some movement made me open them again.

Beldar stood framed in the doorway, his avid gaze fixed upon us, his arms piled high with sheets, a large bowl balancing on top, a jar dangling forgotten from one hand.

I stiffened with a cry of distress and pushed against Amber's chest, scarlet with mortification and embarrassment.

The look Amber shot Beldar had the slighter man turning abruptly away and averting his gaze.

I clamped my lips tightly shut, suppressing another moan as Amber slid out of me and rolled to his side, shielding me from view with his larger body.

The touch of his large hand against my face stilled my mad scrambling.

"Thank you." Simple words, but his eyes . . . Amber's blank shield of control was down, revealing emotions that were almost overwhelming in their intensity.

"You're welcome," I whispered, distressed by what I had glimpsed.

This had been a one-time deal as far as I was concerned. I had to let him know that, but the words blocked in my throat, unable to come out with him looking at me like that.

Gryphon brought the gown to me and I gratefully pulled it over me. Amber stood up with a total disregard for his nakedness, with a casualness that I envied. I kept my eyes carefully averted from that part of him still wet with our mixed essence, that part that bobbed and swayed with his movements, and made my way determinedly to the door.

Beldar backed away at my approach as if I were dangerous. It brought a twisted smile to my lips that seemed to make him even more nervous. Good.

"I need to shower," I announced. "We all do."

～⁌～

SOME OTHER MALES ended up escorting Gryphon and Amber to their rooms, their shocked gazes swinging from Amber back to me, while Beldar remained at my side, careful to keep at least five feet of distance between us, which was fine by me. All I cared about was getting my shower. That, and feeding my men. It seemed I had two of them now.

"Amber and Gryphon need to eat," I pronounced when I was done showering. The room I had used was simply furnished, in sharp contrast to the opulence of the main floor, the pink towels that I dried myself with the only feminine touches of beauty in the stark room.

"The kitchen is down the hall to the left." Beldar indicated that I proceed ahead of him.

"What, don't trust me at your back?" I sneered, walking toward him, feeling perverse, cruel satisfaction as he backed away. "Afraid I'll jump you . . . or that you'll jump me?"

Beldar grinned, his hands spread placatingly wide. "Exquisite though you may be . . ."

I snorted.

". . . I have no desire to fry in the sun or die in some other painful manner."

And I had no real desire to get into any more trouble. Things were going our way. I didn't want to screw things up. Really, I didn't. I stopped crowding him and walked to the kitchen, where Sonia and two other women were washing dishes and doing what women all over the world do in kitchens. To my relief, there was no irritating abrasiveness or attractive rush in their presence, just a comforting recognition of like to like.

"Mona Lisa." The warmth in Sonia's eyes made my heart tighten painfully.

"Amber and Gryphon didn't eat," I said more bluntly than I intended because I felt awkward in her presence.

"Amber is well enough to eat?" Sonia asked, surprise and relief evident in her eyes.

I nodded.

"I had some food set aside for them. Just in case. Where are they?" Sonia asked.

"In their rooms," Beldar replied. "Cleaning up and packing for the trip."

"Lily, Roselyn," Sonia said to the other women. "Could you please fetch the two of them down to the dining table?"

The women left silently. Sonia took out two plates of food that had been warming in the oven and brought them into the next room. I followed her with Beldar a silent shadow behind me. There were no marks or bruises evident upon Sonia. Either they were hidden beneath her clothes or they had already healed.

"You don't resent Amber?" I asked, confused. Amber had raped her, hadn't he? I knew him intimately now, knew how much damage he could inflict with his incredible size.

"How can I?" Sadness laced her words as she placed the plates of food down upon the table. "He was a victim as much as I. And he was as gentle as he could be."

There was so much I needed to ask her, to say to her. But Beldar's presence burned like a restraining brand. He was Mona Sera's eyes and ears, and I could only look at Sonia in uncomfortable silence.

She felt no such constraint. She took my hands into her smaller ones and squeezed feelingly. "Oh, Mona Lisa. I am so glad you are well."

"I . . ." Sliding my hands from hers, I laid my hand over my hidden cross. "Thank you."

Sonia smiled. "You are most welcome," she said softly with understanding.

The male escorts delivered Gryphon and Amber into the dining room, then left, casting me wary, speculative glances that had me gritting my teeth.

"Oh, my," Sonia said, looking at the healed Amber with amazement. Her gaze dropped down to his hands, then flew back up again. His eyes met hers briefly, awkwardly, acknowledging her politely then looking away, busying himself with the task of eating. Gryphon likewise started in on his dinner, his appetite good though he looked a little tired. We were all tired, for that matter.

"You are a healer and quite powerful for one so young," Sonia said with quiet awe.

"I don't know that I healed Amber, per se," I admitted. "He may have just acquired my tolerance of the sun. Do you have a healer here I can speak to?"

"No, which is why we all thought Amber would surely perish."

"Is that why everyone looks so surprised?" I asked.

"That and the extent of his recovery." Sonia paused and I had a feeling that she had left something unsaid. "There are few healers who could do what you did. There are some at High Court where we are going. I am sure they will be as eager to converse with you as you with them."

SIX

How did Moonies travel? Wealthy ones, that is. They flew. In their own private jet. We didn't need to pass through the other Queens' territories; we simply passed over them. Solved a lot of problems.

Mona Sera sat up front in her well-appointed private jet. Marble gleamed and gold trim sparkled. Surrounded by her eight guards, she swiveled around in her reclinable seat and studied us with a smug, calculating expression like a cat who had just swallowed clotted cream. Or perhaps more like a snake that had just downed a rat whole and was digesting it while it still squirmed, alive within her. I sat in the rear with the whole distance of the plane between us, snug between Amber and Gryphon, and yawned.

"Sleep," Gryphon told me, lifting the armrest between us and drawing me against his side.

Ignoring Mona Sera's reptilian eyes making a cold study of us,

I snuggled into his arms and rested my head against his shoulder. "Amber and you need to rest as well."

"We'll take turns."

"Turns?"

"One of us needs to remain alert. I shall take first watch."

I blinked. "Oh. I'll take the next then. Wake me when it's my turn."

Gryphon and Amber exchanged a look. "An honorable notion," Gryphon said, "but that won't be necessary. Amber and I will suffice."

"Men. Still the same. Full of macho crap," I muttered, too tired to argue with them. My lids closed, much too heavy to lift back up, so I missed the smile my men shared.

I awoke three hours later as we were descending, my head in Gryphon's lap, his hand stroking my hair. I sat up, tucking the loose strands behind my ears. "Did you two get any rest?"

"Yes."

I turned to Amber. "How are you feeling?"

"Better, milady," he replied politely, that cool control back in place. His normal defense and demeanor, I suspected.

My hand automatically reached out to assess him, then stopped. I hesitated, uncomfortable about touching him so freely. "May I?"

Amber nodded, his firm lips unsmiling.

I gingerly freed one button and slid my hand over his bare chest. My palm tingled and I smiled happily as I read him. "You are well." I buttoned him back up awkwardly while he sat there gravely, letting me perform the small task.

I turned to Gryphon and he lifted his shirt without my having to ask. My palm tingled and itched but didn't heat as I covered his wound. There was no happy smile with him. The poison was spreading slowly, insidiously, and there was not a damn thing I could do about it. I removed my hand without looking at him.

"It's all right," Gryphon said with a gentleness that moistened my eyes.

I shook my head. It wasn't. It wasn't all right at all. I looked up to meet Mona Sera's black moribund eyes. The plane thudded lightly as we landed and she swung her chair back around, that morose, calculating mind of hers computing all she had seen, no doubt.

We had landed on a nicely appointed private airstrip in Bennington, Minnesota. A generous expanse of black tarmac was visible under the bright night-lights that lined the airfield. Whatever the Monère were, they did not seem to lack money.

"Why is the High Court here?" I asked as we descended the steps. "What's in Minnesota?"

"Exactly," Gryphon said dryly. "We own hundreds of acres of wooded land here and the climate is cool year-round. Canada abuts us less than twenty miles to the north and we are encircled by private Indian reserves and state parks on all other sides. Ideal, is it not? If one wants isolation."

Three new generic gray vans awaited us. Two drivers were Full Blood males, but the third was a Mixed Blood with red hair and ginger-red freckles sprinkled across his young, perky face. I knew he was a Mixed Blood because he radiated much less power, barely any at all, in fact. We stared at each other with equal fascination. There was no pull between us, only a sense of recognition, as with the women, but much fainter.

"Are there many Mixed Bloods here?" I whispered to Gryphon as they loaded our luggage into the vans.

"Very few. They are rare among us. Almost all live among the humans, unaware of our existence."

"Why?"

"Mixed Bloods are essentially human, more fragile, requiring more care, and they often die if left among us. Most are abandoned at human hospitals, orphanages, or such facilities at birth."

As I had been. My hand unconsciously rose to finger my cross.

Beldar approached, handing me back my knives and returning Amber his sword. I gazed at the sword closely. It was full length, quite long, in fact, but looked almost toy-sized once strapped to Amber's girth.

We rode for five long minutes along a private paved road, the only disturbance to the otherwise natural, pristine land, before reaching a sprawling compound where several smaller buildings flanked a large, three-storied stately manor house. Untamed forest surrounded and enclosed us in wild, peaceful serenity. The sky began to lighten as night slowly ebbed into rosy dawn.

An impeccably groomed man not much taller than I bowed to Mona Sera, his black hair touched with silver strands at the sides though his face remained unlined. "Welcome, Queen Mona Sera. It has been too long since you last graced us with your presence." A small army of attendants stood at attention behind the neat little man.

"Thank you, Mathias," Mona Sera replied with a true enigma of a smile. It told you fucking nothing. "This is my daughter, Mona Lisa."

Mathias swept a low bow. "Most welcome, young Queen. We are pleased you have come. My title is that of steward here in the Great House. If you have any needs or questions, please do not hesitate to seek me out. Some of the other Council members have arrived but have already retired for the day. More shall arrive tomorrow. I will show you to your quarters for now and let you seek your rest."

Under his efficient guidance, the luggage was separated and carried upstairs. Mona Sera and her eight guards were taken down one hall, and I, gratefully, down another hall. I was given a large, luxuriously appointed suite with two separate but adjoining bedrooms, normal but for the fact that there were no windows. Sure beat sleeping in coffins, I guess.

The door closed, leaving the three of us alone in the larger bedroom in sudden silence.

"Where would you like the luggage?" Amber asked, his strong, rugged face carefully blank.

I swallowed. Well, hell, maybe the coffins wouldn't have been so bad after all. Would have solved the dilemma of where we were all going to sleep. "Um, they're all yours, right? I didn't bring anything."

"The small trunk belongs to you," Gryphon said. "Sonia packed you some clothing and other such items."

"Bless her. Then you can leave that here. And your things, Gryphon, if you'd like." The latter was added on softly, a shy afterthought.

A beautiful smile lit Gryphon's face. "I would like that."

Without a word, without any change in expression, Amber hefted his trunk easily and carried it to the next room. I threw Gryphon a troubled look and followed Amber into the other bedroom, closing the door behind me. "Amber?"

He set the trunk down at the foot of the bed. "Yes, milady." Reserve colored Amber's voice and face. But I remembered that burning flare of emotion in his eyes.

"What we did . . ." I chewed my lip. "I know the greater part of me is Monère, but I'm still human, inside me, in my mind." My voice softened. "You are a magnificent lover."

The blueness of his eyes heated, causing me to rush on hastily.

"But I want what other human women want. Just one man. And for me, that's Gryphon."

Amber's eyes, so terribly expressive when he allowed it, lowered to the ground. "I understand, milady."

"I know it's horribly unfair to you." I took in a deep bracing breath and released it. "Amber, you are free to go to another Queen. Is there any particular one you wish to go to? If there is, I will try to intercede on your behalf."

Amber's head snapped back up and an intimidating scowl darkened his face. He shook his head. "It has been over twenty-three years since a Queen last took me to her bed."

My brows creased together. What the heck did he mean by that? That he was willing to forgo sex? Or that he didn't mind waiting that long to "mate," as they seemed to term it, with me again? Dammit, I'd never been good at guessing games. I struggled on. "Is there a certain Queen you wish . . ."

"No," he responded brusquely.

"Do you guys date or something?" I ventured tentatively. "Other Full Blood women?"

"Mona Sera did not allow it." His voice was a low growl. He seemed as uncomfortable with the topic as I was.

"Oh. Well, it would be fine with me," I said, backing toward the door. "More than fine. If you saw them, you know. Other women. Not *rape* them," I added hastily, just for definite clarity. "But you can sleep with them. Have sex with them. Consensually, that is." I was babbling like an idiot, I realized, and shut my mouth.

"I understand, milady."

"If at any time you, uh, change your mind about going to another Queen . . ."

"I will not change my mind," Amber said sternly.

"Well, if you do . . . just let me know." I had my hand on the orknob and was turning it, blissful escape only a moment away, when he spoke again.

"Milady?"

"Yes?"

"Why did you save me," he asked, his voice a deep quiet rumble, "if you do not desire me or wish my protection?"

Escape had been so freaking close. I blew out a breath, releasing my grip on the knob, and turned back to face Amber and the incredibly awkward discussion that I so badly wanted to drop. "It's not that I don't desire you. I do. But I am not going to sleep with every male I lust after."

"Other Queens do."

No statement could have set me off more. "I'm not like other Queens!" I almost shouted. "Nor do I wish to be," I added more quietly. "I do value your protection, Amber. Don't misunderstand me. You are more than three other men. I just wanted to give you a choice. I want you to be happy."

"Why?" he asked.

"Why?" I repeated, incredulously. "Because everyone deserves to be happy."

It seemed an alien concept to him. And that honest bewilderment almost broke my heart.

"Why did you save me?" Amber asked again.

I ran my fingers through my hair. "I don't know. Because you did nothing to warrant your punishment. Because it was hard for me to just stand by and not at least try to save you if it was within my power to do so."

He looked at me like an intricate puzzle he could not reason out.

I'd done everything short of ripping open a vein with that little speech. It would have to be enough. "Good night, Amber. Are you sure . . ."

"I will not leave you, my Queen," he said testily.

For some perverse reason, it pleased me that Amber sounded so vexed with me.

"I'm glad." I flashed him a warm, grateful smile, trying to convey to him that I did value him, that I was happy he had chosen to stay with me.

I closed the connecting door gently behind me.

Gryphon had unpacked and stored the trunks somewhere. He sat waiting for me on the bed, my beautiful wounded creature of the night.

"Are you tired?" I asked.

"Do you wish to seek your rest?"

"After I eat. I'm hungry. It was hard to eat with Mona Sera watching me. Do you think they have any spaghetti or pizza around here?" I asked wistfully.

His brow furrowed. "I do not know. Let us go see."

Amber was waiting for us out in the hallway, a towering grim-looking guardian angel. I grimaced.

"The doors just give the illusion of privacy, I guess," I grumbled.

"I will accompany you," Amber said.

"It will be more prudent, milady," Gryphon added, forestalling any protest from me.

I blew out a breath, letting go of my irritation. "I'm sorry, guys."

"Not at all," replied Gryphon most solemnly. "It is our duty to see to the care and feeding of our human."

Even Amber cracked a smile.

"Ha, ha. Very funny." But my stomach was making its demands felt and it was letting me know that bad jokes would not fill it.

A footman met us at the bottom of the stairs. "How can I serve you?" Acute hearing had its uses.

"Milady wishes for some food," Gryphon replied. "Do you perchance have some spaghetti or pizza?"

"Anything but steak," I said.

A brow raised as if to acknowledge what odd requests humans make. "I shall see what we can do. This way, please."

It was a lovely old house, decorated with antiques and delightfully ancient portraits of dignified men and women, some in the Elizabethan style of dress, one bearing the red cross of the Crusades, another in actual armor with a helmet resting in the crook of an elbow. One portrait of a slim, elegant man with dark hair, silvered at the temples, stood out, his bronze skin glowing like a warm beacon among all the other pale faces. He looked quite ordinary otherwise but for his long, pointed nails.

The attendant brought us to the dining room, seated us at one of the smaller tables, and disappeared into the kitchen. A moment later the door swung open and the redheaded Mixed Blood who had fascinated me so much earlier, entered bearing—God bless his part-human soul—a tray of cheese, crackers, and fruits. Yum, yum.

"I had it ready," the redhead said, giving me a toothy grin. "Just in case."

"Oh!" I exclaimed with delight, and gestured for him to sit and join us. He did so readily, watching with enjoyment as I proceeded to stuff my face.

"Mmm, heavenly," I declared, the sweet juice of a grape bursting in my mouth.

Amber leaned down and sniffed the cheese, his face creased in a frown. "It smells of decay."

"That's cheese—mold. Try some," I mumbled, my mouth full.

Amber answered politely enough though his lips curled with distaste. "No, thank you, milady."

"I have to seal up the cheese airtight or it drives everyone crazy," the man—boy, really—said.

"What's your name?" I asked.

"I'm Jamie. You?"

"Mona Lisa."

"How old are you?"

"Nineteen. You?"

"Twenty-one."

"I have an older sister," he lobbed back, his freckles practically dancing on his lively face. "Tersa. Five years older than me."

"Is she also . . ."

Jamie nodded. "Yeah. I'll bring Tersa and my mom to meet you tomorrow."

"Great! I'd like that."

Amber and Gryphon followed our mad volley of words back and forth until Jamie and I just stopped and grinned idiotically at each other.

"This is so cool," I exclaimed, happy to be in the presence of someone like me. Even better, someone who talked like me.

"Cool?" Amber rumbled the word testingly in his deep bass baritone.

"Yeah, cool. Like neat, wow, nice," I explained. "How old are you, anyway, Amber?"

"A hundred and five."

My eyes grew nicely rounded. "Really?"

Jamie whistled. "Ancient, man."

Amber eyed him repressively.

"We'll get him to lighten up," I whispered.

Jamie eyed the big man doubtfully. "You think?" he whispered back.

"Sure. The bigger they are . . ."

". . . the harder they fall," Jamie and I chortled together.

"And boy, does the ground shake when this guy falls," I said, laughing.

"How do you know?"

" 'Cause I threw him."

Jamie's eyes almost popped out. "Nah, you're kidding me."

I put my right hand up in the air. "I swear."

"Really? Can you teach me? My sister, too?"

"Sure."

"Cool," Jamie breathed.

If we'd had tails, they would have been wagging.

Gryphon winced. "Enough, children."

Jamie glanced at Gryphon and whispered, "Another old guy?"

"Yeah. Seventy-five."

"What's up with you and older guys?"

"Don't know." I shrugged my shoulders. "But you gotta admit. They're interesting. And they sure do talk pretty."

Gryphon sighed and Amber wore a pained expression as Jamie and I smirked at each other.

I pushed back my chair, blissfully replete. "Okay, bedtime. Thanks, Jamie. That was great."

"What would you like tomorrow?"

"Got any spaghetti?"

"Meatballs?"

"Nah, just plain old noodles and tomato sauce."

"You got it."

We trudged up the stairs.

"Children, huh?" I said later, nestled contentedly against Gryphon's chest. It was fast becoming my favorite spot.

"Sometimes I forget how young you are," Gryphon murmured,

lightly stroking my hair. He seemed to enjoy playing with the long strands, rubbing them between his fingers.

"Thanks, I think. 'S not so bad here."

"You seem to have found a friend."

"Isn't he great? Can't wait to meet his sister." A jaw-cracking yawn escaped me. I covered my mouth and giggled. How unlike myself. *I never used to giggle,* was my last thought before sleep blanketed me like a downy quilt. "Good night, Gryphon," I said, closing my eyes.

"Sweet dreams, Mona Lisa," Gryphon murmured, stroking my hair as I drifted off. "Sweet dreams."

SEVEN

THE SUN WAS a low fireball in the sky with sunset still hours away when I awoke refreshed, content, luxuriating in the feel of my lover beside me, the gentle beating of his heart, the soft soughing of his breath. I lifted my head from Gryphon's chest, stared down into his face, and my breath caught anew at the heartrending beauty that he had been graced with. I wanted to run my hands through the thick waves of his hair, taste his mouth, feel the downy softness of his nape. But I let him sleep, let him rest, and eased slowly out of the comfortable bed.

I listened for a moment and sensed no movement in the other room. Amber was still sleeping. I opened my senses even wider and detected no discernable stirring in the house below. I donned the silver cross I had laid on the bedside table, slipped into the black gown that was too formal for my taste, and eased quietly out of the room and down the stairs, escaping outside.

It was a beautiful day, cool and crisp with the coming winter, with the ebbing sunlight gentle against my eyes. It had been a while since I had seen the brightness of day since working the evening shift at St. Vincent's. How far away that all seemed now, that life, that job. Yet only two short days had passed. And all had changed.

The forest beckoned me and I stepped into its woody embrace, breathing in the scent of the damp earth beneath the carpet of leaves, free and safe in the sunlight. It was not animals that I worried about, but others of my kind. They were by far more dangerous. But they slept now and I was safe in my solitude.

The sound of running water tickled my ear and I followed it to a small clearing, delighted with my find. A gurgling brook ran before a sprawling tree with the perfect sitting branch, the grass flattened by creatures that had stopped to slacken their thirst. I knelt and sipped the cold water, sweeter than any that flowed from the faucet, and laughed with delight, lifting my face to the sky.

There was no sound, just a feeling that had me whirling around. A golden-skinned man stood there across the clearing, with hair so dark brown that it was almost black. He was dressed oddly for woodside wandering, wearing a flowing white silk shirt. The sparkle of diamonds flashed from his cufflinks. His long, pointed nails were sharp and lethal, and he bore a startling resemblance to the golden man in the portrait, only his hair was free of silver; an ancestor, most likely. Most curious was the absence of pull between us. There was no overwhelming attraction. No abrasion. Just some faint sense of like recognition but different from what I had felt with Sonia or even with Jamie.

"Hello," I said. "Have I taken your spot?"

His elegant brow arched. "My spot?"

"This clearing. I followed the sound of water here and found this lovely hidden spot. Is it yours?"

"I come here upon occasion when I am at court."

"Are you one of the Council members?"

"My father holds a seat. I represent him." He had an odd way of speaking. His words were more commonplace, but some faint phrasing, a slight accent, made them quaint and bespoke of great age. His black midnight eyes studied me with interest. "You are Mona Lisa, I take it. The reason we are all gathered here."

I grimaced. "It seems I am. My apologies for any disruption to your schedule."

"Were all disruptions as lovely and fascinating." He bowed, a neat trick, all fluid, graceful motion so that it seemed entirely natural. "Prince Halcyon at your service." His gaze dropped to my neck. "You wear the holy cross."

My hand flew to where it rested beneath the gown. "How did you know? Oh, you must have heard that silver does not bother me." I tilted my head curiously at him. "The sun doesn't seem to bother you, either."

"No," he said gravely. "Heat is of no bother to me."

There was something in that tone, some flicker in his eyes, and I realized with that strange perception I seemed to have acquired that it was loneliness, sadness.

"I'm different, too," I said softly. "Part human. Part Moonie. Not fully either."

"Moonie?"

"It's what I call the Monère."

Amusement danced in Halcyon's eyes for a fleeting moment, then faded. "Where are your guards?"

I sighed. "Why is it that every male I meet asks me that same question?"

He eyed me curiously but otherwise remained silent, as if knowing that was the best way to prod me into an answer. He was right, darn him.

"They're still sleeping. They need their rest." I lifted my chin belligerently. "They went through a lot yesterday. One of them almost died and the other is . . . the other is ill."

Halcyon's lips pursed, half in amusement, half in exasperation. "I do not believe they will see it in quite the same light when they awake and find you gone."

My hand waved dismissively. "I'm safe enough during the day and I'll be back before they wake up." I winked at him, which took him aback. "This'll be our little secret."

"I think not, my little wayward Queen," he said to my chagrin.

"Come on, there's no harm done," I wheedled. "What'll it take for you to keep quiet?"

"A drink of your blood?" he asked silkily. My wrist was suddenly held lightly in his hand. One moment he was a clearing away, the next moment he was beside me. There hadn't even been a blur of motion that I could follow.

"Oh, my. You move fast," I said with surprise but no real alarm, sensing no menace in him toward me.

He brought the pulse point of my wrist to his nose and drew in a deep breath, as if inhaling some invisible fragrance. "What say you, little one?"

"Don't be silly. I know we don't drink blood." I giggled and twisted my wrist lightly out of his grasp.

Surprise lit his eyes once again, eyes the color of dark chocolate. Those eyes warmed me to him. I happened to like chocolate.

The corners of his mouth tugged into a grin that brightened his face, changing it from attractive to handsome. "We don't?"

"No. Gryphon told me there's no such thing as vampires.

You're just teasing me. You really don't need to tell Gryphon or Amber that I came outside without them, do you?"

"Amber belongs to you as well?" Halcyon asked with no small amount of amazement.

"If you're thinking of the big tall guy, built like a giant oak tree, then yeah." My eyes darkened. "It would have been cruel to ask him to step out into daylight with me when he'd almost died yesterday from sun poisoning, don't you think?"

Halcyon gazed into my earnest eyes and shook his head. "You are most unusual."

I grinned. Familiar ground. "So I've been told. I think it's a good thing, don't you? Come on, be a pal. I won't tell if you won't."

He smiled with startled, twisted amusement. "A pal, is it? If that is what you desire. As a 'pal,' I shall now escort you back to your room. I shall also require your solemn promise that you tell your men of your little adventure."

He was going to be a stick in the mud about it. I gave in with pouting ill grace. "Oh, all right. I promise."

He presented his arm and I took it with a huff. "Let me guess," I said as we headed back. "You're over a hundred, right?"

He gazed at me in a most peculiar manner. "That is correct."

"Figures." I waved my hand at him. "Your manners. The way you talk. The only person I've met that is my age so far is Jamie."

"Jamie?"

"The redheaded Mixed Blood."

"Ah. The son of one of the house cooks, I believe."

"He's great. Talks just like me."

"Does he, indeed? Many of the young Queens do not come to High Court unless they have something to petition."

"Great," I said grumpily. "Which means all the Queens I'll be meeting today will be mean, nasty old crows."

He threw back his head and laughed, no doubt at the accurate image, a true belly laugh with nothing held back. It made me happy to see him so. Like Gryphon, I had a feeling that he did not laugh often.

"Ah, Mona Lisa. I shall enjoy watching you. Very much indeed."

GRYPHON AND AMBER burst out the front door as Halcyon and I were crossing the lawn and making our way up to the porch. One glimpse at their grim, set faces and I knew I was in big trouble. Bigger than I expected, even, when their faces blanched as they saw who accompanied me. They froze into a dangerous predatory stillness. Amber drew his sword.

"Hi, guys," I said brightly, my nerves shimmering in the sudden ratcheting tension. "I was just coming back."

Beside me, Halcyon gently eased my hand from his arm. Moving with deliberate slowness, he stepped away from me. "She is unharmed," he announced calmly.

"Prince Halcyon was escorting me back," I said. "You can put the sword away, Amber."

The gleaming sword remained in Amber's hand.

"Oh, for heaven's sake." I stomped over to the giant, tilted my head back, and glared up at him. "Put the sword away, now!"

The blade slammed back into its sheath, screaming protest all the way home. His eyes never leaving Halcyon, Amber lifted me like a doll and put me behind him. I hated being treated like a child. Hated being made to feel in the wrong, especially when I knew I was.

I stepped out from behind Amber and whacked the big lug's arm. "Stop it. Halcyon's a friend."

All three men, including Halcyon, who had been smiling with

sardonic amusement up till that moment, turned to look at me with equal parts horror and shock.

"What?" I asked them.

Eyes swung back to Halcyon as if to ask, *Is this true?*

I rolled my eyes. "Oh, come on. He made me come back to the house and promise to tell you that I had, um, slipped outside for a little while."

There was a moment of stunned silence.

"If that is true," Gryphon said slowly, "then we are indeed indebted to you, Prince Halcyon."

"Not at all. Just being of service to the new Queen," Halcyon returned, then added more kindly, "She is young. It will take her time to learn our ways."

"You have our sincere thanks, Prince Halcyon." Gryphon bowed.

Halcyon dipped his head in acknowledgment and took his leave.

I watched Halcyon's departure with deep regret, especially when Gryphon turned and fixed me with his piercing stare. "Upstairs, now, milady." It was not a request. He gripped my arm and hauled me inside. We moved at a fast clip up the stairs and didn't stop until we were back in our room. Amber remained out in the hall.

"Did he touch you?" Gryphon bit out.

"Not really. Just my wrist."

Both my wrists were grabbed in a blur of motion and examined minutely.

"I'm fine, Gryphon." I laughed shakily, a little frightened by his brittle intensity.

He looked up and his dark turmoil struck me full-force. He was furious, as I had never seen him before. He grabbed my upper arms and shook me hard. "Don't you *ever* leave without us like that again. Do you understand?" He shook me again, then wrapped his arms around me and squeezed me so tightly that it almost hurt.

"Sweet Light. Sweet Light," he muttered hoarsely, trembling.

My arms went around him and stroked his back soothingly. "I'm sorry," I whispered. "I'm fine."

Gryphon shuddered and buried his face in my hair. "Never do that again. Promise me."

"I promise," I whispered. "But I was never in any danger outside."

He drew back and eyed me incredulously. "Never in any danger? Do you know who you were with?"

"Of course I know. Prince Halcyon. He's different, like me."

"Different." Gryphon gave a harsh bark of laughter. "He is one of the demon dead."

I looked at Gryphon, stunned. "Oh. That's why I didn't hear him. He had no heartbeat."

"His father rules the underworld and Halcyon is his only son. Do you know what that means?" Gryphon demanded fiercely. "Halcyon is the High Prince of Hell."

"Oh," was my faint reply. "He was still a gentleman."

Gryphon sank down onto the bed; his laughter sliced with a raw edge.

"Do they drink blood?" I asked timidly.

The laughter stopped abruptly. "Yes. Did he take yours?" Both of his hands fisted tight.

"No," I reassured him. Then could not help asking, "Would it have been dangerous if he had?"

Gryphon closed his eyes briefly. "It is not unheard of for demons to drain their donors dry, though I have not heard that of Halcyon."

"Can they control you?"

"No. But the pain or the pleasure they can make you feel . . . many are willing to do anything to either stop it or have more of it. It is not an experience I would have you endure. Just seeing him touch you . . . those nails against your skin . . ." He raised his tortured eyes to me. "I have seen him rip a man's heart out from his chest with those nails. And you were not even afraid."

I swallowed at the sudden disturbing image he had painted. It was hard to imagine the quiet, elegant man I had seen, doing something that bloody, that brutal. "He held no malice toward me."

"How do you know?"

"I . . . I just sensed it. He seemed sad. And lonely."

Gryphon reached out and reeled me to him, gripping both of my arms. He was trembling. "Mona Lisa, he is not someone you need to save like Amber or I. Our powerful Warrior Lord Thorane, even our Queens, fear Halcyon for good reason. Halcyon is not bound by the laws of our land. All that holds him back from the slaughter he is capable of is his own sense of honor. He is powerful. And dangerous. And I do not want his attention focused in any way upon you. Do you understand?"

I nodded, more shaken than I cared to admit. "I'm sorry. I just . . . I'm just used to taking care of myself."

He sank down until his cheek rested against my belly, his arms holding me tight. "I am yours, heart and soul, committed to you wholly until my last dying breath. But you cannot ask me to live and then carelessly risk your own life so."

"No," I murmured, remorse flaying me.

"As our Queen, you hold our lives, our well-being, along with yours. When you endanger yourself, you endanger us all."

My breath soughed out. "Yes. Yes, you're right. I will try to do better."

"You are doing incredibly well. Beyond what anyone would have ever expected. Just . . . let us protect you," he finished helplessly.

I sank down until I held his face in my hands. "Yes, I will," I promised and kissed him. With the touch of Gryphon's lips against mine, his fear, worry, and anger transmuted into vivid sensual urgency.

He tugged the gown frantically off me, unsnapped my bra, and yanked my panties down in a fast blur. My hands tugged his shirt out of his pants just as urgently and slid beneath, seeking the smooth muscles of his back, feeling them against my palms with aching relief as I planted wild kisses over his cheek, his jaw, down his neck. Gryphon's shirt sailed to the far corner and his pants were roughly shoved down. And then I had him, warm and hard and vibrant in my hand. I stroked the length of him, squeezed, and watched with dark satisfaction as his head tossed back, the cords of his neck taut, and he moaned, color slashing his cheeks.

Gryphon opened his eyes, met my knowing smile, and something flared deep in those blue depths. He spun me around, facedown, so that I was bent over the bed, my feet still touching the floor. The position made me feel vulnerable and submissive with his hard length curved behind me, over me, his breath beating hotly against my neck.

"Lift up," he rasped coarsely, his hand teasing along the sides of my breasts. I pushed up, bracing myself on my elbows, allowing him access, crying with relief as I felt his hands cup my breasts, his fingers lightly pinching my aching nipples. I rubbed back against him and mewed as I felt him throb against my bottom, so close to where I wanted him to be. One hand glided down, slid over my curls, and parted me. Two long fingers pushed into me, then slid out. They circled that most sensitive part of me, wetting me with my own moisture, plunged in deeper. Pulled out.

"Oh." I groaned. "More."

He nipped my neck, letting me feel the edge of his teeth and I whimpered. Holding my hips steady, he plunged his hot length into me, going in so deep, so deep at this angle. He started thrusting hard, moving me, moving the entire bed and I watched as my arms and hands began to glow.

"No," I said suddenly and he froze deep within me, so still that I was able to feel his cock throb once, twice. The silken muscles of my sheath shivered and clenched in uncontrollable response and his fingers tightened on my hips. "Let me face you," I rasped.

He withdrew and I turned and looked full upon Gryphon's ivory perfection, his striking beauty, the pure loveliness of his male form thrown into brilliant illumination from within. I opened my arms and body to him. With a hoarse cry he surged back into me, all restraint loosened, pounding into me again and again, wildly, furiously. His lips covered mine. His tongue thrust into me, in and out, in time to his rapid rhythm below. I felt the roiling wave within me grow higher and higher, and still yet higher, until it felt as if I would surely crack and burst. And then I did. With my right hand covering his wound, I prayed in my mind, willed with all that was within me, *Heal, dammit. Heal!* I cried out Gryphon's name and felt my palms tingle, felt a faint surge of warmth.

Gryphon's own satisfaction claimed him and he shuddered, ejaculated into me, and then literally collapsed unconscious on top of me, his body released from the too-heavy strain he had imposed upon it.

Touch had been so rare in my life. I held Gryphon's weight against me for a moment, savoring the contact before rolling him off me and easily lifting him fully onto the bed. All redness from his ordeal in the sun was gone, leaving behind skin the color of burnished teakwood. His wrist and ankle abrasions were completely healed. But sullen blood oozed angrily from his poisoned wound, unchanged, perhaps worsened. Slowly spreading.

I wiped the blood off, covered Gryphon, and lay beside him. And almost didn't notice the tears that silently fell.

EIGHT

THE SUN HAD set when I heard the rest of the house begin to stir. I slipped from the bed, showered, and perused my pitiful armoire. Sonia had packed me one blue dress, a simple frock like what the other women wore, and another of Mona Sera's formal gowns. Black, of course.

"The black gown," Gryphon said as he padded up behind me. I leaned back against him as he slipped his arms around me and kissed my cheek.

"How do you feel?"

"Rested," he said ruefully. "I used my body most harshly earlier."

"In a most wonderful way." Turning, I was delighted to see him blush. "I'll see the healer today, after the meeting," I promised, rubbing my thumbs against the back of his hand where it covered my waist.

He angled my head, kissed me lightly on the lips, and released me. "I shall shower and dress and be ready shortly."

Amber was waiting just outside the door, his hair parted neatly and combed back from the strong lines of his face. He was dressed in a forest green tunic with loose, flowing sleeves and snug black trousers, a style more common a century or two ago. Altogether dashing, really.

Gryphon had brushed out my hair, insisting that it be left loose. More feminine, he had said. Long dresses and loose hair; it wasn't just their speech that was archaic.

"You look lovely, milady." The edges of Amber's mouth curved up in a grimace. It took me a moment to realize he was smiling at me.

"Thank you, Amber. You, uh, look handsome as well."

Redness colored his cheeks. Taking pity on the poor giant, I slipped one hand into Amber's arm, and the other into Gryphon's. "Shall we, gentlemen?"

Ever the efficient steward, Matthias met us at the bottom of the stairs and assigned a young male attendant to lead us to the Council Hall. The young man was quite fascinated with Amber and Gryphon and kept glancing at their hands. I realized why now. With their unusual sun-rich tans they looked like the demon dead. That explained all the startled looks we'd been receiving since yesterday.

We waited half an hour before the heavy doors were opened and we were ushered into a high-domed circular chamber where a dozen somber men and women sat arrayed on a raised platform in chairs spread out at even intervals, encircling the edge of the room. I glimpsed Halcyon's dark face to my left. Over half the seats, though, were empty. Walking in, I felt like a Roman gladiator entering an arena full of hungry spectators. Nor was it reassuring to see Mona Sera in the center of the room, gesturing for me to come stand beside her.

Gryphon and Amber remained back by the doors, along with Mona Sera's guards. I strode alone to the center of the Council

Hall, keeping several yards of distance between Mona Sera and myself. Always prudent, that, and not just for comfort reasons.

"Esteemed Queen Mother." Mona Sera bowed before a woman with proud, regal bearing, whose hair was utterly and completely white. White with age. I'd never seen that before in a Monère. There were Queens, I found, and then there were Queens. She looked like a matriarch of old. *Old* being the key word. Or perhaps *ancient* would be a better word. Really, really ancient. And powerful. It exuded from her like a strong, pervading aroma. The vast lines of age marking her face were mere camouflage for that power. And those eyes. *All-seeing* was a creepy term, but it fit her. Those eyes looked as if they could see into your very soul, weigh and pass judgment and never look back once that judgment was carried out. Scary eyes, those. Too objective. Too knowing.

"Honorable ladies and gentlemen of the High Council," Mona Sera continued in her rich, sultry voice, "I wish to present to you my daughter, Queen Mona Lisa, a child I bore from a Mixed Blood union."

I felt the tension in the room kick up a level as I bowed before the Queen Mother in the manner Gryphon had instructed me—lifting my skirts, kneeling with head bowed, then standing once more. The men looked at me with interest—Halcyon with amusement—but the two Queens, marked by their black gowns, glared at me with cold, unwelcoming eyes. No surprise there. Yup, nasty crows. The Queen Mother studied me with detached curiosity, like one studied a fluttering butterfly that had just been captured and pinned.

"There has never been a Mixed Blood Queen in our history," stated the Queen sitting next to Halcyon, an icy blonde with equally cold eyes. She was striking in her beauty, a real true Ice Queen.

"Exactly, Mona Louisa," Mona Sera said mockingly. "Which is

why I called this special Council Meeting. I wish to have my *daughter*"—she purred the word with rich satisfaction—"recognized and acknowledged as the first Mixed Blood Queen before the High Council."

"An abomination!" hissed another Queen to my right whose hair was the color of orange flames. A Fire Queen in temperament as well as in coloring.

"No," Mona Sera replied with a taunting smile, "she is a *Queen* that everyone here, including you, Mona Teresa, can sense and feel."

"Can she Bask?" asked the man sitting to the Queen Mother's immediate right, an older gentlemen with salt-and-pepper hair who wore a gold medallion chain. A sense of solid power emanated from him.

Mona Sera inclined her head. "I have witnessed her Basking myself, Warrior Lord Thorane, this last full moon. She drew the light down from the moon and shared its glory with her new guard, Gryphon, formerly of my court."

The Council members murmured among themselves. Lord Thorane inclined his head to the Queen Mother, spoke softly to her. The Queen Mother nodded.

"What other gifts does your daughter possess, Mona Sera?" the Queen Mother asked, addressing us for the first time. She spoke slowly, with care, her voice rich and resonant with authority.

"Most venerable Queen Mother." Mona Sera bowed ceremoniously low once again, then flung her arms dramatically open as if presenting a gift. A real showman, my mother. "She can wear silver against her skin and not have it affect her strength. Neither does it contain her. She tolerates sunlight as humans do and has passed on this ability to one of her men, for certain. Perhaps both of them." All eyes turned toward the doors to study Amber and Gryphon.

They were easily picked out. Their brown skin made them look like sun gods against the paleness of Mona Sera's men. A few brave souls turned to look at Halcyon also, as if to compare the color of their skin with his. Halcyon smiled sardonically and clicked his long, sharp nails gently together. They looked nervously away.

Mona Sera's dark eyes glittered with pleasure as a new wave of muttering arose. "Of most interest," she continued, delivering the coup de grâce, "she bears the Goddess's tears."

All eyes suddenly stabbed me like sharp knives. I had to brace myself against the intensity of their gaze.

"Show us your palms, child," Mona Louisa, the pale blonde Queen, commanded. I gritted my teeth at the condescending order but chanted to myself, *Befriend. Not alienate.* I needed the Queens' help for Gryphon. I took a deep breath of control and smiled. I could be every bit as good a showman as my mother. After a brief, deliberate pause, I threw out my hands, presenting my palms with a graceful flourish.

Gasps. A sea of murmurs. A muttered "Unnatural!" from fiery Mona Teresa. And the sharp, assessing gaze of the Queen Mother and the two men present. The Queens eyed me with cold hostility. But the other women—some dressed in gold-trimmed white robes, the rest in rich maroon—looked upon me with speculative interest.

A lady in maroon addressed the next question to me. "Have you any special abilities with these?"

"I can determine injuries below the skin's surface. I also have a minor ability to ease pain."

"How old are you, child?" the lady asked kindly. Somehow it didn't grate as much when *she* called me "child."

"Twenty-one."

She turned to Mona Sera. "Have you borne any other children?"

"Only a Mixed Blood male child from the same father," Mona Sera said dismissively.

Her answer made me jerk in surprise. I had a brother?

"And where is this Mixed Blood who fathered your children now, Mona Sera?" Lord Thorane asked.

"He died fifteen years ago," was Mona Sera's devastating reply.

Tears stung my eyes and I looked down at the floor. One given, one taken in a casual statement of fact. She hadn't told me, damn it. She hadn't told me. And she should have.

"A pity," Lord Thorane murmured. Coming to a decision, he straightened. "I second Mona Sera's petition that Mona Lisa be recognized and acknowledged before the court as a new Queen."

A count was taken with a majority vote cast in my favor. The Queen Mother abstained. The two Queens were against me— surprise, surprise. But despite them, I was now, officially, the first Mixed Blood Queen, ever.

"Several of our laws regarding Mixed Bloods will have to be amended," Lord Thorane broached carefully.

"Any change in our laws will unfortunately have to wait until our next session, when we have at least two-thirds of the Council present," Mona Teresa said in a pleased purr that subsided under the Queen Mother's stare. "We have less than half the Council here today," she finished in a whine.

"It *is* our Council law," Mona Louisa spoke up, supporting her.

"So it is," the Queen Mother acknowledged slowly.

I had a feeling I was missing something important here.

Lord Thorane cleared his throat. "Mona Sera, the Council deeply thanks you for the addition of this new Queen to our ranks. Mona Lisa will abide here at High Court until the Council next meets twelve days hence, at which time a territory shall be assigned to her. Council is adjourned."

Outside the Great Hall, Mona Sera turned to me with pleased satisfaction. "Fare thee well, daughter. I return to my territory tonight."

"She needs more guards, milady," Gryphon said quietly beside me.

"She has two of my gowns and two of my strongest men. More?" Mona Sera's lips twisted. "I think not."

"It is your responsibility as sponsor to provide her with protection," Gryphon dared say.

"And I have done so. Her protection is now your problem."

"Where is my brother?" I demanded.

Mona Sera's gaze turned to me with cool amusement. "He was given over to the humans as you were, at birth. I do not remember when. And I do not know where."

"My father's name?"

"I do not remember," she said, and somehow I knew that she lied. Mona Sera tossed me a little smile. "Do your best to stay alive."

"That's it?" I said. "Why did you bring me here?"

"To have my fertility and Queen-bearing status recognized, which will weigh heavily in any future concessions I may desire from the Council. Whether you live or die now is of no concern to me."

Plain-speaking, indeed. For some reason, that made me think better of her, twisted though that may be. Perhaps I was indeed her daughter—scary thought, that—looking upon that beautiful, heartless countenance with her flat eyes more dead than alive.

"One last word of advice," Mona Sera said, glancing from me to my men. "Only the strongest survive in our world. Rule them. Or they will destroy you."

A real cozy mother-to-daughter chat. And then she was gone.

∽⌒∾

THE COUNCILWOMAN IN maroon attire who had addressed me was a healer who invited me to her abode. Amber accompanied us while Gryphon begged off, saying that he wished to rest and give me the chance to talk freely with the healer.

Janelle was her name. She had kind, brown eyes like Sonia, with a few gray strands sprinkled in her sandy hair. She lived in a small, comfortable cottage a few buildings away from the Great House. Dusty, musty books lined floor-to-ceiling bookshelves and several heavy tomes lay open on the long center table, buried beneath various herbs and flowers scattered among pungent jars and bottles filled with interesting-looking concoctions. She remarked upon some of their medicinal purposes, then took my hand and rubbed her thumb over my mole, making a *hmm*ing sound.

"You have potential, undeveloped as of yet. But you are young. Quite young, actually. Most healers do not begin to develop their powers until their third cycle of ten seasons. Some even later."

"Can you teach me some of your healing art?"

"With great pleasure," Janelle answered with a smile. "We may begin tomorrow, if you so desire."

I nodded eagerly. "Please. There is much I wish to learn."

"And there is much I wish to teach you. It is rare to find a Queen with the gift for healing."

"There is one thing that cannot wait, though. One of my men, Gryphon, suffers from silver poisoning."

Janelle's eyes narrowed thoughtfully. "Ah. I sensed wrongness with him but did not know of what nature it was."

"I have come here to seek a cure for him. Can you help him? Do you have the antidote?"

"I know of no cure for silver poisoning," Janelle said sadly.

Well, shit. Two people now had told me that. Not good news. "Might the other healers be able to help?"

She considered it. "Perhaps. But I trained the others in the craft myself. Still, it will not hurt to inquire of them."

"I've heard some say only Queens have the antidote. But somehow I don't think the two Queens here will be eager to help me."

Janelle's eyes glinted with dry amusement. "We have few enough Queens so that every new member is a true treasure to our people. Unfortunately, other Queens will look upon you as competition and a reason to lessen their own territory as each new sister is added to their ranks. In their eyes, there is no reason to aid you. Mona Rodera, who should be here when the Council next meets, is the only other Queen who has some small healing talent. Healers are more apt to share with each other. Perhaps she will be willing to lend you aid if an antidote truly exists, though I have never heard of the existence of one."

"Thank you, Healer Janelle." I took my leave of her.

What I had learned disturbed me greatly, but not enough to keep me from noticing that Amber was unusually tense as he escorted me back. He kept his hand within easy reach of his sword hilt the entire short trip.

Gryphon and five other men awaited us in the foyer. It took me a moment to notice that Gryphon's wooden trunk sat by the doorway and an even longer moment to register its significance.

"Milady." Gryphon, my beautiful Gryphon, knelt before me. "I ask that you release me from your service."

His words were like a stab to the chest, knocking the wind out of me, coming out of nowhere. It was the *last* thing I would have expected. And they say women are fickle. "What?"

He stood upright, his blue eyes fixed solemnly on me. "Milady. Mona Louisa has graciously invited me to join her. Her plane awaits me. She has promised me the antidote," he explained gently.

"You're . . . leaving me?" I asked, stunned and suddenly lost, cast adrift from the one solid thing that had anchored me in this new life.

"If you will release me."

That new inner, possessive demon within me shouted: *No! Never!* How could I let him go? Dear God, how could I not? Mona Louisa offered him *life,* the icy bitch.

"If . . . if you wish to go." Idiot, I berated myself. Of course he wished to go. He was *asking* to go. And yet, he had held me so tightly, kissed me with such tender love . . . at least, I had presumed it was love or some deep emotion similar to it. But then, he had never said the words. . . .

Gryphon knelt again and bowed his dark head, graceful even now when leaving me. "Thank you, milady. Mona Louisa has kindly agreed to loan you four of her guards for your protection until the Council next meets."

I choked off hysterical laughter. I don't think kindness motivated Mona Louisa in any way. Lust, maybe. Not kindness.

He stood and his sky-blue eyes and the wayward lock of hair that fell over his brow were so familiar, so dear. *Don't go. Don't go.* The words choked in my throat as he pressed a last final kiss on the back of my hand. One of the unfamiliar men lifted Gryphon's trunk onto his shoulder in an easy motion.

"Fare thee well, Mona Lisa," Gryphon said softly.

Don't go. Don't leave me. Gryphon, I love you. . . . But the words were locked shut behind my clenched teeth. I swallowed, watched him exchange a glance with Amber. *Please don't go. Oh, God. Gryphon . . .*

Then he was gone.

My harsh breathing filled the hallway, too fast, too deep. Everything seemed surreal. There were four new puppet guards standing before me, their new puppet master. Only I'd just had my own strings cut.

A pretty blond man flashed me an eager smile. They were all pretty, for that matter. One of each individual hair color: blond, brown, jet-black, and one the shade of a colorful carrot. Again, that hysterical laughter threatened me.

Blondie bowed. "I am Miles, milady, and this is Gilford, Rupert, and Demetrius. We are most eager to serve you." I had a feeling somehow that they expected to do so in bed, not that that was going to happen.

Numbness was creeping over me and I welcomed it. It hurt too much to hurt so much. I don't know if I grunted, nodded, or just walked straight past them. All I knew with certainty was that the stairs were suddenly beneath my feet. I flew into my bedroom, shut the door, and sank down onto the floor, my back pressed against the wall. And just sat there, not knowing what else to do.

NINE

HELEN HAD BEEN my human mother's name. Her and her husband, Frank, had taken me home from the orphanage. I had called them *Mama* and *Papa*. They'd been an older couple in their fifties with no children.

Helen loved curling my hair and arranging them into two pigtails that swung and bounced as I moved. She loved adorning my dark hair with pretty pink ribbons or blue bows. Those had been her favorite colors. "Give me good old-fashioned pink or blue any day," she used to say with a laugh that shook her plump, solid frame as she cuddled me in her big arms, enveloping me like a soft, huge teddy bear, squeezing me against her generous bosom. I still remember how she smelled. Like talcum powder, love, and laughter.

She bought me a goldfish named Joey that wriggled around awkwardly in a bowl and had big, fat cheeks that fascinated me to no end. With her big hand over mine, she'd guide me in pinching up little flakes of fish food and dropping them into the water before I snuggled into bed each night. I would watch Joey dart his fat body around, greedily gulping down the flakes while Helen read me a bedtime story.

Helen's pain started when I was four. A sharp twinge in the lower abdomen that made her bend over and gasp. I put my hand over her belly and my palms warmed and tingled for the first time.

"Mama. Bad here."

"Yes, baby. Some bad gas. But it feels much better now."

The pain had gone away but had come back six months later, hurting so much that she had to squat down. And I realized even then that that bad thing inside of her had grown just a little bit more.

"Bad inside," I said. "Mama go see doctor."

"Ah, baby, you've got magic hands." She kissed and buzzed my hands, blowing air against them until the funny noise made me giggle. "Now why should I go see a doctor? They just find things wrong with you."

Quiet and steady Frank, a postal worker, finally started to worry when I was five-and-a-half years old. The pains were growing worse and coming more often. Ignoring his wife's blustery protests, he finally dragged Helen to the doctor, but by then it was too late. Colon cancer. It had spread to the liver and lungs.

Helen underwent chemotherapy and radiation treatments and I fed Joey on my own each night. There were no more bedtime stories. She grew gaunt and laughed less frequently, though she still cuddled me. I'd lay my hands on her and she'd sigh and say, "That feels much better, baby."

She lasted a year, ten months more than what the doctors had predicted for her. When she was gone, Frank was an empty shell and I was sent from the only home I'd ever known.

⟨⟨⟩⟩

THE DISCREET TAP on the door pulled me back from past memories. "Yes."

"It's time for dinner, milady," Amber said through the door.

"You go on. I'm not hungry."

He opened the connecting door and I caught a glimpse of Miles's curious eyes and shiny blond hair before Amber closed the door behind him. "Why are you sitting on the floor?"

I shook my head mutely. How could I answer him when I didn't even know the answer myself? My eyes fell on the bed where Gryphon and I had lain, propelling me into motion. I scrambled up, tore the sheets off the bed, and pressed them into Amber's large arms, mumbling, "Please have them wash these."

"Yes, milady." He left and I sank back down against the wall and closed my eyes.

⟨⟨⟩⟩

I WAS TEN when I bought a goldfish with the money I'd earned from weeding and raking neighbors' yards. It had fat cheeks and wriggled around arrogantly like a little empress in the round bowl I had also purchased. I named her Josephine in memory of Joey. I'm sure he would have liked her.

I'd drop in a pinch of food for her each night, watch her gulp and gobble down each flake, and cleaned her bowl and gave her fresh water each and every week. I shared a room with two other foster girls younger than I. They'd been taken in by Mr. and Mrs. Jackson for the government check issued in the mail to them the first day of each month for their care, same as I.

Mrs. Jackson was a thin woman, perpetually tired. She had worked hard all her life, and it showed in the stoop of her shoulders and in the dullness of her lank hair. Her faded blue eyes regarded us children as extra hands meant to help with the extra work that we brought along with the government check. I'd been with them for several months and had been content to look after the other two girls, my responsibility since I was the oldest. Dutifully, I performed the chores assigned to me.

Things changed, however, when my breasts started to bud and develop later that year. Mrs. Jackson refused to waste any money buying me a bra and Mr. Jackson started looking at me there strangely. He began taking more of an interest in us, kissing little Carlotta and shy Nicole and tickling them on his lap.

"I bet you're ticklish, too, Lisa," Mr. Jackson would say and try to tickle me as well. I'd dart out of reach and though he'd laugh, his eyes would be mad.

He'd have the girls sit on his lap, give him a kiss on the cheek, and reward them with a candy bar.

"Your turn, Lisa," he'd say, and wave the chocolate bar tantalizingly before me. I'd shake my head, knowing only that his smile never reached his mean eyes.

When my breasts grew to the size of small peaches, he grew more surly and demanding. My chores were doubled and I barely had enough time each day to finish my homework.

"The garbage's not taken out, Lisa," he bellowed one day after coming home from his construction job dirty and sweaty and reeking of beer.

"I was going to take it out after I swept the kitchen floor," I said with wide, apprehensive eyes, broom clutched in my hands. Mrs. Jackson was wearily peeling potatoes and didn't even spare us a glance.

"You useless piece of trash!" Snatching the broom from me, he jerked me by the hair into the living room where little Carlotta and

Nicole were watching TV. They glanced up at his red face and fled to their room. "I'll teach you to be lazy," he said, breathing heavily as he put me across his knee.

I didn't fight him as his big hand lashed my bottom again and again. It wasn't the first time I'd been beaten. But when his hand lingered over my rear, stroking the sensitive painful flesh and one of his fingers slid down my crease, I struggled wildly and twisted out of his lap, falling onto the floor. He leaned down with glittery eyes and threatened in a mean low voice, "You better be nice to me, little girl, or you'll be sorry."

Christmas came and Mr. Jackson put on a fake white beard. Carlotta and Nicole sat in Santa's lap, gave him a kiss, and got their candy cane.

"Your turn, Lisa," the fake Santa said. His breath, as usual, stank of sour beer.

Bracing myself, I gingerly sat on his lap and pecked him quickly on the cheek. He gave a *ho, ho, ho*. Under the guise of giving me a hug, he ran a hand over my breasts. I jumped off his lap, candy cane in hand, and saw the knowledge of what he had done in Mrs. Jackson's weary, resigned eyes. She bought a bra for me the very next day during the after-Christmas clearance sale. "Don't make him mad," was all she said.

He came home early from work one day when Mrs. Johnson was out of the house grocery shopping. Carlotta and Nicole's schoolbooks were spread out on the kitchen table, their school bags at their feet, and I was helping them with their homework.

"What's this crap?" Mr. Jackson roared, his eyes drunk with alcoholic outrage. "I don't bust my back all day to come back to this mess in my home!" He kicked their schoolbags out of the way and with one violent swipe, swept the books off the table, sending them flying. The girls darted out of the kitchen but he snatched my arm before I could run off.

"Clean this garbage up!" he shouted and shoved me to the floor. I scrambled on my hands and knees, picking up the scattered books and loose, flying paper. Only when I heard his breathing grow harsher and his heartbeat quicken did I look up from the floor and catch him staring down my shirt, which had gaped open in my bent over position. My only bra was in the laundry.

"Whore!" he breathed and I froze.

I broke for the door, too late. He lunged and tackled me back down, scraping my elbows and banging my head hard enough against the kitchen floor to addle me a bit. Yanking up my shirt, he started roughly pawing my breasts, squeezing them painfully.

"No! Get your hands off me!" I screamed. Instinctively I jammed the heel of my palm into his nose, sending him staggering back.

"Bitch!" he cursed, clutching his bleeding nose. "You'll be sorry for that."

He made good on his promise. Josephine was dead the next day when I returned from school. Her fishbowl had been upended and she lay orange and lifeless in a puddle of water, her fat belly still, her eyes unseeing.

I never dared keep anything for myself after that, even when I moved on to other homes. I learned a painful lesson that day: Don't love things. Don't grow attached to things. It hurts too much when you lose them.

~

A YOUNG HOUSEMAID fixed my bed with clean sheets, eyeing me curiously. She came and went and I barely noticed. I shut down my senses, went somewhere deep inside where I hardly felt anything. Nothing hurt when you couldn't feel it.

Time passed meaninglessly by. At some point I dozed off and big, gentle hands lifted me up, put me onto a soft mattress, and covered me with a blanket. I continued to sleep and dream.

T EN

"Y ou have to eat something, milady," Amber said with pugnacious persistency.

I looked past him. Through him. I'd told him already that I wasn't hungry enough times during the past ten minutes.

"Jamie's mom made this spaghetti especially for you," he coaxed.

I had only two words for him. "Go. Away."

"Not until you eat something," Amber snapped. His tone softened. "Three mouthfuls and I'll leave you alone," he wheedled.

I opened my mouth, chewed and swallowed the allotted times. He left and I sank back within.

A nother day. More murmurs that I tuned out. A loud knock I ignored. Persistent rapping that wouldn't stop.

"What?"

"Prince Halcyon has come to see you," Amber said through the door.

"No."

"She doesn't wish to see you," I heard him say.

Silence. Then the door swung open and Halcyon walked in with Amber shadowing him.

Halcyon came to the bed and sat down beside me. He turned on the lamp and I blinked, dazzled by the sudden light.

"How Victorian," Halcyon said with a flash of pearly teeth. They were startling white against his golden visage. "Your lover leaves and you fall into a sad decline."

I stared beyond him. Didn't blink when those long nails passed in front of my eyes. Didn't flinch when they brushed against my skin as he pushed a lock of hair back from my face.

Amber growled.

"Down, boy," Halcyon said, amusement in his words. "I will not hurt her."

His amusement fled when I turned my face deliberately into those lethal nails. His hand was suddenly gone.

"Go away," I said. No heat. No emotion.

Halcyon's eyes softened. "It is hard, yes. But you will get over it. You are young and beautiful. You will have many more lovers."

"No," I said with certainty.

"Yes," he returned just as surely. "And I will be the first in line."

With effort I stirred myself. "No."

"Are you afraid of me?"

I shook my head.

"Then why not?" he asked.

I looked at him with my hollow eyes and let him see down into me, into my bleeding, gaping soul. "Because I could care for you. And I do not wish to. It hurts too much."

He bowed his head. "Ah, my fascinating Queen. You stir feelings inside me that I had long thought dead." He let out a deep breath and stood. "I will give you time," he said, and I did not know to whom he made that promise. To me, or to himself.

⁂

MY LETHARGY WAS shattered the next sunset by a woman's piercing screams. I sat up, looked out the window, and watched with disbelief as a man threw up a young woman's skirts, ripped off her panties, and began raping her in plain sight. People were staring, but no one made any attempt to stop the brutal violence or rush to her aid.

"Stop!" I opened the window, jumped to the ground twenty feet below, and rolled to my feet. A wave of dizziness hit me as I stood up, weak and light-headed from my days of bed rest. Impatiently, determinedly, I shook it off and raced toward them. "Stop it, you bastard!"

The man's pale buttocks worked obscenely over the woman, pumping up and down like an enraged piston. He did nothing to prevent her screaming. In fact, he seemed to encourage it. Only when she tried to rake his face with her nails did he swat her. The woman's face snapped to the side with almost neck-cracking force, stunned from the blow. *My God,* I realized. *She is a Mixed Blood.*

I ripped him off of her and he landed on the ground twenty feet away, his engorged penis stained red with her blood. He stood up with a smile, casually pulling up his pants. "Not a bad pot of cream for a Mixed Blood."

The woman moaned and fumbled with her skirt, trying to cover herself, and I saw her face clearly for the first time. Her hair was a darker shade of red, but the freckles and pert nose were just like her brother's. She was Tersa, Jamie's older sister. And she had been a virgin.

With a roar I leaped for the man and found myself jerked up short.

"Let me go," I snarled at Amber. My four other guards were behind him, and like all the others watching, doing nothing to help. Useless creatures.

"He did nothing wrong, milady."

I stared at Amber with amazement. "He just *raped* her!"

"She is a Mixed Blood. There is no law against it."

Rage swallowed me up so terribly that I trembled with it. "You're saying he won't be punished."

"No, milady."

"Then I'll see to it."

Amber's hands kept me chained. "Think. They did this to draw you out." He shook me slightly. "Raping is nothing. There is no law against *killing* a Mixed Blood. And you are a Mixed Blood. You are not protected even though you are a Queen. Until they amend our laws, you are vulnerable. Do you understand?"

"Does the little Queen wish to come and play with Samson?" the rapist taunted. He grabbed his dick and pumped it lewdly. "There is enough of him to please two Mixed Blood whores."

"Release me," I said coldly.

"Milady . . ."

"Release me."

Amber did so reluctantly. "It is against our law for a Mixed Blood to kill one of the Monère."

"Your laws suck."

"That is a splendid idea," the man said, strolling toward me. "Maybe I'll have you suck Samson."

I smiled at the walking piece of carrion before me. "Oh, yes. I want to play with Samson. Come to Delilah," I crooned.

Amber shifted behind me. "Milady . . ."

"Don't worry. I understand. If he starts to hurt me, you can jump in and defend your Queen. Your law allows that, right?" I walked forward to meet the bastard, and he was too stupid to be scared. "What Queen do you serve?" I demanded.

"Mona Teresa."

The Fire Queen. That fact somehow didn't surprised me.

A large, dark-haired woman wearing an apron burst from the main house and rushed over to Tersa, sobbing. I closed it off and focused on the leering man before me. Insolently, he reached out his right hand and ran his fingertips over my nipple.

I leaned forward, gently pressing his hand to my breast, my fingers over his, and bared my teeth at him. "You know your problem? You're used to raping women who don't fight back." With a casual twisting upward jerk I broke his fingertips. The sound of bones snapping was the sweetest of melodies.

He screamed with great pain and even greater surprise.

I *tsk*ed in sympathy. "Hurts like a bitch, doesn't it?"

He swung at me with his good hand. I ducked and, sweeping his foot out from under him, rode him down to the ground, knife in hand. His head hit the ground with a loud crack and he lay beneath me, stupefied and stupid. I sliced open his pants and bared his organ, still semihard.

"Now what exactly happened to Samson?" I mused. "Oh yeah, Delilah cut his locks off." I grabbed his offending organ. My knife flew and blood spurt over me. His scream was horrendous.

I stood up, stepped aside, and watched him with a cruel smile as he rolled on the ground, clutching his bloody dickless groin. The missing piece drooped flaccidly in my hand.

"If something offends me, I break it, cut it off, or destroy it." Calmly, I dropped his severed prick—it hit the ground with a wet *plop*—and methodically mashed his manhood to a pulp beneath my heel. All the watching men winced and many hands flew protectively up to cover their own groins.

"Will it grow back?" I asked.

"Yes," Amber said. He stood by my side and stared dispassionately down at the screaming, writhing, bleeding man.

"A pity. I may have to cut it off again."

Someone whistled in admiration. I turned and stared into Prince Halcyon's golden visage.

"How terribly brutal," he declared. "I'm in love."

The neutered man was screaming, one long breath after another, his eyes filled with horror as he gazed at his mashed pride and joy. His broken fingers were cradled against his chest, oddly bent and swollen quite nicely by now.

I leaned down and buried my blade in the dirt, millimeters away from his face. "Shut up!" I roared.

The screams ceased abruptly. He whimpered as I whipped the blade out of the ground and wiped it on his white shirt.

"Now return to your Queen and tell her what I said."

He crawled away from me, stark terror in his eyes, and it pleased some dark part of me to see it there.

Then the smell of blood and raw meat hit me suddenly, along with the knowledge of what I had done. My stomach revolted violently. I bent over, gagging, and heard my heartbeat slow down. I barely had time to remember the medical term for the reflex—*valsalva maneuver*: stimulating the vagus nerve by gagging or holding your breath, causing the heart rate to decrease—before the world spun and darkness overtook me.

ELEVEN

BACK IN MY room, once I had revived, I celebrated the small victory with a big, bloody T-bone steak prepared for me by Jamie's mother. My five men winced as I chewed the beefy chunks with relish and licked the plate clean. I had let myself get dangerously weak. Not a smart thing to do among a crowd of carnivores.

I stripped out of my bloody gown and showered, lathering up and scrubbing myself completely from top to toe three times. Too bad I couldn't wash away the stain within me as easily. There was a cruel, sadistic part of me that was emerging that scared me to death.

The dirty gown was gone when I stepped out of the bathroom. Adrenaline still pumped in my veins and the room was suddenly too small; I had to get out. I threw the other black gown over my head and knocked on the adjoining door. Miles opened the door, his eyes wary. "Milady?"

"I'm going for a walk," I informed him curtly.

"We will accompany you," Amber said from behind Miles, towering over the other man.

There was no smell of blood in the forest, just the clean scent of pine and the earthy smell of damp leaves and woods. It should have made me feel better. Instead, I began to cry, uncontrollable sobs that choked my breath and jerked my body. Amber's strong arms swept me up. He sat down on a fallen tree trunk and cradled me against his chest. The comfort and bigness of him reminded me of Helen, my human mother, and I wept even harder.

"It's all right," Amber murmured, awkwardly patting my back. The Four Colors, what I called my loaned guards, stood a cautious distance away. Men either wanted me or were afraid of me. No middle ground, it seemed.

"No, it's not." I gasped. "They hurt her because of me."

"You returned the pain doublefold back to the assailant."

"I'm glad," I said with ferocious pleasure. "I wanted to kill him!"

"Next time," was Amber's calm reply.

"I don't want there to be a next time." I sobbed and buried my face against him. "I hate it here. I thought coming here would give me everything I wanted. Instead, it's taken everything away."

A twig snapped, jarring me from my grieving, careless disregard of the area around me. I expanded my senses and heard it—seven, no, eight other slow heartbeats. Amber set me on my feet, drew his sword, and moved silently forward, signaling to the other four guards who surrounded me in a circle as the intruders glided into view. Eight of them armed with knives, dressed with tattered, patched tunics and worn boots. A ragged lot.

"Amber," I said, my voice tight and peculiar.

He glanced back and froze as he saw the silver blade held to my throat over where my pulse beat. Miles stood behind me, holding the knife. Another man, Gilford, I think was his name, stripped me of my knives while the other two held my wrists.

We were outnumbered and betrayed. "Run," I said roughly to Amber. "Get out of here."

Amber hesitated, his face as hard as stone. Instead of running, he came rushing toward us. Damn it! The stubborn gallant fool never listened to me.

"I wouldn't, if I were you," Miles said with silky menace, "or we shall test how fast she can heal silver."

The threat halted Amber.

"Drop the sword," Miles instructed. When Amber didn't move, the blade sliced lightly, professionally, and my blood sang in the air. Amber threw down his sword.

"Very good," Miles said, praising Amber as if he was a dog being trained. "Now kneel. Lace your hands behind your head."

Amber dropped to his knees and one of the bandits moved quickly behind him, clamping a silver cuff around his wrist. Twisting his arms roughly down behind his back, he fastened the remaining cuff. They'd had it all planned. Bastards.

"Hand her over," said the bandit who had secured Amber so efficiently.

"Patience, Aquila. You shall have her as promised after we have sampled her charms first. It is our Queen's most ardent wish. She greatly desires the ability to withstand the sun." And it seemed the way they were going to acquire that gift was by having Mona Louisa's men mate with me and carry my potency back to her.

Miles yanked my hair back and swiped his sharp blade down my front. My dress parted open almost down to the knees, the fabric yielding like butter to the slicing knife.

"Fancy yourself an artist with the blade, huh?" I gritted.

"Oh, yes." Two more swift movements and my bra and panties fell away. "And I am as much an artist with my other knife."

"See, that's your trouble. Too much emphasis on your dick."

"With good reason, as you shall soon see."

Not liking the sound of that, I started to struggle. Miles squeezed his arm around my neck and hooked a leg around one of mine. Rupert, to my right, trapped my other leg. Arms and legs held open, I was on wide display. At least I was still standing up.

Rupert, the carrot-top, approached me holding a small vial similar to the one I had found in Mona Sera's bedroom. The one that Gryphon had made me wash my hands three times after touching. Uh oh. I squirmed, wriggled, and twisted, but was held fast.

"No!" Amber roared, lunging. Aquila jerked his chain back ruthlessly, throwing Amber to the ground.

With great care, Rupert opened the vial. Ensuring that none of the fluid touched him, he carefully swiped the stopper over my nipples and between my slit. The men all looked at me with avid expectancy, Amber, with anguish. I swallowed, waiting for something to happen. But nothing did.

"Give her more," Miles ordered harshly.

Rupert looked at him with wide eyes.

"Uh, you really don't have to. I'm starting to feel something," I lied.

"Do it!" Miles screamed.

Rupert jumped, spilling half the bottle onto my chest.

"Sweet Goddess," Amber whispered.

The oily, sweet-smelling substance dribbled down to soak in the hollow between my legs. Nothing for one blissful second. And then heat engulfed me like a rabid fire. I was surprised I didn't burst into flames. It felt as if fiery ants were crawling over my entire flesh, stinging me, eating me alive.

I gasped and collapsed, held up only by the men restraining me. They lowered me to my knees and stepped back.

"Wipe the excess oil off of her!" Amber said hoarsely. "Quickly!"

Gilford sliced off a chunk of my hem—I guess the dress was already ruined—wadded it up, and wiped it down between my breasts, down my stomach, so close to that area that was suddenly the focus of all that heat and burning fire, a place that throbbed and wept demandingly. I moaned and whimpered. Gilford threw the cloth hastily away from him.

"You feel it now, don't you, whore?" Miles shoved me from behind and I fell forward onto my knees and hands. "Unnatural cunt. Even the Demon Prince lusts for you."

I heard the rasp of his zipper going down.

"That's right. On your hands and knees like the bitch in heat you are." His hand trailed down my back, over the curve of my buttock, and I nearly wept at his touch. It felt so good, so *necessary*.

"Light up for me, you mongrel strumpet."

I felt the head of him probe me in an unimaginable spot. And it felt so good, stretching me. Pleasure that edged into pain. My body screamed for him. I needed him in me. Now. Any way. It was the hardest thing I'd ever done in my life, to roll onto the ground, away from him, onto my back. To stare up at that beautiful, hard, ready cock that my body so desperately craved. I wept, above and below, shaking with need.

Grabbing me by the hair, Miles yanked me to my knees and jerked my head to the side where he stood waving before me in rampant glory. "Open up." He nudged my lips with his hard staff. "Be a good girl and I might touch you. You would like that, would you not?"

I whimpered. My lips parted and he pushed in a little.

"That's a good little whore. Suck me."

I gathered myself—how hard it was to do so—and slammed my clasped hands up hard into his balls. "Suck that," I panted and fell limply onto my side.

Miles screamed with pain and rage. He squatted over, clutching himself. "Bitch! Unnatural mongrel bitch!"

In outraged masculine fury, he threw himself onto me, forgetting himself, his hands wrapped around my throat. The weight of him over my flesh, the rub of his fabric over my nipples—God. I needed that more than I needed air. If my body had its way, it would have gladly let me strangle to death as long as he didn't move off me. I writhed and rubbed against him uncontrollably, wetting him with the excess oil from my body while he glared down at me, that once beautiful face now a twisted, evil, grimacing mask as he squeezed and squeezed and shook me with violent rage.

"Miles!" Aquila said sharply.

"Do not worry," Miles snarled, breathing rapidly. "I won't kill her. I'm just choking some of the fight out of her."

That's true, came a distant floating logic. Choking couldn't kill one of our kind. But I wasn't entirely Monère. I was also part human. And humans *could* be choked to death. It took longer, since I didn't breathe as much, but I began to feel the lack of air—a desperate clawing sensation. I was gasping, trying to draw in air. Suffocating. And over it all, I was burning, burning, burning!

That terrible aching, throbbing need was only worsened, not relieved, the more I rubbed against him. My vision began to fade. I pushed weakly against his chest, my strength ebbing as the tremendous need for air and the desperate need of my body to be filled built and built and became too much. Something had to give.

My hands tingled, burned, brightened with true heat. Every electric, pulsing, desperate sensation that I felt poured out of me in a frothing rushing gush through my palms.

The smell of burning fabric and singed flesh polluted the air. Someone was screaming. My throat was suddenly free and I gasped in sweet, life-sustaining air. My vision cleared and I lifted my head and saw Miles rolling madly on the ground a few feet away. The red imprint of my palms were seared into the pale flesh of his chest like a horrendous macabre brand. The fabric of his shirt was whole but for a neat outline where my hands had burned through, like two imprints of cookie dough that had been cut out with a cookie cutter.

"See how long it takes you to heal that, prick." I gasped, using up the last of my strength. My head fell back onto the ground and my eyes closed. I felt that hot, burning torment creep back over my limp body, tightening it once again, and I wanted to weep and cry and throw myself onto the nearest man.

I heard the others gather Miles up and leave. His cursing and weeping grew fainter.

When I opened my eyes, Aquila stood above me, the other seven men a safe distance away. He was handsome in a severe, stern-looking fashion, older, with short, dark curly hair. The neat appearance of his thin mustache and Vandyke beard was at peculiar odds with his ragged clothing.

If he raped me now I wouldn't be able to resist. Frankly, I might even welcome him with open legs. But he didn't fall on me as I expected, to my sharp relief and despair. There was no lust in his eyes, just a flicker almost of pity.

He showed me the hand restraints he held. Had been holding all along, actually. Only I hadn't noticed them until he drew attention to them, so fractured was my concentration on the desperate clamoring of my traitorous body.

"Are you able to hold out your hands, Lady?" Aquila asked.

I didn't know. Could I? I grunted and lifted one hand up to sway feebly in the air. Aquila clamped the cold metal around it and

I gratefully let my arm sag back down, leaving him with the burden of holding up the obscenely heavy weight my arm had suddenly become.

"The other," Aquila said. He enunciated his words in a gentleman's precise, clipped manner. What the hell was he doing with these bandits?

Making a Herculean effort, I lifted the other arm to waver in the air. Aquila snapped the restraint closed and used them to pull me to my feet. I teetered but didn't fall. He pulled gently, keeping five long feet of chain between us, and my legs moved.

The slitted dress had fallen almost completely off, held up only by where it caught at my arms. It didn't matter that my breasts hung free in their meager glory or that the only things covering me down below were my inadequate curls. It took all of my dwindling strength just to hang on to the fast unraveling threads of my control. To keep from begging and pleading to be fucked. To just put one damned foot in front of the other in what seemed an endless march.

We finally halted and the sound I had heard for some time registered at last. Water. We were at a small brook, a different one from where I had met Halcyon a short lifetime ago.

I stood, swaying, not knowing what else to do.

Amber's voice drifted distantly to me. "Release me. I pledge my solemn oath that I shall not attempt to escape or resist when you restrain me once again. I just wish to care for her."

A short man with a large head and wide shoulders snorted. "Like we would take your word."

"Do *you* wish to care for her, Greeves?" Aquila asked blandly.

Greeves shook his head and remained sullen and silent.

"Your pledge," Aquila demanded of Amber.

"My solemn oath," Amber rumbled, "upon my honor as a warrior."

His chains fell away and he walked to me.

"Amber," I whispered, need huge and monumental in my eyes.

He waited patiently for Aquila to unshackle me. Then, grasping my wrist, led me to the little brook. He slid the gown off my arms and ripped off a clean piece, untainted by the oil. Methodically, Amber removed his shoes and socks, and then mine. With rag in hand, he led me into the shallow streaming water.

I gasped. The sensation of cold, prickling water flowing over my flushed, heated skin was almost beyond bearing. He urged me to sit and I resisted him for one useless second before my strength gave out and I collapsed. Supporting me by my arms, he sat me carefully down in the running water. Cool, tickling droplets ran over that most heated, most sensitive part of me, licking me like a thousand wickedly soft tongues. I convulsed in an explosive orgasm and cried out helplessly. I felt the solid presence of Amber squatting behind me, shielding me from the others' eyes, and slumped against him, tears leaking out from beneath my closed lids.

Amber's arms bunched and moved and the wet cloth smoothed down my chest. I gasped as he rubbed over the excrutiatingly sensitive tips of my breasts. He washed me thoroughly while I dug my fingers into his knees until my knuckles whitened and threatened to split, trying to make neither sound nor movement. He cupped water and splashed it over me. I endured it in silence, but when the cloth dipped down to that part of me immersed in water, electric shocks stabbed me and I could not help the moan that escaped my lips. I leaned back harder, and opened my legs wider in a desperate plea. He stopped before I reached my peak and I whimpered, wildly shaking my head. *No!* I wanted to plead. *Don't stop!* He dropped the cloth in the water and guided my hand down into the water to stroke myself. I jerked and resisted him for a moment, then let my head fall back heavily against him in surrendering need. Let him guide my other hand up to squeeze and pinch my nipple. I exploded, literally. A brilliant shower of light fell behind my closed lids. He eased two of my fingers inside me while I was still yet convulsing and pressed my palm against my painfully oversensitive, swollen clitoris, where it seemed every nerve in my body had gathered. That light contact, that touch, was almost too much. My head thrashed and my third orgasm ripped through my body, hard. Then I fell blessedly limp, free for a moment from that terrible racking tension. I tasted blood and vaguely realized that I'd bitten my lips.

Amber swung me into his arms and set me down on the grass, still shielding me from the others. He took off his shirt, slid my arms into the shirt, and buttoned it back up. I was asleep before he had finished, unaware, unknowing, unfeeling when he swung me into his arms and carried me.

Twelve

I FLOATED IN and out of consciousness, pulled into awareness first by the unnatural warmth of my body, followed viciously by icy chills that wracked my body. The chilling coldness had somehow heated my body until it seemed that blue flames licked my skin, burning worst between my legs, and swelling my breasts so uncomfortably full and tight so that I tossed and turned and moaned and whimpered.

Fingers would guide my hands to those places that needed stimulation most desperately. My body would spasm and I'd sink back into sweet oblivion until the next time. When I became too exhausted, gentle fingers would sink into me and I'd cry out and fall back into blessed unconsciousness.

At times cool water bathed me. Other times a spoon would push between my lips and he'd gently rub my throat until I swallowed some broth. He . . .

"Gryphon?" I whispered and felt a deep rumbling response.

Not Gryphon. That's right, he had left me, I remembered, and the pain would tear at me sharply once again until I escaped back into peaceful unawareness.

Gradually, the demands of my body lessened so that I came less and less into awareness. I was content to remain in the soothing darkness. So tired. I was so tired of hurting.

"You must not tarry long in this place, my child. It is dangerous." A soft hand smoothed my brow. I opened my eyes and looked up into Sonia's sweet face.

"You should have been my mother," I told her.

"Ah, sweet child. You are the daughter of my heart. You must return to me."

"I'm tired, Sonia. So tired."

She smiled and cast her lure. "Your brother shall need you soon."

I tossed my head fretfully in her lap. "I don't know how to find him."

"But you do. I have given you the information." Then she was fading.

"No, don't go. . . ."

But she heeded me not and left me so that I could no longer feel her touch.

"Go to him," she called softly. "Find him."

I reached for her but she was gone.

No! I wouldn't let her go. She was my only comfort.

I staggered to my feet, determined to follow her, but I was so weak. *Too weak,* a voice whispered.

I heard a child's voice. My brother?

I whimpered in pain and weakness. Such effort it required simply to stand. But Sonia had said that my brother needed me. So sweating, trembling, I fought my way upward, one step at a time, out of the deep abyss.

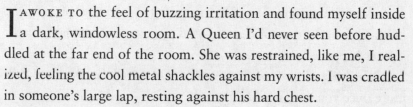

I AWOKE TO the feel of buzzing irritation and found myself inside a dark, windowless room. A Queen I'd never seen before huddled at the far end of the room. She was restrained, like me, I realized, feeling the cool metal shackles against my wrists. I was cradled in someone's large lap, resting against his hard chest.

"Milady?"

"Amber," I croaked, surprised at the terrible rusty sound I had produced and how weakly it had come out, a bare whisper.

"Thank the Goddess." He heaved a shuddering sigh of relief, leaned forward and brought a glass to my lips, his movements made awkward by his own wrist restraints. "Drink. It is but water."

Cool liquid moistened my mouth and eased down my parched throat. I swallowed painfully twice, then pushed it away.

Amber set down the glass. "Can you eat some meat?"

"Not hungry."

"A tiny piece." Who knew such a big, harsh-looking man could be such a coaxing shrew. "Well-cooked, the way you like it." He lifted a spoon to my mouth and I opened up, chewed, and swallowed, knowing he would not relent until I had taken some sustenance. It felt like a brick going down.

"You look awful," I rasped.

And he did, haggard, thinner, with dark bruises of exhaustion and worry puffing his eyes. Amber smiled tiredly at me, his hair uncombed, his chest bare.

"Where's your shirt?" I asked.

"It is covering you."

I looked down. His shirt shielded me down to my knees. The sleeves had been rolled back so many times that it was a thick bundle of cloth against my wrists, just above the metal restraints. My socks and shoes looked peculiar against the bareness of my legs. "Oh. Thanks," I mumbled and closed my eyes, so damnably tired. "What happened?" I slurred.

"You were ill but you are recovering now. Sleep. We shall talk more once you have rested."

⁓

THE NEXT TIME I surfaced, the sun was up. Amber blinked his eyes open, brought to awareness when I stirred in his lap. I drank more of the water this time.

"Here, eat."

"What is it?" I asked, chewing what he stuck in my mouth. "Doesn't taste like beef."

"Venison."

Deer. I'd never tasted it before, and didn't particularly care for the taste—too gamey—but I swallowed a few chunks, knowing I had to regain my strength. Exhausted from the effort, I tumbled once more back to sleep.

⁓

A CHILD'S VOICE roused me from my slumber the next time. Inquisitive eyes that were oddly familiar peered at me from beneath a tangle of matted brown hair that looked as if it had never known the touch of a comb. Dirt smudged her cheeks and browned the little hands that clutched a tray bearing three bowls of aromatic soup.

"She's awake," the girl whispered.

"Yes," Amber said, taking two bowls from her. "My thanks, Casio."

Simple statements, simple actions, and yet not.

My big man or little giant—both aptly described him—was acting most peculiar. Amber was such as I had never seen him before, and it finally came to me. The oddity was in the way he looked upon the wild child, the manner in which he spoke to her, in the tenderness of his tone. It was different even from the manner in which he treated me, without the wary deference or cautious constraint that usually marked his gestures and words unless he was vexed with me.

The timid little creature brought the remaining bowl to the Queen who eyed us warily from across the room. Then she darted out, dashing quickly past Greeves, who stood leering by the door.

"Sandoor wishes to see you and the new Queen after dinner," Greeves said to Amber. "Perchance she will serve as dessert." Laughing nastily, he shut the heavy metal door.

I ate half of my stew and insisted that Amber partake of the other half. No wonder he had lost weight. The little meat that was in the bowl would barely sustain a woman, much less a man of Amber's size.

"Who's Sandoor?" I asked when he had finished eating.

"My father."

My eyes widened in shocked surprise. "He's still alive? But I thought he raped and killed his Queen."

"Raped, but he refrained from killing me," came a bitter voice from the far corner, the other Queen. "He wouldn't kill the golden goose that lengthens his life."

Only there were two golden gooses now. Did that make one of us expendable?

"He made it appear as if he and I had perished and everyone apparently believed it so. Fools!" the Queen said.

"How could he have done that?" I asked.

"There were two piles of ashes and empty clothing," Amber explained. "That is all that usually remains when we die."

I stared at the Queen. "How long ago?"

"Over ten years ago," she said, her eyes burning with bitter emotion.

God! I couldn't imagine being kept captive that long and still remaining sane.

The door creaked open, bringing a wave of fresh air into the staleness of the room. "Outside, you two," Greeves said.

Amber lifted me up into his arms and carried me out into the cool night. Back in the room, cloth rustled.

"Not you, Mona Carlisse," Greeves said. "It is Balzaar's turn to see you tonight."

I craned my neck and saw a tall, heavily built man slide in past Greeves's thin, wiry frame. The door closed behind him ominously. Greeves looked at me and smiled. The cruel lust burning in his small eyes made the hair on the back of my neck stand up. Really good incentive to regain my strength.

I pushed against Amber as he walked into the night. "I can stand," I protested.

His arms tightened warningly around me as we entered a clearing where the other six men, and one other, a man who stood a head taller than the others, waited. Then again, I considered, looking at Amber's father, the paternal giant to my little giant. Maybe it was in my best interest to look weak and ill. Too bad it happened to be true.

"So, she has finally awoken," boomed a deep voice. Sandoor. Amber's father. He was a big man, though less heavily framed and an inch or two shorter than his son. Silver streaked his brown hair and years of harsh, unpleasant experiences lined his rough face. His blue eyes, so like his son's, were darker, harder, and much, much meaner. He felt powerful.

"Is she sane?" Sandoor inquired in a tone that implied that it didn't matter if I was or wasn't.

Amber nodded.

"That is of good fortune, although not particularly necessary." Sandoor's dark eyes fell on me like a nasty caress. "We just need the use of her body."

They might look the same, but he was nothing like Amber.

"She almost passed from this life. She requires a few more days to recover fully," Amber warned in a low rumble, "or you may yet lose her."

"Ah, yes. She is a Mixed Breed. More fragile, though quite gifted, I am told." Sandoor's dark eyes probed me, a singularly unpleasant experience. "Very well. She has one day longer before I break her in." His smile—the look in his eyes—creeped me out most ardently.

Amber turned to go.

"Not so readily." Sandoor's perverse words and tone stopped Amber cold and I felt renewed tension sing in the arms that held me. "I did not give you leave to go yet. Do tarry. Set her down here." He gestured to a log, which served as furniture here, apparently, in this sparse, barren domain.

Amber placed me carefully down on the ground, propping me up against a fallen tree trunk. Much better than being supine, among this pack of wild and hungry rogues.

"How carefully you handle her, Amber," his father mocked. "How diligently you have tended her these past six days."

Six whole days! The revelation staggered me. No wonder I felt so weakened.

"How tenderly you continue yet to care for her," Sandoor continued, his voice a deep, unhappy taunt. He came to tower over me.

"That is not the manner with which we treat women here, Amber. If you are to stay amongst us, you must learn that we do not serve women, they serve us."

"I do no more and no less than what she did for me when illness befell me," Amber returned carefully, no challenge or inflection in his words.

"And what caused you to be ill, Amber?"

"Mona Sera punished me by having me withstand the rays of the sun."

"For what length of time?"

"Four hours."

The other bandits muttered with anger.

"Then it was not punishment," Sandoor remarked with dangerous softness. "It was an intended execution. Not because you did not serve her well. Oh, no. You no doubt foolishly served her to the best of your ability, as we all served our Queens. And like you, we were to be rewarded for our utterly stupid loyalty, our years of thankless service, with death." Sandoor glared down at me with pure, undiluted hatred that was quite unsettling. "Why? Because inevitably we grow too strong for our Queens and threaten their power. Hundreds, thousands of our best and strongest warriors have been slaughtered under the guise of punishment, and will continue to die in this merciless manner unless we wrest control from the Queens and have them serve *us*."

"Mona Lisa saved me," Amber protested.

"Because she needed you, a vulnerable new Queen."

"She is not like other Queens, Father."

Sandoor smiled upon his offspring most pityingly. "Have you not learned yet, son, that they all begin most sweet. But eyes that gaze upon you with warm eagerness and affection those first few fleeting years, quickly become hard, wary, and fearful as your power grows until, alas, they banish you from their bed." He bent down to Amber, whispering into his face. "And then they destroy you."

Sandoor drew back and raked my body with cold, hating eyes. "How sweet you must be to draw such loyalty from my son, a man fully grown, who should have learned much better by now the harsh lessons of life. And yet, most interestingly, you were able to save him, when he was but as good as dead. Show us your hands, girl."

If that was all he wanted, I was most happy to comply. The restraints prevented me from turning my palms up, requiring me to bring my arms up and bend them at the elbows, so that my palms were displayed outward.

"So you have the ability to heal as well as harm with those unseemly blemishes," Sandoor mused. "Perhaps we need not sever your hands, after all."

Dear sweet God in heaven. My hands fell weakly back into my lap and curled protectively into impotent fists as fear dried my throat so that I could hardly even swallow.

"And let us hope, for your sake, that you breed better than that other bitch and contribute something more besides another useless female," Sandoor said sneeringly. A bush rustled and the little girl, Casio, who had been hiding behind it, darted away.

And I suddenly knew why her eyes had seemed so eerily familiar. They were Amber's eyes. And Sandoor's, as well.

"She's your daughter," I said to Sandoor, dazed by the sudden knowledge. His and Mona Carlisse's. Casio, that little shy, wild creature, was Amber's half sister.

"She is nothing. Not a Queen or a warrior, although she may serve some use to my men in a few short years."

Sweet Lord in heaven, he meant sexually. Her own sire.

I did not blame Sandoor or any of the other men here for fleeing their Queens, for becoming rogues. They were doing nothing more than merely surviving. Not after Sandoor's revelation, confirmed by my very own eyes and through my own mother's carefully planned actions. She had been cleaning house: killing off her strongest threats, her strongest men. I saw it clearly now. But I did hold Sandoor accountable for all his actions since then, for the needless unkindness that he deliberately inflicted with relish to those in his captivity, for his cruel actions to his very own flesh and blood. For that, oh yes, I held him most accountable.

"You are a monster," I rasped. "Far worse than any Queen who may have done you wrong once."

Sandoor's eyes narrowed in dangerous warning. "*I* determine whether you shall live or die. Do not forget that most pertinent fact." He whipped away, crossing to the other side of the clearing, and threw himself into the only seat present in this most rustic abode, a chair roughly hewn from wood. "Come forward to the center, Amber," he demanded from his crude throne.

Amber rose and walked to the middle of the clearing.

"Aquila. The lady, if you please," Sandoor said, and the man with the neatly trimmed Vandyke beard knelt behind me and held a silver dagger to my throat.

Sandoor smiled most unpleasantly as Amber stiffened. "Behave, and the knife shall not touch her."

There was a deep, lusty groan and a faint feminine cry in the distance. Light flashed out from beneath the door where we had been imprisoned.

"Ah, good. Balzaar will be in attendance shortly," Sandoor said. "You may remove Amber's restraints, Romulus."

A blond man of average height, with handsome unsmiling features, walked to Amber and began removing his cuffs. The door swung open and Balzaar emerged. Greeves secured the door with a heavy chain and both he and Balzaar joined us in the clearing. It was impossible to ignore the heavy tang of sweat and sex that clung to Balzaar's heavy frame.

"You have been most careful around your new Queen, my strong son. She does not fear you," Sandoor said in a careful, considering voice. "And I wager she does not know the reason why she should fear you, does she, Amber? Why Mona Sera feared you. Why she wished to destroy you. I believe—yes, yes—I do believe you should enlighten her. Show her. Show all."

Amber's face became set like stone.

"Come, come. So shy," Sandoor said in a provoking tone. "Let us see if we can make it worthy of your while, then. All present here are free to challenge my son one at a time. Any who are able to defeat him may have first stab, shall we say, at the new Queen. Tonight. All night long."

Every eye turned upon me. I felt like a helpless, tender rabbit trapped among a pack of starving wolves.

"If you are able to defeat all who wish to challenge you, Amber, you may remain with your Queen and let her have the rest you believe she so desperately needs one last night. If you can muster control of yourself, afterward." Sandoor smiled most nastily. "It may even be better for her if you do *not* win. A small consideration for you to chew over."

I had an unpleasant feeling, like I was missing something vital again. Then it was too late. Balzaar was pulling off his clothes. Amber kicked off his shoes and stepped out of his pants. A prickling surge of energy and they were changing, shifting, falling onto all fours, their faces distorting, heads flattening, muzzles growing, a wash of heavy fur flowing.

All the men backed away, including Sandoor, creating a wide circle fringing the perimeter of the clearing. Aquila lifted me to my feet, his grip unbreakable but not bruising, in that conscious strength that strong men used. He dragged me backward, almost into the trees. My legs quivered but held me upright. I damned my weakness.

Before my eyes, in a transformation so quick and complete, Amber became a vicious mountain lion of enormous size. His civilized façade was stripped away, and lethal razor-sharp teeth glistened as he snarled savagely in that chilling, purely animalistic manner seen only in creatures most wild. Deadly muscles rippled under that sleek, tawny coat. Yet strikingly cold intelligence glittered in those crystal-clear amber eyes. Those same eyes that had looked upon me during the heat of passion. Eyes that looked so right on the vicious creature he had become.

With a scream that curdled my blood, the big cat launched itself at the towering black bear that had risen onto his hind legs. With a roar, the bear's thick, powerful upper limbs wrapped around the cat as they rolled to the ground, with Amber's razor-sharp teeth buried in the bear's throat.

Sharp claws slashed, a heavy blow, and blood streaked obscenely on Amber's tawny coat as he tumbled away. The cat's sharp teeth had broken through his opponent's skin, but the bear's coarse, thick hair had prevented deeper damage.

It became a game of strategy: the mountain lion's speed, agility, and pouncing quickness against the bear's slower but more powerful strikes, deadly strength, and thick protective coat. Amber springing and attacking, again and again, slashing, biting, inflicting superficial but not serious damage. Balzaar defending, retaliating, landing fewer but more damaging strikes that drew more and more blood.

I swallowed the cries that rose to my throat with each landing blow, knowing they would serve no purpose but to distract Amber.

Balzaar was playing a game of endurance, his greatest strength, waiting for Amber to weaken. A smart strategy, particularly when Amber's strength had already been greatly lessened by six days of slow starvation from caring for me day and night.

The sounds of battle filled the quiet night. I turned to face Aquila and was stopped by the warning press of his blade against my skin.

"Face forward, Lady, and kindly keep your hands lowered," he issued quietly from behind me.

That's right. What I'd done to Miles with my hands, branding him, had apparently frightened the men enough to have Sandoor consider cutting them off.

I shivered. We had to get out of here. Amber was fighting with body and flesh. I was too weakened to battle that way, so I would fight another way.

There seemed to be no real meanness in Aquila, no hatred of women that I could detect, unlike Sandoor. Though I did not particularly like Sandoor, I believed without doubt what he had stated. All of these men had become too powerful for their Queens and had joined Sandoor, outcasts, rogues, because there was no other place where they could go and still live.

I issued my invitation to Aquila in the barest of whispers. "All who come to me with an honest and willing heart, I will accept into my service."

Battle raged before me but it was the silence behind me that held me. I knew Aquila had heard me.

"The offer expires in twenty-four hours. Tell the others, but not Greeves or those of his ilk."

Aquila's non-answer was answer enough. He would consider it and would not tell Sandoor—yet. It was enough for now. It had to be enough. But it was damnably hard convincing myself of that when Amber, visibly slowing, gave a screaming shriek of pain as Balzaar delivered another slashing blow and charged at his tired opponent, sensing his weakness.

With a sudden burst of speed, Amber leaped over Balzaar and ripped at his unprotected rear. Balzaar spun around with a raging roar and slashing paws. Amber ducked, but instead of springing away he surged forward, slashing the bear's vulnerable face, blinding one eye and ripping through the tender nose. With a bellow of pain, Balzaar spun away and loped into the forest.

The big mountain lion stood alone in the clearing, an injured predator, flanks heaving, blood slowly oozing from deep gouges on his left back, shoulder, and right belly, waiting for the next challenge.

With a vicious snarl, his next challenger attacked. It was a silver wolf. Teeth clashed, claws ripped, and more blood flowed. The wolf danced around the large cat, darting in and nipping at his flanks. A powerful, retaliating blow from Amber's sharp, ripping claw and the wolf was rolling away. The wolf sprang to his feet in lightning-fast movement and leaped again. They clashed in the air, heavy bodies impacting one against the other. The wolf's teeth sank deeply into Amber's throat. With a cry of fury, the big cat jerked free. Tawny fur and a chunk of meat ripped away was the price of that freedom. Blood oozed but didn't spurt.

He missed the artery, I told my thumping heart, but it continued to hammer away mercilessly in my chest so that my head spun and the ground swayed. The hand gripping me became supportive rather than restraining. I ground my teeth and desperately clung to consciousness with dogged determination. I would not faint.

With a sudden pounce, Amber grabbed the wolf by the throat. With casual, almost disdainful strength, he threw the smaller animal in the air. The animal sailed for some distance—his blood *did* spurt—and landed ten feet away with a yelp of pain. Tail tucked down between his legs, he fled into the woods, leaving behind a trail of pumping blood.

There was no waiting in the next attack. A flash of spotted fur rushed at Amber. It was Greeves. Top-heavy Greeves, whose big head and wide shoulders looked quite natural in his other form—a massive hyena with a most frightening, smiling grimace twisting that intelligent face. His weaker hindquarters were compensated by his massive head and powerful jaws. He attacked with sly cunning, darting in with sudden lunges, teeth snapping, pulling back, circling, twisting, and lunging again each time Amber evaded those deadly jaws.

Hyenas were better known as scavengers and carrion feeders. People often forgot that they were active and skilled predators in their own right. I knew I would never forget that oft-overlooked fact as I fixed my eyes upon those vicious teeth, dark pigmented lips curled back in a sly, snarling smile.

Amber twisted and slipped on a patch of blood-soaked grass and Greeves lunged for his throat. Sharp teeth locked together like a steel trap in a deadly grip. I gasped and cried out, unaware I had stepped forward until I was pulled back and locked securely against Aquila.

Amber twisted and struggled. He slashed deep furrows in the hyena's powerful chest but those mighty jaws remained deeply clenched. Greeves shook Amber, tossing him back and forth until the mountain lion's struggles lessened, grew more feeble, then finally stopped. Sobs choked my throat and tears poured down my face as those beautiful amber eyes closed. The once majestic cat became dead weight, dragging the hyena forward until it stood breathing heavily over him.

"No! No . . ." I moaned in the sudden quiet. "Amber . . ."

Amber's yellow eyes suddenly flashed opened and four razor-sharp claws swiped with great force at the hyena's vulnerable underbelly, slashing it open with ripping ease. Rich, tangy blood spurted. Intestines bulged and swelled and pushed out. And those viciously strong hyena jaws unlocked and released. With a chilling howl of outrage and pain, the hyena loped away.

Amber rolled slowly to his feet, precious blood dripping from the gaping wound at his throat, his breathing harsh and belabored. No one moved.

Sandoor broke the silence. "Next challenger?"

No one stepped forward.

"Amber wins," Sandoor declared, his voice rich with satisfaction and pride.

I moved to go to Amber but Aquila restrained me, shaking his head warningly.

A shimmer of energy and Amber was kneeling in the clearing, tan skin above the waist, pale white flesh down below, both colors ribboned with red blood. Flesh had been torn from his throat, and his chest, torso, and legs were ripped open from slashing claws. With effort, Amber staggered to his pants, and pulled them on. He lifted his eyes with tired alertness as Romulus approached him, restraints in hand.

Amber turned and sought me out, casting me a wild pleading glance, his eyes still that unsettling yellow color. I desperately wished I knew what he wanted me to do. Break free? Try to escape? Even if I could, it would be a futile attempt. More than half the men were still present, rested, whole, healthy, uninjured.

When I made no move, Amber held out his hands, despair flooding his eyes as the manacles clamped shut about his large wrists. He turned his pleading gaze to his father.

"Return them back to join Mona Carlisse," Sandoor commanded.

Romulus took hold of Amber's arm. Amber resisted.

"Allow me to stay here, outside, tonight," Amber asked Sandoor, his ragged voice a low harsh sound.

"No." His father shook his head. "I am sorry, son."

As if the words had released a sudden trigger, Amber began struggling in quiet earnestness. Another blond man joined Romulus and helped subdue Amber. Together they dragged Amber forward.

Aquila removed the dagger from my throat. "Can you walk?"

"I can certainly try." My quivering legs felt like jelly but I was able to walk back to the stone hut that would imprison us. Sandoor unlocked the thick metal door and I hobbled inside.

"Father, please do not do this," Amber said hoarsely. "I beg of you."

Sandoor's voice was chillingly sincere. "It is for your own good, son." The terrible thing was that he truly meant it.

Amber's roar shook the air. "Do not do this to me!"

But they pushed him inside.

The door clanged shut behind Amber, locking him in.

THIRTEEN

"AMBER," I CRIED, moving toward him.

"Don't!" he said, his voice terribly strained.

"But you're hurt. . . ."

"Do as he says!" Mona Carlisse snapped from across the room. "Back away slowly from him," she instructed more quietly.

Amber leaned with his back slumped against the door, fear and rage filling his eyes, a potent combustible combination. "Do as she says!" he rasped harshly.

I eased into the corner where he had nursed me, kept me alive, and sank onto the blanket. "Amber." My voice came out small, timid. "What's wrong?"

Mona Carlisse's voice floated out in the darkness, her voice tight with strain. "He is fresh from battle and from shifting. His blood still pounds with bloodlust and his body demands relief."

"How can he gain relief?" I asked, already knowing I would not like the answer.

"Blood or sex. They usually hunt afterward to burn off the powerful tension."

But they hadn't allowed Amber to hunt. They had locked him here inside instead, with two Queens and his natural powerful attraction to them, allowing it to stir and stimulate his already violent emotions. They had only allowed him one outlet. Sex.

I understood it now. They expected him to be violent. *He* expected himself to be violent and he feared it. Mona Carlisse feared it. Her alarm pulsed like an audible call in air that was already thick with the smell and scent of spent passion.

Amber trembled. His muscles locked. His arms and thighs bulged with threatening strength. He gasped in air desperately like a drowning man. Spinning, he violently struck his shackles against the door so that it shook. Metal rang against metal in a sickening, angry desperate clanging.

"Let me out! Let me out!" His rage was terrible. He pounded the door, smashing metal again and again until it dented. He spun suddenly, taking a few steps forward, making Mona Carlisse gasp in fright. He threw a viciously bitter look of hatred at her then threw himself against the door. Unbound by silver, he could have ripped the door apart. Even just human strong, he could do a lot of damage. Three hundred pounds worth of damage. He battered the door, battered himself mercilessly, shaking the metal, rattling its hinges, coating it with his blood. But it held. He slid down to the ground, his face pressed against the door.

"Amber," I called to him, my voice low, calm. "Come to me."

He stiffened, his ragged breathing the only harsh sound. Then he burst into explosive motion once again, pounding himself against the stone wall this time, against the weakest point where the wall abutted the door. He battered himself over and over like a ram. Dust flew but the stubborn stone held. He braced his great weight against the wall and pushed, grunting, straining. His arms bulged and trembled, his back rippling so that all his muscles were thrown into sharp delineation. But he was no Samson, no mythical Hercules. With a sob he collapsed, unable to escape, a wild animal caught in an unbreakable trap.

Welling up within me was an undeniable, instinctive urge to soothe and comfort, to ease his horrid suffering. You could get your well-meaning hands ripped off trying to help a wild beast. I knew that fact well. Oh, yes. But I was more than willing to risk it.

"Amber. Come to me. Trust me."

He shook his bowed head, his matted, disheveled hair flung wildly across his face like a madman. "Don't! Oh, Goddess. OhGoddessohGoddess . . ."

What his own father was doing to him with knowing deliberation was far worse than what Miles had done to me with the aphrodisiac. How could a father do this to his own son? *How could a mother give away her own child to strangers?* a small voice within me whispered. I let my eyes fall down to the pitiful suffering animal huddled on the dirt floor before me and had one of those sudden insights. Perhaps, by giving me away, Mona Sera had done me more good than I had realized. At least I'd had Helen and her warm love for those first six years of my life.

Amber's head slowly lifted. Feral amber eyes, inhuman eyes, gleamed in the darkness at the huddled figure in the far corner—at Mona Carlisse. Crouching on hands and knees, he took a gliding step in that direction, his belly low to the ground, a great cat stalking his prey.

"No, Amber," I said.

His voice rumbled deeply in his chest with effort, as if it was hard for him to form human words. "I'd rather hurt her than you."

And I was struck again with another insight. Sandoor had known, had deliberately left Mona Carlisse here knowing his son would choose this, knowing that once Amber raped a Queen, he could never go back, that then he'd *have* to stay with this band of outcasts forever.

Grim resolve tightened like a drawn arrow within me. I would not lose Amber. Not him, too.

"Watching you hurt her would hurt me worse," I said to him. "Come to me."

He stopped, shuddered, took a sobbing, sobering breath. "It would destroy me to see fear in your eyes. I would not be able to stand it. Not now."

"Look into my eyes, Amber. You will not see fear." My voice deepened and the right words came to me from somewhere deep inside. "I am your Queen. It is my right to aid and comfort you. Heed me now. Come to me."

Almost against his will, he turned to me, his cat eyes a frightening gleam. I held out my hands to him and he slowly flowed to me on all fours, using muscles that no human possessed. He was beautifully, dangerously graceful, even with restraints hampering his movement.

I reached out to him, wanting to lay my hands on his terrible wounds. To heal him.

"No!" he cried desperately. "I shall not be able to control myself if you touch me."

"All right." I lay back, offering myself to him freely.

"You're too weak."

I laughed. "I don't need much strength to just lie on my back. I promise I'll let you do all the work this time." My eyes twinkled up at him.

The sound of my laughter eased some of that terrible tension in him.

He turned his head toward Mona Carlisse. "Don't look," he rumbled warningly.

Her head whipped around to face the wall, and my heart grew soft and warm at the realization that even now, wracked with such terrible need, Amber remembered my discomfort, my odd modesty.

I smiled tremulously up at him as he crawled over me, careful not to touch me.

"Oh, Amber." His name was a soft sigh upon my lips.

He crouched above me, straddling my thighs. His hands reached beneath my shirt, between my legs. One thick finger tested me. My eyes fluttered closed for a moment and I bit back a welling moan.

"You're not wet enough." He breathed harshly, a faint trembling shaking his entire frame.

I was wet, but not enough for him, for his size. "I'll be fine."

"Give me your hands," he gritted, opening his pants and freeing himself. Licking both my palms, wetting them with his saliva, he wrapped my hands roughly around his spearing length, one atop the other, leaving room yet for still another hand had I had one, so thick around that my fingertips did not meet. He groaned harshly and levered over me, his forearms braced above my head. I held him tightly, my hands creating a sheath between my thighs.

"Squeeze me harder! Yes!" He pumped himself above me, hard, vigorous, violent strokes, not pausing or hesitating even when my hands started to tingle and heat and my power started to flow. He lit the dingy room with incandescent light that shone from within, outlined above me in brutal, savage glory.

I turned my face and licked the wound at his throat, my tongue going deep, causing him pain, causing him pleasure. He cried out and slammed his lower body into my hands even harder, faster, more urgently, propelling us several inches up the blanket with each pounding stroke. His muscles tightened and he roared his release, spilling his hot essence between my thighs.

"You're glowing," he said with gritty surprise, lifting his head, his eyes still that animal amber. But the desperate wild edge in them was gone.

"I love your pleasure," I said, purring, noting with rich, hot satisfaction the smooth, perfect skin that now covered his neck where that deep wound had been.

"Your hands are hot," he whispered.

"And you're not afraid."

"You would never hurt me."

"Oh, Amber." I sighed and brushed him against my hungry opening, drenched wet with his ejaculation. He was smaller, semihard in my hands. I moaned and lifted up against him, sliding in his broad tip. "I'm wet enough now," I enticed. My hands dipped down, coating and caressing him with his own fluids.

He lifted his upper body up, freeing my hands, and I stretched my arms over my head, moving my shackles out of the way. I writhed against him. Opened my legs wider. With his beautiful, dangerous eyes clinging to mine, he pushed slowly into me, so gradually that there was no discomfort, just a feeling of being wonderfully stretched. It was easier now that he was smaller but he still had to work his way deep with gentle, small thrusts that weren't enough. Not nearly enough. Once he was seated in me fully, he stilled. I felt him grow, lengthening and thickening within me to full arousal, filling me deliciously, painfully full and then some, until I felt as if I would burst if he moved, until I felt as if I would burst if he didn't move. I whimpered and arched up against him.

"Shhh," he soothed roughly. "You said you would allow me to do the work."

"Then do it," I snapped.

His rough laughter warmed my heart. His deep thrust suspended my breath. "Oh." The wildly pleasurable tearing sensation that ripped through my body hazed my vision.

"I love giving you pleasure," he rumbled and stroked strongly, leisurely, setting a slow, steady rhythm that was almost but not quite gentle. He surged steadily, relentlessly, like the tide, building the wave of our pleasure until the light emitting from us was pure and blinding. My wave crested and broke and I spasmed on endlessly. He loosened his control and with one forceful plunge that stole my breath, buried himself hilt-deep in me, all the way to my womb, and held still, letting my strong squeezing contractions milk him to his own glorious release. He groaned sweetly and collapsed over me, his arms still bearing most of his massive weight, and I savored the moment, the closeness, and the triumph. I had come so close to losing him.

I rubbed my cheek against his in simple affection. "I love your strength, your bigness."

I felt his passion-slashed cheeks heat even more and I giggled when I realized that he had mistook my meaning.

"Down there, yes. But also your size, your height. You make me feel safe," came my whispered confession.

Amber pulled out of me, the slide of his withdrawal making me quiver. He rolled with me onto his back so that I sprawled atop him. Covering me with the blanket, he brushed his lips sweetly, tenderly, against mine. "You make me feel safe, too," he said.

I smiled, happy, tired, and relaxed, and willingly embraced the bliss of sleep that called to me.

FOURTEEN

THE SUN WAS a high ball of fire in the sky when I awoke. Amber's large hands slid up my spine in a slow, savoring stroke and I lifted my head and smiled at him.

"How do you feel?" he queried softly.

"Better," I said after a moment's consideration, "and stronger, oddly enough." I tested the restraints at my wrists and they snapped apart easily. Perhaps when I had healed Amber, I had healed myself as well. Or maybe I had just recovered quickly after some much-needed rest. Or perhaps Amber had imparted some of his own great physical strength to me. That raised another question. Did Queens receive some of their lovers' gifts or did it only work the other way around? Whatever it was, I was too grateful for the return of my strength to question it much now. I stripped off the manacles, freeing Amber.

With ease, he rolled to his feet with me cradled in his arms and set me down. "Let us depart," he said.

"Take me with you." Mona Carlisse's quiet voice coming from the corner startled me. She had been so quiet and still that I had actually forgotten she was there.

I hesitated. "The sun is at its hottest now."

She stood up. "I care not. I would rather die free in the sun than submit to another rutting pig one more day."

I looked askance at Amber.

"They will be less inclined to hunt us if she remains. A good chance, in truth, that they will simply depart to another hiding place. If we take her with us, they shall have no other choice but to come after us."

What he said made good sense, and yet . . . I had only been here one week, and awake and aware but only one day. And what I had seen that one day was enough to make my skin crawl. She had been here, at their merciless mercy, for over ten long years.

"How much sun can she take?" I asked.

"She can withstand up to one hour of direct sunlight," Amber answered. "After that, I can perhaps try to shield her with a blanket and carry her if necessary."

"What about you?" I asked softly. "Will you be able to tolerate the sun?"

Amber shrugged. "We shall see shortly. If not, we will have at least an hour's start."

I turned to Mona Carlisse. "I have extended a twenty-four hour offer to accept any man here if he comes to me with an honest willingness to serve. Not Greeves or his like, but men like Aquila. I do not know if any will accept, but if they do, I must have your promise that you will not seek retribution personally or through the Council for what they have done to you here."

Her face was a shuttered mask. "Only to those you accept," she finally said.

I nodded.

"Agreed," she said.

"Where is your daughter?" I asked.

"Casio shelters in a nearby cave when she does not sleep here."

"Can you lead us there?"

She nodded.

"Good," I said. "Let's go fetch her."

Mona Carlisse bowed her head in deep formality. "Thank you, Sister."

I inclined my head. A shrug seemed too impolite. "No thanks needed."

There was nothing to gather in the primitive structure but the two blankets. A gentle push and the chains gave with a snap that sounded quite loud in my ears, but no alarm was raised from the two huts in the distance.

The door swung open and Mona Carlisse ran soundlessly into the wilderness, the blanket over her head, only a small part of her face exposed. She led us to a small, well-hidden cave, crawled into the little hole, and emerged a short time later with Casio wrapped in the same manner as herself with the other blanket.

The little girl blinked wide, beautiful blue eyes at me. I smiled reassuringly at her. She looked behind me and craned her neck back to peer up at Amber. He squatted down to her level and let her study him.

They had the same brown hair, though his was much cleaner, the same cerulean eyes. I wondered what other like features we would discover behind all that dirt. Amber bestowed a warm, gentle smile upon the little creature that shared his own blood. Casio returned a fleeting smile that stuttered on her lips for a moment, then died. Shyly, she wriggled out of her mother's arms and hid behind her skirt.

We traveled in total silence. After the first mile, Amber picked up the pace, uncaring of any rustling or disturbing noise we made as we traveled through the dense brush and wild foliage.

I tapped his arm and gestured to his bare chest.

"I'm fine," Amber replied quietly.

"Doesn't hurt?"

Amber shook his head.

He looked well. No redness, no sign of discomfort. Mona Carlisse and Casio, on the other hand, were already flushed beet-red and sweating profusely, their faces pinched with soundless discomfort. But they pushed on without a word of complaint, Casio having to run, at times, to keep up with our longer strides.

We had passed an hour and were nearing two when Mona Carlisse and Casio reached their endpoint. Amber stopped us by a small stream. Casio collapsed on the ground, panting, while Mona Carlisse dragged herself to the water, sipped it, and splashed it over her heated face. She submerged her arms up to her elbows in the cool water for a moment, then picked up Casio, brought her to the water's edge, and made her drink while she splashed water on her red little face.

So Mona Carlisse did care for her daughter. I wondered if other Queens were like her or more like my mother.

I was a little winded and my eyes were tearing from the irritating brightness of the sun, but otherwise I was holding up well. Amber stood guard while we rested, comfortable in the sun except for its bright glare, teary-eyed like me.

"That one is not like his father," Mona Carlisse said quietly, looking at Amber.

"No," I replied, "not within."

"He serves you with a devotion beyond a reach that I have never seen. Few men would refuse a life where their will was served by a Queen."

She turned to Amber. "Why did you still care for your Queen when there was no longer any need to, when it was even in your detriment to do so?"

"We are drawn to Queens," Amber replied. "It is our nature to desire to serve you, protect you. We require your warmth, your presence, as much as you require our strength. She is the Queen I have dreamt all my life of serving."

Mona Carlisse gazed at him wonderingly. "Why?"

"Because she loves and cherishes us as much as we love and cherish her," he said, his eyes fixed upon me.

I squirmed a little at the word *love* but did not deny it. I did love them, both of them, even now. My heart twanged at the thought of Gryphon, a soft ache.

"And she shows it by her actions, as you yourself have so witnessed—what she does, how she cares for us, how she foolishly puts our needs ahead of her own safety." He said the latter with sharp acidity.

"It was worth the risk," I declared. "*You* were worth the risk."

Amber's eyes caressed me with surprising gentleness. I smiled tenderly back, aware that a strong elemental bond between us had been forged.

He turned and addressed Mona Carlisse. "If you will carry Casio, I can then carry you both."

"I can carry Casio," I offered.

Amber shook his head. "No. If you deplete your strength, then I shall have to carry you as well."

I didn't like it but his logic was inarguable.

Mona Carlisse covered Casio completely with the blanket and

picked her up. Amber arranged Mona Carlisse's blanket so that it shielded her and the child, then lifted them both into his arms and started off at an even faster pace than before.

Two hours later, he put them down, breathing heavily.

He glanced at me, assessing my state. My heart beat a little faster and my muscles were starting to protest the abuse, but I could still go on.

"The sun goes down in one more hour," Amber informed Mona Carlisse. "Are you two able to walk now?"

She looked no better—worse, actually—despite her rest. Her heart was pumping fast and she panted with her mouth open—her body's way of cooling itself. But she lifted her chin up, a true Queen. "Of course."

They stumbled along doggedly, Mona Carlisse picking Casio up whenever she fell and pulling her along. The little girl trudged valiantly on as the sun slowly set with lazy ease. I was wondering how many more miles we had yet to cover when a giant bird swooped down and landed nearby. It was an eagle, bigger than its natural normal variant, with gray intelligent eyes. Amber's sword hung about the bird's neck along with a cloth bundle. In the distance, a wolf howled in joyful hunt, catching our scent. A hyena gave a laughing, chilling cry. I shivered.

Amber moved protectively in front, putting himself between us and the eagle, but he did not attack.

A shimmer of energy, of light, and Aquila stood before us. He tossed Amber his sword and calmly stepped into his clothes and shoes that he had wrapped within the bundle.

When Aquila was fully dressed, he knelt, facing me. "Milady. I wish to serve you if you will have me."

I stepped out from behind Amber's protection. Amber tensed but did not stop me as I went to the kneeling man. Gently, I cupped

Aquila's neatly bearded chin with both hands and lifted his face so that I could peer directly into his eyes. He stared up at me unflinchingly and allowed me to search those gray depths that slowly swirled back to their normal green-brownish hazel even as I watched. An extraordinary transformation to behold.

"I can only promise to do my best to protect you," I told him solemnly, "but I cannot guarantee it. If the Council rules otherwise for what you have done . . ."

"Then so be it. I have lived long enough. It would be a good way to go, an honorable way, serving you."

"Then I gladly welcome you," I replied in formal acceptance.

Aquila took a deep breath, let it out in a gentle gust, and placed a light kiss upon my hand. Standing back up, he bowed deeply. "My Queen."

"How far back are the others?" Amber asked him.

"Several hours' distance," Aquila replied. "But they will close that length rapidly once they change." He paused and smiled. "None other than I, however, can fly."

Amber turned to Mona Carlisse. "Do you have another form, milady?"

"No," Mona Carlisse said with regret.

Amber turned back to Aquila. "If you are able to carry Mona Carlisse and Casio in your eagle form, I shall see to Mona Lisa."

Aquila nodded and I saw the look of unspoken understanding pass between them. Amber would not entrust my safety to Aquila just yet.

Shoes and clothes were wrapped in blankets and hung around my neck and Mona Carlisse's. I looped Amber's sword and belt over my neck and one shoulder, allowing the blade to rest behind me. It was much heavier than it had looked in Amber's hand. Aquila shifted once more into a majestic eagle and waited patiently for us.

"He does not feel bloodlust?" I asked.

"He is a bird," was Amber's simple reply, "and he has not just battled."

Amber hesitated before shifting. "Do not fear me when I change."

I laid my hand on Amber's chest and smiled up at him. "I won't."

He pressed a tender kiss into my palm and shifted. Wild amber eyes lined in black kohl stared back at me, eye-level with my standing self. I reached out and stroked his furry head. He lazily blinked those golden eyes and turned his head so that I could scratch behind his ear, making a deep rumbling sound, purring.

The great cat crouched down before me and I clambered onto his back, my arms twining securely about his neck. A few gliding steps to make sure I had my seat and then he was running in smooth, loping strides through the thick brush, darting among the trees.

Aquila soared above us, his sharp talons wrapped carefully around Mona Carlisse and Casio. The little girl lifted her hot face to the cool blowing wind and smiled wonderingly as they flew over the trees above us.

I clung and buried my face in Amber's tawny fur, inhaling that feral musky fragrance that was him. Powerful muscles bunched and uncoiled beneath me in a smooth, steady rhythm. Leaves and branches whipped rapidly by us. He ran on tirelessly in that loping, ground-covering run that did not falter, did not slow, even as hour after hour passed and darkness descended fully, and his breathing grew harsh and labored.

Amber finally came to a halt beside a pool of water. I slid off him, unburdening him, and let him lap the cool water. His flanks heaved in and out, panting, as he rested fully upon the ground, those golden eyes blinking tiredly in that lazy-cat way.

Aquila glided down, dropped Mona Carlisse and Casio gently to the ground, and came to rest on a nearby stump.

"How are you doing?" I asked the other Queen.

Mona Carlisse rubbed her waist. "He grips us tightly but carefully. The wind, at least, feels good upon our faces." She bent down and scooped up some water to drink, then splashed water over her face. It was less alarmingly red than before, I saw with some relief.

"Are you having fun, Casio?" I inquired.

The little girl nodded. "It is fun to fly."

I smiled. "I shall have to try it myself one of these days."

I stretched out upon the wonderfully cool ground, relaxed my muscles, and closed my eyes. It seemed but a brief moment later when a cold wet nose nudged me. I reached out and stroked Amber's white whiskers. They felt like thin wires, but his muzzle was surprisingly soft and silky. His panting had slowed.

"Time to go, huh?" I climbed back on top of him.

The wolf howled again, much closer. They were covering the distance faster than we were, unburdened, unhampered. How much longer, I wondered, did we have to travel? It would be a close race, determined solely by the remaining distance.

We broke out of the forest into the safe, familiar clearing several hours later. Lights around the compound and from the main building brightly welcomed us.

In the forest behind us, so close that it made me shiver and hasten my pace, animal howls of gnashing rage lifted and filled the sky.

We were back at High Court.

FIFTEEN

THE YARD MILLED with a sea of people—an overwhelming number of guards, maids, footmen, and healers who looked curiously upon us, ragged lot that we were and much the worse for wear. The other Council members had arrived, it seemed.

Murmurs were loud and continuous as we made our way up to the Great House. I could imagine what they saw: two guards, one of them shirtless; a wild dirty child; and two Queens, one dressed in a ragged, torn gown, whom all had long thought dead, the other wearing only a man's shirt. It covered all that needed covering, really. But all those many male eyes made me vividly aware of the long bare length of leg I was showing. Frankly, I was too tired to care much. They could look as long as they did not touch. Amber's flashing sword ensured that they did not. Heeding the blade's warning, the watching men stayed back, giving us a clear path up the most welcomed steps.

We were met within by Mathias, the impeccable steward, who

did not even bat an eyelash at our less than regular attire, although his eyes did widen impressively upon seeing Mona Carlisse.

"Mona Carlisse and her daughter, Casio, shall be staying with us until other arrangements are made," Amber announced.

"Very good, sir," was the good steward's reply.

"Has the Council met yet?" I asked.

"They began their session a short while ago, milady."

I heaved an inward sigh. At least it wasn't over yet. "For how long do they usually meet?"

"Several more hours yet."

"Good. So we have some time to wash up. Mathias, would you be so kind as to rummage up some clothes for Mona Carlisse, Casio, and my man, Aquila, and have it brought up to our quarters immediately?"

"Of course, milady."

I smiled as I ascended the steps, amused at the bristling edge in Matthias's reply that I dared doubt his efficiency. "Oh, and could you have something brought up for all of us to eat as well?"

"Yes, milady."

Amber stayed behind a moment and bent down to whisper into the steward's ear. The little man's eyes grew even wider. "I shall make Lord Thorane aware of this immediately," Mathias uttered, faintly.

Back in my splendidly comfortable furnished room, I grabbed my one other black gown from the closet, detestable though it was, and hit the shower immediately, leaving Amber to sort out the bedding arrangements. Under the shower's spray, I groaned with deep appreciation. I'd forgotten how marvelously good it felt to be clean. The tiny pellets of water hitting me were wonderful. I washed myself twice and shampooed my hair thoroughly.

My little group was standing around stiffly when I emerged

from the bathroom. Mona Carlisse hovered in one corner with Casio. Amber and Aquila claimed the other end of the room, a wary distance between the two men. I lifted my brow but forbore saying anything other than "Please feel free to use the shower next, Mona Carlisse. There's a robe in the bathroom you can use until they bring up some clothes. The men will shower after you and Casio are done."

She nodded and escaped into the bathroom without a word, Casio in tow.

Someone knocked on the door. Amber opened it and three footmen bore in several trays of delicious-smelling food. Two maids entered behind them, their arms filled with clothes.

Rare meat didn't taste that bad, I decided a short time later, my stomach blissfully full. I'd eaten half my steak and pressed the other half on Amber. He wolfed down three steaks in addition to that. Aquila restrained himself to two large pieces of the lightly cooked meat.

Mona Carlisse stepped back into the room, looking young and vulnerable wrapped in the fluffy robe. So much so that I wondered exactly what her age really was. Her wet dark brown hair hung loosely down to her hips, its length a surprise. It hadn't looked that long, secured in a bun. Another surprise was her stunning looks. She was beautiful, I realized. Even now, too thin, with lines of fatigue and strain pinching her face, she was a striking woman. And strong, with a great force of will to have survived those ten years. When Amber had been locked in with us, filled with bloodlust, she had warned me and tried to help. Her daughter clung to her leg, wrapped in a towel, wet hair the color of spun gold covering her face. Automatically, Mona Carlisse put a protective, comforting arm about the girl.

She was downright decent for a Queen.

"There are some clothes in the other room for both of you," I said kindly. "You can change in there then join us for some food."

Mona Carlisse hesitated a moment, then nodded and went into the other room, closing the door behind her.

Aquila took his shower next and emerged wearing pants that were a tad too long and a simple loose shirt, no doubt borrowed from one of the footmen. Still, they were neat and clean, and much better than his old patched clothes. "The facility is yours," he said to Amber.

"I need not wash," Amber replied, his face cloaked once more in its usual impassive sternness.

I looked at Amber in surprise, then narrowed my eyes when I realized the reason for his reticence. He did not trust Aquila alone with me.

"Go ahead and use the shower, Amber," I said flatly.

"There is no need," Amber replied, a ferocious scowl on his face.

"I insist."

We locked in a short silent battle of wills before Amber dropped his eyes. Nodding curtly, he stalked into the bathroom.

"You cannot blame him, milady," Aquila said softly. "I would do the same were I in his position."

"He will have to trust you sooner or later. I'd rather it be sooner."

Aquila gave a short, surprised laugh. "You truly do not fear him."

"No. I know he would never hurt me. And I know you wish me no harm, either."

"No, milady. I do not," Aquila affirmed most solemnly in his precise, clipped manner of speaking.

The adjoining door opened and Mona Carlisse returned wearing a gown—black, of course—with a shy Casio clinging like a burr to her mother's skirt, in a dress much too big for her. The little girl finally lifted her head to peek at the food, her small delicate nostrils flaring, and I beheld her face clearly for the very first time. She was a lovely girl with exquisite, pale skin. All the heated red that had flushed her face was gone now, healed quickly. She had Amber's strong features—a bold nose, wide mouth, his beautiful sea-colored eyes—but more refined, like her mother. My heart twisted upon seeing her. A little girl.

The bathroom door opened and Amber stepped out abruptly, a towel wrapped tinily around his waist, barely covering him. He shot a sharp assessing glance at me and Aquila.

My lips twitched. "Less than a minute. Did the water even touch you?"

He ignored me and walked past Mona Carlisse and Casio into his bedroom to dress. Mona Carlisse shrank back against the wall as he passed.

"You shouldn't bait him," Mona Carlisse warned me.

"But it's so fun," was my lazy reply.

Her eyes were fearful. "You do not know what it is like when they turn that strength against you."

I thought of my foster fathers, of nasty Miles. "You're wrong. I do know what it is like." And I let her see the bitter knowledge in my eyes. "But Amber is not like those men. He would never hurt me."

"How can you trust them?" Mona Carlisse whispered and I knew she was asking that question more for herself.

"Sometimes you have to trust your instincts and just risk it. You will know soon enough if you made the right choice." My eyes softened. "Was it all bad? Did you not find pleasure with some of them?"

Mona Carlisse gave a harsh, tearing laugh. "I *had* to find pleasure. That is the only way they gain power through us, did you not know? The punishment for not glowing . . ." She shuddered and her eyes filled with terrible memories. "Last night was not the only time I was locked in with a warrior filled with bloodlust."

What a horrible, horrible image. I shook it off. "That time is over for you," I said firmly. "You were strong enough to survive it. You are strong enough to put it behind you."

She shook her head almost violently. "I shall never forget it."

"I did not ask for you to forget. That would be impossible. I only ask that you give yourself time to heal. Don't let it twist or warp you. There are good men as well as bad, just as there are good and bad Queens. You just have to give the good guys a chance."

Mona Carlisse bowed her head. "I will think upon what you have said."

I gestured to the food. "Eat. Then we go before the Council."

SIXTEEN

WE DID NOT have to wait this time, and were shown immediately into the great chamber. Almost all the Council seats were occupied and all the new faces were women. The Demon Prince and Warrior Lord Thorane were the only two men on the Council, I saw as we strode in.

The Ice Queen, Mona Louisa, was there. And so was Gryphon. I'd known that as soon as I had entered and smelled the stench of purulent, decaying flesh. He knelt at her feet like a prized pet on display, a jeweled collar around his throat. The leash was held casually in Mona Louisa's white hands. His chest was bare, allowing all to see the poisoned, rotting flesh low in his stomach. Purplish-red streaks of drainage marked his skin, spreading out from the stab wound like an aggravated sunburst. His heart beat too quickly and his breathing was too shallow. I saw the knowledge in Gryphon's eyes. He was dying.

Mona Louisa stiffened involuntarily for a moment when she

saw me, before her face smoothed into a blank porcelain mask. I swallowed back my fury. *Later*, I promised myself. I would see that she paid for her treachery.

The Council members gasped as Mona Carlisse entered behind me and walked to the center, escorted by Amber and Aquila. The only faces not twisted with surprise were that of Lord Thorane and the old and wise Queen Mother.

"Queen Mother." I curtsied deeply before her. "Ladies and gentlemen of the Council. I wish to present Queen Mona Carlisse, whom many of you recognize. She did not die as you can see, but has been held captive these past ten years by Sandoor." I moved aside and let Mona Carlisse step forward.

The chamber erupted in an uproar of angry voices.

"Silence!" Lord Thorane thundered, bringing the room back to order. "Queen Mona Carlisse, if you will explain, please."

Mona Carlisse stepped forward and addressed the court, telling them of her staged death, the birth of her daughter, the years of imprisonment, the growth of the band of rogue warriors under the leadership of Sandoor, and finally of their rescue and flight here. Her recitation was dry, given almost in a monotone, her back rigid with a dignity that dared others to pity her.

"Queen Mona Carlisse, you have endured much," Lord Thorane said most gently. "We have but a few more questions for you. I ask that you bear patiently with us." He paused, clearing his throat. "Am I correct that, according to your testimony, the man beside you, Aquila, was one of these rogues?"

"Yes."

"And that he aided you in your escape?"

Mona Carlisse nodded. "That is correct, Lord Thorane."

"How, then, would you have us punish him, milady? His life is yours by right."

Mona Carlisse's eyes glittered with an emotion I dared not try to read. I held my breath.

"I ask that he go unpunished," she finally whispered. "I forfeit his life into Mona Lisa's service. And I pray that he serve her well."

The room grew abuzz, flying with whispered comments.

"Thank you, Sister," I said quietly.

Lord Thorane called for silence once more and looked to the august Queen Mother, who gave the barest nod.

"It shall be as you asked, milady," Lord Thorane pronounced.

"But the other eight men," Mona Carlisse said with cold hatred. "I wish to see them hunted down and executed in the most painful manner. Sandoor, in particular."

"It shall be as you request, Queen Mona Carlisse," Lord Thorane declared.

She hesitated. "My men from before . . ."

"Your people will be called back from wherever they dispersed to and your territory shall be restored unto you, Queen Mona Carlisse. The court will provide you with guards until that time when your own men return."

She bowed her thanks and stepped back.

My time had come. I shot a feral smile at the treacherous Mona Louisa and stepped forward. "I have yet to explain to the court how I came to be captured by Sandoor's men."

The Council members followed my gaze to Mona Louisa. Her blond iciness calmly endured their scrutiny.

"Indeed, Queen Mona Lisa," Lord Thorane said. "Please do so now."

"Mona Louisa promised one of my men, Gryphon, the man at her side, the antidote for silver poisoning if he went to her."

"She lies," Mona Louisa countered smoothly.

I turned to my former lover. "Gryphon?"

"I deliberately misled you so that you would allow me to leave," Gryphon said, his rich, resonant voice unweakened. "There is no cure for silver poisoning."

In a sudden flash, it all became clear to me. "You traded yourself for four of her men to guard and protect me," I said flatly.

"Yes. I was dying anyway."

And Gryphon had traded with the only coin he'd had to barter to ensure my protection—his beautiful body and the rare gift of walking in sunlight that he had gained from me.

"It was a poor bargain, my love," I said, my heart crying bitter tears. "They betrayed me to Sandoor's men at the very first opportunity."

The room buzzed once more with agitated speculation.

"She lies," Mona Louisa repeated, her calmness unruffled.

Aquila spoke up for the first time. "A blond warrior, Miles, brought the new Queen to our attention and agreed to turn her into our hands within the forest. He and his men did as promised, standing by while we took her. Only Amber tried to aid her."

"Queen Mona Louisa," Lord Thorane interjected after the sudden bubble of silence that met Aquila's statement. "Were four of your men given the task of guarding Queen Mona Lisa?"

Mona Louisa nodded, her blue eyes unrippled calm. "Yes. But they informed me they were surrounded and outnumbered and she was snatched away."

"They *informed* you," I mocked and turned to the blond, slippery shadow trying to hide in the back. "Did you hear that, Miles? Your Queen is going to throw you to the wolves. Come out, come out, wherever you are," I crooned in a sing-song voice.

"Step forward, Warrior Miles, and approach the Council," Lord Thorane ordered.

The other guards stepped away from him, leaving Miles no choice but to make his way reluctantly forward.

Lord Thorane eyed Miles sternly. "Let me remind you that false testimony before the Council is punishable by death."

Miles visibly swallowed and looked to Mona Louisa. She gazed back at him impassively.

"Warrior Miles," Lord Thorane said. "Did you contact the rogues regarding Queen Mona Lisa?"

"No," Miles said, his voice trembling.

"Did you report to Queen Mona Louisa that you were outnumbered and surrounded, and that Mona Lisa was abducted?"

Miles did not look at his Queen. "Yes."

"Is that true?"

"Yes," Miles said, his voice low.

"Lord Thorane," I interrupted. "Perhaps you should ask him if he tried to rape me." I heard Gryphon draw in a sharp breath. "After he ordered Rupert—I believe that's his name, the redheaded one—to smear a liquid aphrodisiac on me."

Amber's voice was a low, ominous, rumbling rage. "He spilled almost the entire vial of witch's brew upon her, leaving her not in her right mind for six days. It is only by the Goddess' mercy that she did not pass from this life."

"Hell's fire!" Halcyon snarled.

Miles glanced nervously at the Demon Prince, sweat dampening his once pretty and now very worried face.

"Warrior Miles, did you order Warrior Rupert to apply witch's brew on Queen Mona Lisa's person?" Lord Thorane asked forebodingly.

"No!"

"Did you try to rape Queen Mona Lisa?"

"No, Lord Thorane!"

I sauntered closer to Miles and asked silkily, "What, did you think I was willing? Is that why you tried to strangle me when I fought you?"

Gryphon let out an anguished cry.

"And did you not say that it was your Queen's most ardent desire that you and the other three guards taste me before handing me over to Sandoor's men?" I bared my teeth at him in a vicious smile. "If you didn't try to rape me, how then do you explain my burn marks upon your chest?"

I was taking a chance that they hadn't healed completely yet. Burn wounds were notoriously slow to heal. It took months in a human.

"Take off your shirt, Miles," the High Prince of Hell said in a dark portending voice. You could almost smell the sulfur brimming.

Miles grew chalk-white. He turned to Mona Louisa, his eyes desperate. "Milady."

"Do as he says," Mona Louisa said, her voice as cold and flat as her beautiful eyes.

His hands visibly shaking, Miles unbuttoned his shirt and slipped it off.

Gasps. Murmurs. All it lacked was applause.

There on Miles's chest were the imprints of my hands, as deep, as brightly red as the day I had branded him. They hadn't healed at all.

I walked to Miles, my hands outstretched. Miles backed away, fear flooding his eyes.

"Hold!" Lord Thorane commanded.

Miles held still, quivering as I fit my two hands over the burns. A perfect match, down to the pearly indentations in the center.

I slid my hand down until it rested over his groin and whispered into Miles's ear, "Next time I'll place my mark lower."

He wet his pants.

I stepped contemptuously away from him.

"I believe Miles and his men require further questioning . . . in private," Halcyon said. "Along with their Queen."

Lord Thorane nodded. "The Council would welcome your worthy assistance in this matter, Prince Halcyon."

"I will be most happy to offer it." Demon nails clicked sharply together.

Mona Louisa blanched.

I turned to the Ice Bitch. "You struck a false bargain with my man, Mona Louisa. Therefore it is null and void." I held out my hand to the man I loved. "Gryphon, come to me."

Gryphon rose and in one easy motion ripped off the bejeweled collar, his eyes filled with sorrow, anger, love, and regret. He took a step toward me.

Mona Louisa rose behind him, a vengeful pale wraith, her eyes narrowed in deadly malice. A silver dagger clutched in her upraised hand, her fingers wrapped tight around the leather-wrapped hilt. "He will never be yours again!" she screeched at me.

Time seemed to stretch out as my vision first narrowed and focused on that descending blade, then expanded until that was all I saw in close, intimate detail. Light glinted off that brilliant blade the color of moonlight. I thought of the taste of silver, remembered that metallic tang in Gryphon's blood. I thought of the feel of my own knives these last few weeks, how they came eagerly to my hands even as I reached for them. I fixed on that reflective silver-bright blade, on the simple, leather-wrapped hilt, and desired it in my own hand.

The hand I held stretched out tingled and throbbed, a giant warm pulse.

The silver dagger flew to my hand, the hilt resting warmly, securely in my palm.

Time continued to move slowly. I saw the shock and fear in Mona Louisa's eyes. Felt my own murderous rage at what she had dared. And knew with sure certainty that I could send that dagger flying straight back into her heart as swiftly as I had called it to me. And I wanted her dead so badly I trembled with the desire of it.

A voice mellowed with age and hardened with innate authority reached me. It was a voice I could not ignore or block out. "Mona Lisa. Attend to me."

Time snapped back, moving swiftly forward once more. I put away the dagger and looked almost blindly to the one who had called me, the august Queen Mother. I dropped to my knees before her and felt Gryphon's warm, tingling presence as he knelt beside me.

"Rise," the Queen Mother commanded.

I stood and lifted my eyes to that proud visage, to those blue eyes that had faded neither in color nor in intelligence or perception.

"You have great gifts, child," the Queen Mother said. "You shall need great control to wield them wisely. Content yourself that Gryphon is yours for however much longer he may live."

I bowed and looked into those wise neutral eyes, neither cold nor warm. "Is there no way to cure him, Queen Mother?"

"What they say is true. There is no antidote for silver poisoning."

My heart wept at her certain words.

With considering eyes, the Queen Mother studied Gryphon and I. "But perhaps there is a way to cure him."

"How?" I whispered.

"You called the silver blade to your hand, did you not? Call the silver out from within his body."

My mind reeled at the simple idea and my heart pounded faster with excitement, with possibility. I could not heal the poison within him, but maybe I could draw it out.

I turned to Gryphon, to his blank face that showed neither hope nor expectation, and traced my eyes down to that gaping, festering hole in his belly that had widened as his flesh had softened and been eaten away. Touching that rotten flesh with my palm, I thought again of silver—the taste, feel, and smell of it. I thought of the silver in his body. And thought of it coming out.

My hand warmed and trembled and the Goddess tear imprinted in the heart of my palm suddenly came to life. It throbbed, pulling on my nerves, pulsing all the way up my arm, shooting to my heart. The embedded tear in my palm began to emit radiance of the purest white light. Light that penetrated into Gryphon's skin. Infused with that light, his skin began to change colors, from deadly gray, rotten, to living color once again.

In that critical, fragile moment, I called even more power out from within, penetrating even deeper into him. With the pull of my palm, one massive blackened clot of blood was sucked out from the wound. Gryphon let out a raw cry of pain. Now with the passage free and uncluttered, I could see. Deep in the gaping hole of his flesh was a tiny puddle of liquid silver.

My hand pulsated. Vibrated. Shook. A sullen, silvery blood-tinged drop oozed from the hole, growing fatter and fatter until it dropped to the floor with a tiny wet *plop*. Another drop welled, this one almost pure silver. It, too, kerplunked to the ground. Two more fat, sluggish silvery drops dived to their timely demise, then the light faded and my hand cooled. I dropped my hand, drained, trembling now with fatigue.

Gryphon's rigid body softened. His eyes opened as if awakening from a deep sleep, refreshed. The wound was still there but the violaceous streaking was gone. His presence felt better, stronger, and I knew that Gryphon's body would heal itself now with time.

Gryphon's parched, trembling lips brushed mine in silent gratitude. I ran my fingers lovingly through his tousled hair, comforting

him. I bowed in deep gratitude to the Queen Mother. She acknowledged me with a kind smile that softened her face for a moment.

Lord Thorane cleared his throat. "Queen Mona Lisa, I could
not fail but notice that one . . ." He narrowed his eyes, concentrating for a moment on Gryphon. ". . . er, two, actually, now . . . of
your men have reached a high enough level of power to . . ." He
paused, then continued doggedly on. "Is it your wish, milady, that
the court recognize Amber and Gryphon as Warrior Lords?"

"Warrior Lords?" I asked, forcing myself to attend his words
despite my tiredness. "Like yourself, Lord Thorane?"

"That is correct, milady."

"If they have the power, why do you ask me?"

"They can only be recognized if their Queen requests it."

Oh. Some dark emotion in those aged eyes of his compelled me
to ask, "How many Warrior Lords are recognized by the court,
Lord Thorane?"

"Myself alone."

Just one. Some Queen had loved him then. But what had become of the many other men that must have reached that same level
of power?

"What is the significance of becoming a Warrior Lord?" I asked.

"First of all, it means that through their servitude to their
Queens, they have attained enough power—that is, the power they
have siphoned off through a Queen's Basking and, of course," he
cleared his throat, "through mating—yes, well, in any case, it means
they have attained enough physical power to live up to the promised age of three hundred years solely by their own life force. They
no longer need to depend upon a Queen's power to sustain their vi-
ability, and they can roam free from your control. They can be in-
dependent, which brings us to the second point. Because they have
attained the above physical power, this rare status allows them to

SUNNY

have the privilege and right of ruling their own territories like a Queen, directly serving the Queen Mother."

So Warrior Lords were as powerful as Queens. *My two strongest warriors,* my mother had called Gryphon and Amber. No wonder Mona Sera had tried to kill them. Not only would they no longer serve her but they would become her direct competitors. Was that the reason why Queens slaughtered their best men or drove them away to become outcast rogues like the ones in the forest?

Lord Thorane was asking me to *free* them.

Should I? Could I? But I'd only just found them. How could I give them up? Should I make the choice my mother and the other Queens made? Should I chain them to my side forever in servitude? Should I be selfish, treating them as my slaves? Or should I do what was right and free them to stand as equals among us all? Would my heart be broken?

I looked at my beautiful Gryphon, at my strong Amber.

"Yes," I said. It came out a harsh whisper. "I wish to have them recognized."

Lord Thorane exhaled slowly in relief. "Thank you, milady. You are a most unusual and generous Queen. Amber, Gryphon, you may approach the Queen Mother."

I stepped back. Amber moved to stand beside Gryphon. They both knelt before the Queen Mother. With slow care, she slipped over each of their bent heads a gold medallion chain proclaiming their new status.

"Rise, Warrior Lord Gryphon, Warrior Lord Amber," the Queen Mother's strong voice commanded, "and tell me what is your desire." She waved her bejeweled hand to a huge map on the wall behind her, displaying all the sprawling Monère territories scattered around the face of the continent. "All is yours just by asking."

Gryphon didn't even look at the tantalizing map and the promise of his own fiefdom. His eyes were on me. In a clear voice he said, "My heart's greatest desire is to continue serving Mona Lisa, revered Queen Mother."

The Queen Mother raised one eyebrow. "Laudable, laudable, laudable. Such a gallant spirit. What about you, Warrior Lord Amber? You have suffered long and hard. I have quite a few lucrative territories for you to rule. Now is the time for you to reach out and take your glory."

Amber's face remained expressionless, an innocent giant. "It is my desire as well to continue serving Queen Mona Lisa, honored Queen Mother."

The room echoed with a hundred whispering voices.

"Quiet!" Lord Thorane ordered.

"How most unusual," said the Queen Mother. "It is to your credit, Mona Lisa, that these Lords have made such a choice. You are a fresh breath of wind. Now, will you, Queen Mona Lisa, accept these Warrior Lords back into your service?"

I knelt, dizzy with relief, weakened with joy. "Oh, yes. Oh, yes, with a most happy heart, Queen Mother."

SEVENTEEN

A HOT SHOWER washed away all my fatigue. Leaving the bathroom, I found Gryphon sitting on my bed, waiting for me, reminding me of the plight I faced. Whom should I choose as my
lover? Amber or Gryphon? I loved them both. They both loved me.
What choice should I make?

"Forgive me," Gryphon said.

"For what?"

"For what you suffered because of what I did. For almost dying."

"Oh, Gryphon." I reached out a hand and he slowly took it,
holding it as if it were so fragile. I pressed his dear hand to my face,
rubbed my cheek tenderly against it. "Your only fault was in trusting that treacherous bitch."

"They question Mona Louisa and her men even now. Aquila
leads a troop of guards back to Sandoor's camp and Mona Carlisse
has moved to other quarters with her temporary guards."

"Where is Amber?"

"He is in the adjoining room. He allowed me to stay here with you."

I closed my eyes for a brief, agonizing moment. How was I to choose between them? I released Gryphon's hand and he drew it away. We looked at each other.

"If you so desire, there is yet time before the Trade Festival ends this night," Gryphon said, breaking the fragile silence.

"Trade Festival?"

"Young men mature enough to serve. Mature men released from their Queen's service. Healers, servants, men and women in trade, looking to serve in new territories. The Council will assign you your territory tomorrow. At the very least, you have need of more guards."

"Oh. I'd better dress," I said, hating the sudden awkwardness that had sprung up between us.

"I will leave you then." He slipped away into the adjoining bedroom.

I opened my armoire, noting with sadness that none of Gryphon's clothes were there, only my two donated dresses. I was so tired of wearing black. I took down the blue dress and slipped it on. Something stiff at the waist pricked me. I examined the seams and saw that something other than cloth had been slipped in there on the right side. A small folded piece of paper.

I unfolded the note.

Thaddeus
Our Lady of Lourdes Orphanage
January 5, 1989

My orphanage where I had been left in a basket on the doorstep. Suddenly, vividly, I remembered the dream where Sonia had come to me as I had drifted in unconsciousness, weakened by the aphrodisiac. When she had come to me and pulled me out of that sleepy abyss.

Your brother shall need you soon. . . . I have given you the information, Sonia had promised.

My brother!

The note was the promised information that would guide me to my brother. He would have worn a silver cross like mine, bearing his name. I had a way of finding him now.

Soon, I promised him. *I'll find you soon.*

◈

T HE TRADE FESTIVAL was held on the front lawn. It was a lavish affair with music and dancers. All the Monère were out there in a great spirit of celebration. Queens strolled along in the accompaniment of their large entourage, a pageantry of colors and coats of arms. There were animals walking freely among us— camels, deer, stallions, and cats. Twined about branches, snakes hissed from the trees. One could not tell if they were truly animals or just warriors having fun, shifted into their other form.

Tents were erected to shelter trade counselors. Under their shade were tables strewn with lists of Queens from various territories seeking people to fill open positions in their courts. There was an even longer list of Monère, mainly men, youth seeking to service Queens for the first time in their lives, and older men cast out of one Queendom, seeking a position in a new one. Several Queens were holding court with a group of young, eager, starry-eyed lads gathered about them. Wary-eyed older men looked enviously on.

Mona Teresa, the Fire Bitch, was there with her retinue of guards. Her maimed rapist was in conspicuous absence. Her flame-colored hair made her stand out easily, as did the free, possessive manner with which she ran her hands over a preening boy's chest, shoulders, buttocks, and thighs. And the boy wasn't protesting. Quite the contrary; he appeared to be almost ecstatic.

"God, she looks as if she were buying a horse," I muttered in embarrassed disgust.

"More like a stud for her bed," Gryphon replied matter-of-factly. "The eager pups are the ones usually chosen by Queens when they are too young, too virginal to have acquired much power. They will serve for several years in the Queen's bed until they begin to grow stronger. Then they are banished from her sheets to serve among her guards."

Two men stood slightly apart, their stronger emanations of power a silent declaration of their age, though their faces were smooth and unlined.

"Any you recommend?" I asked.

"The light-haired man on the far right," Amber said, gesturing toward the two men I had noted. "Not a bad lad."

A strong recommendation, coming from Amber.

Men's eyes landed curiously upon us. Noting Amber's and Gryphon's medallion chains, they grew more alert, then became confused as we neared enough for them to sense me. I felt like a Queen, but wore a simple blue dress a maid or a servant girl would wear.

The younger boys dismissed me, but the fair-haired man and the other man who stood apart observed me with sharp interest.

I stopped before the "lad" Amber had indicated. A man, really, but no doubt thought of as a boy to someone who numbered over a hundred years in age. He was plain-looking, of average build, with wheat-colored hair and light brown eyes, a few inches taller than I. Nothing extraordinary but for the strong power he radiated about his person, rivaling that of Aquila.

"Milady. High Lords." The man bowed respectfully.

"What is your name?" I inquired.

"Tomas, milady." He pronounced it an odd way, with a slight inflection on the last syllable.

"Why are you here, Tomas?"

"My Queen no longer wished me to serve her," Tomas said, his voice rich with the flavor of the South. The soft twang, along with the color of his hair, brought to mind sun-kissed wheat fields.

I liked his direct gaze. Opening my senses, I looked deeper. A simple man, I noted. An honest man at heart, with a clear trait of loyalty. I was satisfied with what I found.

"My name is Mona Lisa," I said, searching for words, unsure of the procedure. "I am a new Queen yet to be assigned my territory. I, uh, have one other guard besides Lord Amber and Lord Gryphon, and am looking for another."

Tomas knelt before me, his eyes eager. "I would be most honored to serve you if you will have me, milady."

I hesitated and some of that hopeful gleam faded from his eyes. "I won't be mating with you," I blurted out, feeling my face heat but wanting to make that particular point clear to him. "Does that cause you to change your mind?"

Tomas' eyes lighted once more. "No, milady."

"Oh, good. Um . . . as long as we're clear on that . . . then I would love to have you join us."

"Thank you, my Queen," Tomas said fervently. "You will not regret this." He kissed my hand and rose.

"Welcome, brother," Amber said gruffly.

The joy of being accepted brightened Tomas's face, chasing away his plainness, making him look almost handsome. He exchanged a courteous, acknowledging nod with Gryphon.

I felt another man's approach and turned.

"Milady." It was the other older man. He was tall and slender,

Gryphon's height but with a wiry leanness and curly brown hair and blue eyes. Something about him felt different, muted somehow. My impression was confirmed when I felt Amber and Gryphon stiffen beside me.

Cautious, painful hope was in his eyes. "I could not help but overhear you, milady. I have had many years of experience as a guard."

It was the hardest thing to say no, I discovered, to someone who looked at you like that. But Amber and Gryphon had not recommended him, and they seemed to know him. "I'm sorry . . ." I said.

"If you will just give me a chance, milady," he urged with quiet intensity.

"I'll give you a chance, Chami," interjected a sly feminine voice.

Chami frowned, dismayed, as Mona Teresa swayed up to him, her guards and new boy toy trotting obediently behind her. "Mona Rosita no longer desires you? Do not worry. I shall find some interesting ways to occupy you, my deadly darling," Mona Teresa purred.

Holding my eyes, casting me a quiet plea, Chami said, "I would be willing to serve as a butler, footman, or gardener if you have no need of another guard, milady. Anything."

"You cannot desire to serve her," Mona Teresa said in an angry hiss. "She is a mongrel! A Mixed Blood!"

I turned stricken eyes to Tomas, my new man, when I realized he might not have known that. "I forgot to mention that to you."

Tomas gazed calmly back at me. "I was already aware of that, milady."

Mona Teresa gave Tomas a wily smile. "I am willing to take you into my service as well, Tomas."

"Thank you for your generous offer, milady," Tomas said politely, "but I have already been accepted into Queen Mona Lisa's service."

"If you wish to change your mind . . ." I ventured.

"I do not wish to change my mind, my Queen," Tomas said firmly.

"You shall regret it!" Mona Teresa snapped with vicious temper. "She will not last long. And when she is gone, you shall come crawling to me on your hands and knees." She turned to go. "Come along, Chami."

Chami didn't move. He beseeched me with quiet passion, his blue eyes pleading.

Mona Teresa's voice crackled with warning rage. "I said, come along!"

"Wait." I spoke the word quietly. "Gryphon? Amber?"

Gryphon released a deep sigh of resignation. "Show her your ability, Chami."

With no warning, Chami dropped his shields and I felt him fully for the first time. He was strong. As strong as Gryphon had been when I'd first met him. From Mona Teresa's apparent shock, she hadn't been aware of it. All the other Queens whose service he had passed through probably had had no inkling of his true power, as well.

Chami gave me only a brief moment to feel his full force before he muted it once more, turning it down, down, down. Before my eyes he disappeared. I gasped and would have doubted my own senses but for a faint presence that I could barely detect. He moved and only then could I see him. A bare outline visible only with movement, and hardly noticeable even then. Chami had not faded so much as taken on the coloration and pattern of his surroundings so that he blended perfectly among them and became invisible.

Then he stood before me, visible once again, eyes downcast.

"What is your full name?" I asked.

"Chameleo."

He was a chameleon. The perfect assassin. *My deadly darling,*

Mona Teresa had called him. I wondered how many Queens he had served. And how many Queens had given him up because not only was he powerful but very, very dangerous.

"Enough!" Mona Teresa screeched. "Come with me now or I shall withdraw my offer!"

Chami's fists clenched but he did not move. "Milady?"

"Look at me," I commanded softly.

Chami lifted his eyes and opened himself to me, dropping his barriers, giving me permission to look deep within him. He was a well of dark complexity, his trait of loyalty a bit blurred. Only time would tell. And I detected a touch of viciousness and cruelty. He would be a gamble.

"I will accept you if Lord Amber and Lord Gryphon are willing to have you," I finally declared.

Hope flared anew in Chami's eyes, deepening the blue almost to violet. Chami turned his face to Gryphon and submitted to Gryphon's probing gaze. Searching with his senses, his power, Gryphon studied him for an intense moment.

Gryphon turned to me. "Do you see what I see in him?"

"Blurred trait of loyalty with a slight propensity for viciousness and cruelty?"

Gryphon tilted his head. "Yes, exactly what I saw. Were you always able to see traits of character within another?"

I thought back. "No, it's something that came to me rather recently. Right after . . ." My words trailed away. Right after I had first slept with Gryphon. "Could I have gotten my gift from you, from your sharp falcon eyes?" I whispered.

"Does it please you that part of me is now a part of you?" Gryphon asked softly.

"Does sunlight please the flower? I will cherish your gift always. What do you say about Chami?"

"It's not wise, but . . . I will accept him with reservations."

"So noted," I said with a small smile. "Amber, how about you?"

"I will abide by your judgment, milady," Amber replied.

I turned back to Chami. "We will be happy to have you join us."

Chami dropped to his knees, kissing my hand with lips that trembled. "Thank you, my Queen."

"No!" Rage spewed from Mona Teresa. "You unnatural bitch! You think you have won? I wish you joy of them. You shall soon find that you have bitten off more than you can handle."

"Well, it certainly would have been more than you could have handled," I said easily.

"You are an obscenity!" Mona Teresa shouted, practically dripping with venom. I was surprised her teeth didn't burst into fangs.

I batted my lashes at her. "Aw, you're just jealous."

Mona Teresa stalked away in a cloud of seething wrath.

"You've made an enemy," Gryphon warned quietly.

I shrugged uncaringly. "She already was my enemy. Nothing has changed."

"She fears you now," Gryphon returned. "That makes her more dangerous."

I arched a brow. "Fears me?"

"How you marked Miles," Amber explained in his deep bass rumble. "There are few injuries the Monère cannot heal."

"In addition to that, five strong warriors serving one Queen . . . unheard of," Gryphon said thoughtfully. "Adding in your own unusual powerful gifts, all the Queens shall fear you now."

"Nor did recognizing and elevating us to Warrior Lords endear you to the Ladies of Light," Amber noted, reminding me of an important fact.

"I am so glad you did not leave me," I whispered fiercely.

"We are not fools. Why would we choose to depart from the

one good thing we have found in over a hundred years?" Amber chided gruffly.

Tomas and Chami observed our brief interplay with wide-eyed fascination.

"Come along," Gryphon said, bestowing a warm smile upon me. "Let us sign the agreements and be done with it."

A counselor was called for the task. He came running with the contracts clutched in his hand and noted down the new placements in his thick ledger. Tomas and Chami both signed their names on their contracts. I signed with bold relish, in large stroking flourish in celebration of my first official act as a Queen. With the transaction consummated, we went to collect their luggage, two small trunks.

Behind us, a voice called out to me. "Mona Lisa."

I turned and saw Jamie. He was with two women, both of whom I recognized. "Jamie."

"I want you to meet . . ." Jamie winced as the two women elbowed him on both sides. "Oops, I'm sorry. I mean, could I have the honor, milady, of introducing my sister, Tersa, and my mother, Rosemary."

Tersa was even smaller than I had imagined, a tiny, delicate creature, half a head shorter than I. I would have felt like an Amazon standing beside her but for her mother. Now there was a true Amazon, standing nearly six feet tall and massive in girth. She had a plump, round face that would probably have been quite pleasant were it not so grim.

"I'm so glad to meet you both." I took Tersa's small hands in mine. She was all delicate bones, like a little bird. "How are you doing?"

"I am well, milady. Healer Janelle attended to me." Tersa's voice was gentle and quiet, like herself. "I wish to thank you for coming to my aid."

"All of us thank you, milady," Rosemary, the Amazon, interjected feelingly. "May the Goddess bless you for coming to my
daughter's rescue."

I squeezed and released Tersa's tiny hands. "I'm sorry I couldn't
have done more." Sorry I hadn't been able to stop the rape. "I regret not killing the bastard. Was he punished?"

Jamie shook his head angrily, sending his russet curls flying.
"His Queen, Mona Teresa, was given a small reprimand. She, of
course, did not punish him." He straightened his shoulders, a boy
shouldering the responsibilities of a man. "Milady, my mother, sister, and I would like to serve you if you will have us."

My eyes widened in surprise. "You all have good positions here at
High Court. I . . . I don't even know what territory I will be getting."

"It doesn't matter where you go," Jamie said passionately.
"We'll follow you anywhere."

"I'm one of the best cooks," Rosemary declared. Not bragging,
just stating a fact. "Tersa is a good maid and Jamie will make you a
fine footman."

"I have five guards now. I don't know if I can support more than
that." I looked to Gryphon for guidance.

"You will have income from various businesses and property
that come with your territory," Gryphon said.

I absorbed that quietly, then spoke plainly to Rosemary, stating
the real reason for my hesitance. "Your children will only be more
of a target if they are with me."

"Being here at High Court did not protect them," Rosemary re-
joined, just as bluntly. "We'll take our chances with you. At least
you'll *try*. No one else will do even that."

Three more lives I would be responsible for. Only they were
weaker, unable to protect themselves, and far more vulnerable.
Could I do it? How could I not? It was because of me that their lives

had been thrown into turmoil. Tersa, a Mixed Blood like me, had been raped to draw me out. If I, a Mixed Blood, didn't protect others of my type, who would?

"Are you *sure*?" I asked.

"Yes!" they answered unanimously.

I prayed to God that I was strong enough for their trust. "Then I gladly welcome you into our family. I promise I will do my best to keep you safe and happy."

They knelt and kissed my hand. I pulled them up and squeezed Jamie and Tersa's hands. "I've always wanted a brother and sister," I told them, smiling.

EIGHTEEN

PRINCE HALCYON WAS waiting for me in the front parlor when we returned. Chami and Tomas studied the Demon Prince warily while Rosemary and her children nodded to Halcyon respectfully. Amber and Gryphon remained with me while the others went upstairs to settle in.

I seated myself in a tailored leather wing chair across from where Halcyon lounged with casual grace on a plump leather sofa.

"We have finished questioning Mona Louisa and her men," Halcyon announced. "Miles has already been executed."

"By you?" I queried.

A brief hesitation. Then an acknowledging nod.

"Good," I said coldly.

"Bloodthirsty, aren't you?" Halcyon's tone was one of approval.

"Yes. The other men?" I asked.

"They are to be punished. But they will live."

"And Mona Louisa?"

"She will lose her territory for her complicity and will be moved to a smaller, less important territory."

"Complicity?" I arched an arrogant brow. "She masterminded it. She should have been executed along with Miles."

"Ah, but she is a Queen, much more precious to the Council. We never execute our Queens. You are the bloodlines and matriarchs of our world," Halcyon said pragmatically. "More good news is that the Council has amended the law so that it is now forbidden to take the lives of Mixed Blood Queens."

"You and Lord Thorane must have pushed hard to pass that through," Gryphon observed quietly.

"The Queens were the only ones opposing it," Halcyon said.

"Surprise, surprise," I said, crossing my legs. Halcyon's eyes followed the gesture, making me suddenly conscious of my body. I felt almost an invisible caress against my skin beneath my skirt that caused me to draw in a quick breath. He lifted his eyes back to mine with a small smile.

"They managed, however, to include in the condition that other Queens may take a Mixed Blood Queen's life, like any other Queen, if she threatened them personally. I would watch myself with the other Ladies. They will no doubt try to draw you to challenge them."

"Are they powerful enough to defeat me?" I asked curiously.

"Some Queens have great powers. Others have even greater treachery," Halcyon said gravely. "Do not underestimate them. They are very dangerous."

"I won't. And the law that Mixed Bloods cannot kill any Moonies?"

Halcyon's lips quirked at my quaint term for them. "An exception was made for you. Try not to kill too many of them."

I blinked my eyes lazily. "Only those who deserve it."

Halcyon threw back his head and laughed with rich appreciation.

I loved hearing him laugh so. Smiling, I went to Halcyon, bent down and kissed him lightly on the cheek. He stood, bringing his body so close to mine that we were almost in an embrace. I felt Amber and Gryphon tense behind me and ignored them.

"What was that for?" Halcyon asked softly.

"For your concern and for your help. You're a good friend."

Halcyon turned my right palm faceup and traced my pearly mole with one sharp nail. My hands remained trustingly relaxed in his grip. "Friend," he said with a half smile. "For now." He slanted a glance at Gryphon. "As I said, I can wait."

I shook my head in amused exasperation and stepped back. "You need to find yourself a nice sassy demon lady, Halcyon."

His teeth flashed startling white against the gold of his skin. "I've already found my hell-cat. None are as sassy as you. Nor as pretty."

I laughed, enjoying his flattery. "How very sweet you are."

"Sweet." Halcyon nearly strangled on the word, a pained expression on his face.

"If I can help you at any time, please come to me," I said softly.

Halcyon's smile made Gryphon shift nervously behind me. "Oh, I will. I most definitely will. That is a promise."

NINETEEN

M Y MEN'S DISAPPROVAL filled the parlor like a heavy dark cloud after Halcyon left. I sprawled on the comfortable sofa where Halcyon had sat, letting my body relax. Amber sat in the great chair across from me. Gryphon stood propped against the wall, a dark glowering presence.

"Go ahead," I said, after the silence had spun out long enough. "You can yell at me."

"Many things have occurred since I departed, it seems," Gryphon said in a carefully contained voice.

Amber snorted, unamused. "If you are referring to Halcyon, yes, he has made his attraction and intentions toward our Queen quite public." He did not look any more pleased about it than Gryphon.

"He does seem to care for her, in his manner," Amber reluctantly added. "It was he who caught her when she fainted after punishing the man who abused Tersa, and carried her to her room.

I must confess, I have never seen the Demon Prince handle a woman so gently before."

Something twisted oddly in my heart. I had not known that.

"He has proven an invaluable ally," Amber pointed out.

Gryphon burst into motion, prowling the length of the room with agitated strides. "You think I know that not?" he snarled.

"Gryphon," I said placatingly. "He knows I want only to be his friend."

"That will not stop him from trying to seduce you."

"If that's all you're worried about . . . he won't be able to."

"How do you know?" Gryphon snapped.

"Because my heart is already given to you and Amber."

My quiet statement stilled Gryphon's pacing and changed Amber's eyes to clear, brilliant yellow. Gryphon sank down to his knees before me. "Oh, Mona Lisa," he muttered, laying his head in my lap, "I have missed you so much."

I stroked his long silky hair. "Then you should not have gone."

Gryphon gave a laughing sob. "No, I should not have gone."

"You must never lie to me again," I said with gentle firmness. "Both of you."

"No, I shall not," Gryphon promised hoarsely.

"Nor I," Amber vowed, his beautiful yellow eyes glittering.

"And I promise to tell you both the truth, always." Starting now, oh God. Swallowing back the selfish raw possessiveness I felt, I took a deep breath and let it out. "You both are free now to do as you wish. You are Lords in your own right. You can go to any Queen's bed with your power and gifts."

"We do not desire to be with any other Queen but you." Amber's deep voice rumbled like thunder.

"We chose to stay with you," Gryphon said, gripping my hips almost painfully.

"But you don't need to limit yourselves to me any longer," I said, pointing out the obvious. "Any Queen would welcome you now that you no longer threaten them and they don't have to worry about controlling you. And you could gain even more power by being with them."

Gryphon's face spasmed with pain. "You no longer desire us?"

"No, I do."

"Then let us be with you," he beseeched.

I looked at him with hot agony. "I love you both. Do not ask me to choose between you. You must make the decision."

The room grew tensely still.

"Why should you have to choose between us?" Gryphon asked carefully.

The words flitted feather-light into my brain before their full import sank home. "You want me to be with you *both*?"

"Humans do so, do they not?" Amber asked.

"Some men do, but they're *cheating*. Being unfaithful," I said. "The natural state is one man with one woman."

"Why do you profess that is the natural state?" Gryphon asked most reasonably. "Human men have taken more than one woman to wife throughout your history, and even still continue to do so to this day in some countries, do they not? And you are more Monère than you are human. We see matters in a different light."

"You both want to be with me *at the same time*?" my voice squeaked.

"Not if you are not comfortable with it," Gryphon added hastily.

"No," I said in a choking little voice. "I would not be comfortable with that."

"Then be with us separately. Allow us to share you," Gryphon urged.

"How?" I asked in a low voice, tantalized despite myself.

"We could take turns," Amber suggested. "Alternate weeks."

"And you both would be okay with that?"

They nodded.

"It would not be cheating," Gryphon declared.

"You would be faithful to us both," Amber said.

For some ludicrous reason, I understood what they meant. "I . . . I don't know. It's such a crazy idea," I said faintly. "I have to think about it."

"We shall give you time." Gryphon's words echoed in the room, reminding us of another man's recent similar statement.

But time, it seemed, would be in short supply.

～⌘～

THE WAIT WAS soon over. We were all called to the Great Hall to hear the announcement of my new territory. Lord Thorane didn't make us wait long. He made a short speech about the glories and responsibilities of being a Queen. An anthem was sung by a chorus of youths, their voices lifted like a choir of angels, and long horns were blown in gallant pageantry announcing the assigning of the new territory to a brand-new Queen.

"After a long and arduous consideration," Lord Thorane said after an acknowledging nod from the Queen Mother, "and wise counsel from the Queen Mother, we hereby assign our fine territory of New Orleans to Queen Mona Lisa. This assignment shall come as the law decrees with its attributes of assets in corporations, holdings in real estates, etcetera, etcetera, all to be listed in its great detail in this Book of Holdings that I shall now present to you. Step forward, Queen Mona Lisa. Put your hand on this book and swear that you will never forget your utmost duty to turn in your tithe and your attributes as also detailed in this book."

I stepped forward and repeated my vows in a clear firm voice. Lord Thorane passed the Book of Holdings into my care.

"Now is the moment of coronation," Lord Thorane announced.

The Queen Mother stood up, holding a gleaming crown in her hands. I knelt before her. Carefully, with full pomp and ceremony, she laid the crown upon my head.

"Behold, all fellow Queens. Behold, all fellow Monère. By the power of the moon, our ancestral planet, I hereby bestow upon Mona Lisa the title of Monère Queen of New Orleans. Hereon, thereafter, all courtesy and respect must be extended to her in accordance to her status by the laws of this High Council." The Queen Mother looked down upon me. "May our Mother Moon always shine upon you. May her light always be your guide."

Tears of joy trickled down my cheeks as the bugles blared and the crowd cheered.

I am a Queen now, I thought, *like my mother.* How ironic. To be born in New York and to reign over New Orleans.

I was joined in the side chamber by my jubilant family.

"Louisiana. Wow!" Jamie whistled with excitement. "The French Quarter, Mardi Gras, jazz, and hot babes."

"Hot, period." His mother grimaced.

"True," Lord Thorane said, smiling. "Aside from being one of our oldest, more profitable territories, it also allows a seat on the Council, milady."

"The Council?" I echoed with faint distress. "I don't wish to become involved in your politics."

"Yours now as well, milady," Lord Thorane pointed out. He continued more gently. "Your presence is sorely needed there. You will not be required to attend more than half the sessions, if you so wish. The Council meets every other lunar cycle on the second weekend after the full moon. But I would urge you to attend all the sessions, milady." He paused then said bluntly, "It will allow us to monitor you."

I frowned. "Why should I want that?"

Gryphon pushed away from the wall where he had been lounging. "He means that it will reassure the respectable Council members and the other Queens, in particular, that your men remain under your control."

"And not the reverse," Amber said in a deep growl.

I was outraged on Amber's behalf. "They would never turn rogue. Especially now." They were tainting the son with the father's sins. "How dare they even think that?"

"This matter with Sandoor has truly upset all of us and will continue to do so until he and his men are captured. Seeing you every other cycle at High Court, milady, with their own eyes will do much to reassure them," said Lord Thorane. He cleared his throat, as seemed to be his habit before broaching anything uncomfortable. "You will need to build an army to guard your new territory and ensure the smooth administration of your court. Never underestimate your power. You will be as powerful as the governor of Louisiana. But always bear in mind, never give the other Queens or the High Council the impression that you are building an army out of proportion to your function, threatening the balance of power among us and among your sisterly territories."

"I thank you for the warning, Lord Thorane," I said stiffly, formally. "I will heed it."

Lord Thorane bowed. "Thank you, milady. Lord Gryphon. Lord Amber. Your new positions also entitle you both to Council seats. I will expect to see you there each and every session."

"Well, hell!" Amber exclaimed. Even Gryphon frowned.

My lips twitched. "I'll enjoy the company," I murmured.

They glared at me.

Lord Thorane watched us with amusement. "Believe me when I say that it will be in your best interest for everyone to see you serving the Council and the Queen Mother in this small manner."

"We understand," Gryphon grated. "One last question, Lord Thorane. Whose territory was New Orleans before?"

"Mona Louisa."

Ah, came the pleasant realization. *Her punishment for trying to kill me.* "Well," I purred, "there's some definite satisfaction to that."

"Let's look at the Book of Holdings," Jamie said exuberantly.

They gathered around me eagerly as I opened the pages.

Page one held the deed of a mansion located on the French Quarter with my name printed on it.

"See, I told you. The French Quarter," Jamie crowed.

The original date of the deed was 1768.

The second page was the certificate of incorporation for a company called Louisiana Power and Electricity.

"A utility company. Steady income," Aquila observed.

The third page was a certificate of holdings in three thousand gold bullions.

"How much would that be worth?" Tomas asked.

"A lot," Aquila murmured. "You never wish to trade that, milady. That is your golden nest egg. Even better than dollars."

"You seem to know a lot about commerce, Aquila," I observed.

"I was a man of business before," he replied modestly.

"Hurry up and turn the pages, Mona Lisa," Jamie urged.

Someone knocked on the door. A footman entered and came straight to me. "A note for your eyes only, milady."

I extracted myself from the crowd busily reading the Book of Holdings and in a quiet corner opened the note.

My dearest Mona Lisa,

Forgive me for dampening your glorious moment of jubilation but I must tell you what is urgent in my heart. You must by now have found the folded note I left for you. Indeed, it is the whereabouts of your brother. That information came from a private diary that I have kept during my long service as a midwife.

Last night, as I was leafing through it, reviewing as I often do, the names and placement of each baby I was obliged to hand over to the care of humans, I detected the presence of a foreign scent lingering over your brother's entry. Upon closer examination, my eyes detected the fingerprints of an intruder of unknown origin. An alarm rang in my heart. I have a sickening sense that your brother's life is about to be intruded upon. I do not know for certain, but I believe it has something to do with your coronation and new status as Queen. As you know, power always draws flies of evil. You must hurry and find him before they do.

With warm love,
Sonia

"You own three casinos," Jamie shouted to me. His excitement dampened upon seeing my somber face. "You don't approve of gambling?" he asked.

"Close the book now," I said. "We must go to New York right away."

TWENTY

IT WAS GOOD to be a Queen. The High Council authorized a private jet for our exclusive use. An hour later, we were winging our way to LaGuardia Airport. But my heart wasn't able to enjoy the luxury, the gold trimmings, the gourmet meals and drinks, the king-sized bed that came with a private shower on the jet—all befitting the status of a new Queen. Neither did anyone else. The mission in our hearts leadened the flight.

"I need your help, Chami," I said as we were descending. "Are you able to gain entry into a locked building quietly and unnoticed?"

Chami nodded, confirming what I had suspected. All of us could easily break down doors and smash windows with little effort, but Chami employed stealth in his practice. He killed quietly.

"Good," I said.

Chami's blue eyes glinted enigmatically. I knew he thought I wanted to employ his deadly assassin skills.

"Gryphon, Amber, and Chami will come with me," I said to them. "Aquila and Tomas, you will stay behind to watch the rest."

"I would like to fight for you, milady," Tomas said. "May I come?"

"Your job watching over the others and our Book of Holdings is just as important a task," I told him gently.

Tomas nodded unhappily.

At LaGuardia we were met by two stretch limousines complete with chauffeurs—hats, uniforms, and all. They looked fine, but looks didn't matter so much as the fact that they could be bought. I couldn't afford the risk. Pulling a stack of crisp one-hundred-dollar bills, I said to the chauffeurs, "Take this and split it between you. You can go home now. We'll do the driving."

"What about our limos?" the taller driver protested.

"We'll take good care of them."

The two looked at their money, then looked at each other and smiled. They walked away, not even bothering to say good-bye, busy counting their money—three thousand dollars exact.

"Aquila, how good are you at the wheel?" I asked.

"I believe I drove one of these things when I was eighteen. That was about a hundred years ago."

"Good enough for me. Take this." I handed him another stack of Benjamin Franklins and whispered the name and address of a hotel in his ear.

"Got it," Aquila said.

Tomas herded Jamie, Tersa, and Rosemary into the limousine and off they went, jerkily, joining the traffic stream.

I got behind the other wheel, and headed toward the Midtown Tunnel, the skyline of Manhattan looming before me.

The East Village was quiet and the orphanage was even smaller and older than I remembered it to be. It was a simple red-brick, three-storied affair with drab, dreary windows. A few sad shrubs huddled around the cracked stone steps as if they had passively absorbed the emotions of the many little lives that had lived in the orphanage. It was a time of true quiet, those few hours before dawn when all slept, even the criminal elements.

It was a simple matter to blend in the shadows and wait quietly as Chami pulled out a small case of tools and fiddled with the back entry lock for a few short moments.

Chami twisted the knob and like magic, the door silently swung open. We slipped inside and I led the way to the lower level office. It was locked as well, and just as easily breached by Chami. I made my way to the cabinet files.

"What are we looking for?" Gryphon asked quietly.

"A boy with the first name of Thaddeus who would have first come here on January 5, 1989, or close to around that time."

Amber and Gryphon began helping me search the countless old folders. Chami, to my surprise—for I hadn't imagined such familiarity with modern human technology—booted up the computer. The screen illuminated the room with an eerie blue glow.

It was a frustrating, unproductive task. All the files in my cabinet were of children in current residence. I moved to the next cabinet—there were five in all—but it only dated as far back as children who had resided here ten years ago. Amber finished the three drawers of his cabinet file and moved on to the next one.

It was Chami who finally found it. "Milady," he called softly, and indicated the computer screen. I took the seat he vacated and read the information eagerly.

A boy named Thaddeus, with black hair and dark brown eyes, had been taken into the orphanage sixteen years ago, wearing a silver cross with his name engraved on the back of it. My heart pounded and a sudden surge of moisture blurred my vision. I swiped my eyes with my sleeve and read on. He had been adopted three weeks later. I committed the name, address, and telephone number of the adopting couple, Henry and Pauline Schiffer, to memory.

"Good job, Chami. Thank you."

"It is my pleasure to serve you, milady."

"Are other Monère computer-savvy like you?"

"Not many, no," Chami confessed. "But I found it necessary and useful in my line of work."

They'd aimed Chami at human targets as well, I realized. The Queens had used Chami in his own lethal way, much as Mona Sera had used Gryphon and Sonia's sexual services in her business dealings, eliminating with cold finality any obstacles that could not be lured with money or seduced.

When we left the orphanage, night was fading and faint light pressed against the thinning darkness. We came out of the building one by one, silent dark shadows. As soon as I hit the street, rounding the block where our limousine was parked, I was jerked into an alley with bruising force.

I'd had no warning because there'd been no heartbeat to warn me of any intruders in the radius around me. The hand that grabbed me was golden-skinned, with sharp familiar nails. But the bestial face I looked up into was not Halcyon's.

One bronze arm wrapped around my waist, lifting me off my feet, pressing me against my captor with a terrible ease, trapping my arms at my side in an unbreakable grip. The demon was impossibly strong and huge, at least seven feet tall. He'd been expecting us.

Amber and Gryphon came around the corner in a blurred rush. I felt the demon move sharply. One quick downward slash of his hand and Amber's chest was ripped diagonally open, ribs breaking, flesh peeling down all the way so that I saw with vivid horror, his slow, pulsing heart. Warm blood splashed across my face as Amber was flung away. He hit the ground some distance away in a crumpled heap. I opened my mouth to scream but all the breath had been squeezed out of my body by that imprisoning grip. Another swipe and Gryphon was sent flying, demon nails ripping deep furrows in Gryphon's stomach.

I called my silver dagger to my hand, the one I had taken from Mona Louisa, and with a twist of my wrist, drove it into the demon's belly. He hissed with pain and his arm squeezed me so tightly that I was in true danger of being pinched in half. With an animal snarl, he ripped out the little offending dagger. Invisible bands wrapped my hands to my sides, and stilled my kicking legs. I couldn't move or break free of the invisible mental force he had wrapped around me.

The demon's mouth twisted in a vicious snarl, his eyes becoming fiery red like a wash of angry blood as another knife plunged into his chest from out of nowhere. The demon's hand swept out and grabbed something. Chami came into sudden view, with the demon's claw wrapped tightly about his neck, his arms banded to his side as if invisible forces restrained him, too.

With a savage drooling snarl, the demon sank sharp teeth into Chami's throat. Deep red blood trickled slowly down Chami's white fragile neck as the demon's throat worked strongly. *Dear Goddess,* I realized with sickening horror, he was drinking Chami's blood, draining him, and growing stronger with the intake. Chami's eyes glazed over and his body fell slack. *No!* With every ounce of force and will within me, I struggled to break free. My hand moved slightly.

With a snarl of rage, the demon discarded Chami, throwing him away like a toy he no longer desired. The invisible vise holding me secure snapped tight once more. With a simple move, the dagger was plucked out from the demon's chest and tossed aside. Blood oozed sullenly from the demon's two wounds.

Gryphon had picked himself back up and thrown himself forward. The demon stopped Gryphon's rush by simply digging the sharp points of his nails into my throat.

"What do you want?" Gryphon demanded harshly.

"Tell Halcyon that Kadeen has his precious Mixed Blood Queen," the demon growled in a guttural voice, the smell of fresh blood heavy on his breath. "Have him come meet my challenge. Or she dies."

The demon carried me deeper into the alley, into a wall of mist, stepping into a terrible buzzing force of energy that I'd never experienced before or ever hoped to experience again. Hot, searing pain lanced me like a thousand vicious stabbing knives and darkness took me.

TWENTY-ONE

I AWOKE IN twilight darkness, terribly weak, chained naked to the ground, my clothes in sliced tatters around me. The air was like the arid heat of the desert. We were outside, in a courtyard of some sort, a ring of faces in various colors shading from light brown to deep bronze watching me with hostile curiosity a short distance away. It took a moment before I realized what it was about the place that bothered me, besides the demon dead, that is. There were no bright colors. No living green grass, no blue sky, no yellow or red leaves. Everything was muted, dampened, darkened, until there was almost no color at all. The only thing that stood out down here was my very white, living flesh and enhoused within it, my very red, flowing blood.

Kadeen paced beside me, a dark creature of menace with red-stained fangs and bloodied nails. He was different from the other demon dead who rather looked like a tanned version of myself. Kadeen bulged with unnaturally strong muscles, more animal than man. His face was oddly distorted, as if a beast was bursting out from within, his forehead large and bulging, his brow jutting. And those red eyes that glowed with an unnatural luster. He was demon unmasked.

"I was supposed to kill you," Kadeen said, his voice grating like rusty iron, as if it was hard for him to speak in that form. "But I decided to use you instead to lure Halcyon, my enemy, out from his lair. I have been challenging him for the last one hundred years ever since he killed my father in challenge, but he never bothered to accept it, considering me far beneath his notice. But now Halcyon will meet me. You are what he fancies. You are my bait to draw him out to this battle for supremacy."

Kadeen stilled. "He comes." He bent down to me. Bloody teeth gleamed and he snapped his fangs viciously at me. I jumped, unable to help myself, and screamed. The chains held me and I could not break free though I pulled and strained until my wrists and ankles were raw and bleeding.

"Scream again," Kadeen commanded and roughly squeezed my breast with bruising force. His sharp nails pierced through my skin like knives.

I screamed with helpless hatred and rage. Then screamed with horror as Kadeen's teeth ripped my throat. The pain was excruciating. He fed voraciously, drinking my blood. There was a curious buzzing in my head and everything seemed to swirl.

"Enough. I am here." Halcyon's quiet voice pierced the night, jerking the demon from me. Kadeen faced the Demon Prince with fierce hatred and grim satisfaction, my blood dripping from his fangs.

Halcyon looked the same here in Hell, I noticed with a distant floating detachment. White silk shirt, black coat, elegant trousers. That same calm golden face I'd first seen in the forest amid the sunshine. Halcyon glanced at me once then looked away.

"I challenge you." Kadeen grunted, seething with eager ferocity, high and powerful on the fresh blood that I had unwillingly donated.

"I accept." With unhurried ease, Halcyon undid his diamond cufflinks, unbuttoned his shirt, and stepped gracefully out of his soft, calf-length leather boots.

"How did you know where to find Mona Lisa," Halcyon asked.

"Mona Louisa told me she would come to the orphanage. She wanted me to kill the new Queen so she would get her territory back."

"Mona Louisa again. What a nuisance she is becoming," Halcyon murmured.

It seemed an impossible match. A slim elegant man facing a towering beast. Then that part of Halcyon fell away even as his silk shirt fell to the ground. I felt a rush of energy and Halcyon grew in size and width, swelling with brutish muscles until he stood monstrously large, even taller than Kadeen. Maybe eight feet. His forehead widened and thickened, a vein bulging prominently down the center. His brow jutted and my comfortable lassitude that I had fallen into ripped away. Halcyon's eyes hazed red and his face twisted in a silent snarl, displaying fangs that were ivory white and impressive as hell. Then the brutish rage smoothed out and his eyes returned to that calm midnight black.

They lunged at each other, a blur of speed almost too fast to follow, their heavy bodies meeting in the air and rolling to the ground a few yards away, shaking the earth beneath me with the impact of their combined weight. Claws slashed and blood ran. Kadeen howled with rage and threw Halcyon off him. The Demon Prince rolled to his feet with fluid grace, at peculiar odds with his beastly appearance, and sprang and tackled Kadeen in a haze of motion. They rolled on the ground, farther away from me, each trying to get atop the other, Kadeen slashing with his claws, snarling and cursing,

Halcyon fighting in a cold, freezing silence that was somehow even scarier than Kadeen's hot rage.

"Enough," Halcyon said suddenly, as if he was tired of playing.

All I caught was a swift sharp movement that abruptly shut Kadeen up mid-snarl. There was a stunned, uncomprehending look on the smaller demon's face for a long, stretched-out moment. Then Kadeen's head fell off and rolled to the ground. Blood, the color of dark burgundy under Hell's twilight sky, seeped out beneath it. I gave a muffled shriek, unable to tear my gaze from that head, from those eyes. Those red, burning eyes that, dear merciful God, still held awareness and watched as Halcyon proceeded to slice off Kadeen's arms and legs with swift, lethal precision. Watched as the severed limbs fell in bloody, chunky pieces to the ground. Watched with fear-wide eyes as Halcyon walked over to him and drove both talons into his skull with one forceful, piercing thrust. Those eyes finally closed as Halcyon cracked open the thick bone of Kadeen's skull several inches to reveal soft, wet brain and oozing cerebral fluid. Just as I was breathing out a sigh of relief, those terrible eyes flashed open once more in awful awareness.

Halcyon tipped back his head and released a blood-curdling howl. Fierce, joyous baying answered in the distance, unearthly cries that made my skin want to detach itself from my flesh and crawl away just to escape whatever was coming.

"Feed him to the Hell hounds," Halcyon ordered. His rough, gravelly voice, a hoarse parody of his usual smooth, cultured tone, made me flinch. And that one involuntary ripple of movement from me tore away Halcyon's cool facade and revealed the seething emotions within. Hot, burning rage poured out from Halcyon in roiling waves until the very air quivered. His flaming eyes burned so hotly it seemed as if they would surely sear flesh. The other demons seemed to think so as well. They faded away, all but two males who quickly gathered up all of Kadeen's many parts and hurriedly took them off into the woods, as if they too could not wait to escape their prince's wrath.

Halcyon walked to me and knelt down, so close and so big that I felt like a small, fragile doll beside him. The chains that I had not been able to free myself from looked ridiculously tiny in his hands. Hands that spanned more than three times the length of mine.

With one yank, Halcyon snapped the chains easily and removed the manacles, his big hands accomplishing the task with unexpected gentleness. I was free, but couldn't seem to move. His red eyes, set deep in that beastly face, touched upon my torn and swollen neck, my bruised and bloodied breast, moving slowly down my body, making me vividly aware once more of my nakedness.

I closed my eyes, unable to do anything else. A moment later, I felt silk touch my skin. I opened my eyes to find Halcyon's shirt covering me.

I sat up and flung myself against Halcyon, hot tears rolling down my face. "I am sick of men stripping away my clothes and chaining me up," I said fiercely, my face buried against the hard ridges of his abdomen.

Halcyon took a deep breath and shuddered. Energy prickled my skin. As Halcyon changed back, shrinking once more to normal size, I found myself held against his chest, my eyes level with his throat now. I gazed up into black midnight eyes, into Halcyon's dear familiar face. He lifted me into his arms and I was never so aware of a man's greater strength.

He carried me out of the courtyard and I had a brief impression of entering an ancient dark fortress that seemed to reach for the sky. I glimpsed a few startled, tanned faces. His servants, no doubt.

Wrapping my arms around Halcyon's neck, I pressed into him, needing the contact, the security, unable to stop my body's tremors.

Ascending a flight of stairs, Halcyon brought me to a rich, comfortable chamber and laid me down on cool linen, disappearing for a moment. When he returned, he wore clean clothing. The blood that had covered him was gone. He held two wet washcloths in his hands. One he gently pressed against the torn flesh on my neck. With the other, he slowly and methodically cleaned my face, wiping off Amber's blood. He carefully washed my raw wrists and ankles, even my breasts, as efficiently as any nurse. When Halcyon was finished, he slid me into a clean silk shirt that smelled faintly of him.

"Where are we?" I asked.

"In my private chambers," Halcyon said, sitting on the edge of the bed.

"He staked me out in front of your own house." I snorted. "He certainly had balls."

"No longer," Halcyon said coldly.

I shivered, remembering the unearthly baying of the Hell hounds.

"I am sorry you had to see that," Halcyon said quietly.

"No. I know you had to set an example. To let others see what they risked if they challenged you. And it's not as if I haven't cut parts off of men myself." My smile cracked and disappeared. "Just not quite to your thorough degree."

"I meant that I was sorry you had to see me in my other form." Halcyon kept his gaze averted. "You fear me now."

Monsters were we all, I thought, and so terribly fragile.

"It would be foolish not to fear demons," I replied softly.

"You did not fear me before."

"I was foolish. I did not know how incredibly strong and dangerous you were." I remembered Gryphon's trembling fear and anger when I had returned from the forest in Halcyon's company. Gryphon had known.

Halcyon's face was a carved golden mask, devoid of any living expression.

"But I trust you still not to harm me." I took Halcyon's unresisting hand, laid it against my face, and drew his long lethal nails gently down my skin.

Halcyon drew in a convulsive breath. His hand tightened against my face for a brief moment, an involuntary spasm, then relaxed.

Something changed. The room suddenly shimmered with sensuality. Halcyon's lips softened in a seductive smile, drawing my attention to them like an irresistible siren call. His lips were pure red carnality. His nails slid down the smooth uninjured side of my neck in a sensuous caress that seemed to touch more than just skin, going deeper, much deeper inside to secret places. Unbelievable pleasure slithered down my spine and loosened my knees.

I shuddered and drew carefully away from his touch. "I don't, however, trust you not to try and seduce me."

"And well you should not," Halcyon murmured, his voice a deep sensuous velvet that stroked all my senses. He bent over me, lowering those erotic red lips down.

"No," I said softly. The small hand I put up to his chest was no match against his greater strength, but he stopped.

"Why not?" he asked just as softly.

"I've given my heart already."

"To Gryphon."

"And Amber," I said in a low voice.

Halcyon's lips twisted. "Then why not me, too?"

"I . . . just can't. I'd feel as if I were betraying them."

Halcyon lowered those tempting lips closer and whispered against my mouth, "I could make you not care."

I did not doubt that he had the ability to make true his words.

"Then you might as well tear my throat out," I whispered against the almost press of his lips. "It would hurt me less."

Halcyon stilled, looked deep within me, and read the truth of my words. He drew away and closed his eyes.

"I'm sorry," I said, not knowing why I was apologizing but feeling as if I should.

He gave a harsh laugh. "So am I. So am I. It's my fault you are hurt. I should have hid my interest in you. My only excuse is that you took me so by surprise. I was not thinking."

"No," I said sharply. "You cannot hold yourself accountable for Kadeen's actions." My voice softened. "Anyway, you rescued me and killed the bad guy."

One elegant eyebrow quirked upward. "You don't think of me, a demon, as a bad guy? After you saw my other self?"

"No. You just make visible that dark part that every one of us has inside of them, especially me."

Halcyon reached out, his thumb rubbing small circles against my hand. "I love that part of you, hell-cat."

"Do you? I sense a beast within me, waiting to be let loose. It scares me sometimes." I smiled tremulously. "But it reassures me to see how in control you are of that part of yourself. You control it. It doesn't control you."

"No, it doesn't control me."

"What you change into is not so different from the forms the Monère shift into."

"Perhaps because we were once Monère."

My eyes widened upon hearing that fact. "All of you?"

"There are some Mixed Bloods among us but not many. Few have enough psychic power to make the transition to Hell."

"Why should that matter?"

Halcyon smiled. "Hell is not the place for sinners that humans believe it to be. After the Monère die, some fade back into the darkness. Those who have remaining psychic power come here and exist in this forever twilight realm for as long as their energy sustains them."

"Would I come here?"

"Yes, if your mind was not burned out when you died."

I searched his eyes. "Then why did it anger you so when you learned that the witch's brew almost killed me?"

Halcyon pressed a soft kiss to my hand, making me shiver, and not in fear. "I value life. Yours especially, hell cat. It was your joyous laughter that first drew me to you, your pure delight in nature's beauty. You were bathed in sunlight and filled with happiness. You captivated me and you lured me in even deeper when you betrayed no fear of me. When you tried to protect me, made Amber sheath his sword, I fell in love with you."

His simple statement lay between us.

I lifted the hand he had kissed and tenderly traced the lean lines of Halcyon's elegant face. "You must try and find someone else to love. For both our sakes."

"You love Gryphon and Amber only because you met them first. But you will love me last. I shall be here long after they have gone," Halcyon said with certainty.

I smiled wryly. "But will I?"

He nodded. "Your psychic power is greater than theirs."

When Halcyon had promised to wait, he had spoken not only of life but of the afterlife. I stared at him. "How old are you, Halcyon?"

"I have lived over six hundred years in this realm."

No wonder he had looked at me so curiously when I'd asked if he was over a hundred years old when we'd first met. What *was* this thing I had for older guys?

"One last question. Can I leave Hell?"

Halcyon's smile did not reach his dark chocolate eyes. "You mean will I let you leave."

"That, too," I said softly.

"Your young man does not expect you to return," Halcyon said suddenly.

He meant Gryphon. I guess seventy-five years would seem young in Halcyon's eyes. "Why not?"

"No human or living Monère ever has. If the descent does not kill them, the arrival certainly does. Their bodies cannot survive in this heat. They become the demon dead or simply fade into the darkness."

So maybe it was not the sun itself but heat that killed the Monère. "But I'm still alive. My heart beats."

"Yes. You can survive here," Halcyon said, looking at me in a contemplative, unsettling manner. "And you were not brought here by my hand. Even the Council would not question me if you never returned."

His dangerous words made my blood run more quickly in my veins. "I am not a captured butterfly you can keep, Halcyon. Do not make me hate you."

"Could you not choose to be with me?" It was a quiet plea.

I gazed at the lonely, elegant man before me. A man who said he loved me. A man who stirred feelings of friendship and more within me. Could I have chosen to remain here with him? Yes, if I had met him first. And to tell Halcyon that would have been the utmost cruelty, because the unalterable fact was I had *not* met him first.

"You must let me go. I fear my brother is in peril. I must find him. Please, Halcyon." I licked my lips nervously, drawing his gaze down to my mouth. His gaze dropped even farther to the beating pulse of my neck.

"A kiss. Or one small taste of your blood," Halcyon said finally. "That is my price for letting you go."

Dizzying relief rushed through me even as my heart pounded faster in fear as I remembered the brutal way Kadeen's teeth had ripped into me.

"I will not hurt you," Halcyon promised gently.

My brief spurt of alarm receded. "A taste then," I said, reasoning that a sip of my blood would be much, much safer than kissing him. Turning my head, I offered my neck to the Demon Prince.

Halcyon bent down over me and sharp awareness of his body over mine singed me though no part of him touched me. I felt his breath against my skin, felt an involuntary tingling in my breasts as he inhaled and drew in my scent. A tingling that turned into an ache as I felt his teeth sharpen against my neck, an ache that began to throb as he scraped his fangs lightly along my skin in an erotic caress that made me suddenly doubt the wisdom of my choice. Sensual tendrils whispered over my body like invisible hands.

He pierced me, a glorious aching pain that made me cry out. Crooning with fierce pleasure, Halcyon drank my blood and I felt his vibration trill over my breasts, trip down to my core and arrow into me with sweet ferocity. I arched up against him as agonizing pleasure burst within me, drenching me until wetness trickled down my thighs and the scent of my satisfaction filled the room. Halcyon released me as my light was slowly absorbed back into my body. I looked up into his dark eyes, limp and dazed, my breath coming fast.

He licked a small drop of my blood from where it rested like an innocent red beauty mark upon his lips. "A small taste of me, as I tasted you."

"I do not believe I could survive more," I said, breathless.

"Would it not be glorious to see if you could?" Halcyon whispered temptingly.

I laughed shakily, pushed him away from me, and sat up on the bed. "Take me back, Halcyon. Please. I need to find my brother."

⤜⟐⤛

W E ARRIVED BACK in the same alley where I had been taken. Halcyon walked out of the misty wall, carrying me in his arms. He had shielded me somehow so that all I felt was minor discomfort.

Gryphon was waiting, slumped against the wall. Grief and despair ravaged his face, twisting it into a harsh mask. He rose to his feet slowly and stiffly. Disbelief shadowed his luminous eyes for a moment then fled as fierce glittering emotions took its place.

Halcyon set me down and I rushed into Gryphon's arms. He held me tightly, uncaring of his own wounds.

"Amber? Chami?" I asked.

"Back in your apartment, not far from here, resting."

They were both still alive. Thank God.

Gryphon set me carefully aside and dropped to his knees before Halcyon.

"My thanks, Prince Halcyon, for returning her back to us," Gryphon said, his voice hoarse with gratitude.

"Do not thank me. It was her choice. Not mine."

"My deepest gratitude, then, most especially because of that," Gryphon said, holding Halcyon's gaze.

The Demon Prince smiled wryly down at Gryphon. "Thought of that, too, did you, lad?" Halcyon sighed and looked at me mockingly. "I would have been the better choice. But he's not too poor an alternative, considering. Until we next meet, milady." Halcyon bowed and walked back into the mist. The swirling white slowly faded and disappeared.

Gryphon stood up and ran his gaze over me in close examination, taking in the silk shirt, the baggy pants cinched tight at the waist with a man's leather belt, the masculine necktie wrapped around my throat. "I thought we'd lost you," Gryphon whispered, loosening the cloth about my neck and gazing at the marks on either side. He retied the cloth without comment.

"Nope. I'm hard to kill."

"That was the only hope I clung to, when I dared hope."

"How badly are Amber and Chami hurt?" I closed my eyes. "Stupid question. I saw how badly. But they'll live, right?"

Gryphon nodded and gave a fierce smile. "We too are hard to kill."

"I'm glad. Terribly, terribly glad. Let me see your wounds."

Gryphon lifted his shirt. The deep furrows, already beginning to heal, arrowed angrily from his left hip to just below his right ribs. The stiletto wound was finally gone, I saw, only to replaced by this new injury. My palms tingled as I ran both of my hands over the deep gashes, easing his discomfort.

"Ah, that feels much better." Gryphon took my hands in his and kissed them. "The wounds will heal quickly enough on their own. I was most fortunate. It was but a glancing blow."

I'd seen up-close and personal what those claws could do and could not disagree with him.

"Let us go quickly to your place," Gryphon said, tucking me against his side as we left the alley. "Amber needs you."

I was grateful for Gyphon's lack of jealousy. Truly I was. But at the same time it bothered me. "You and Amber. You're amazingly generous with each other about me."

A hard gleam came into Gryphon's eyes. "I do not share you lightly, Mona Lisa. Only with Amber. He is my equal and shares with you his strength and helps shield you from our enemies. We belong to you." Gryphon touched the necktie, his fingers unerringly finding the spot where Halcyon had bit me. "Halcyon does not belong to you. He is not one of us. And being with him does not strengthen but endangers you."

"I asked him to find someone else to love."

"That would be most ideal," Gryphon said dryly, "and make you less of a target. Will he do so, do you think?"

I shrugged unthinkingly, jarring my wounds, above and below. "I don't know. Will there be other demons?"

"The fate of the demon who took you will surely serve as a deterrent but . . . few demons are powerful enough to leave Hell."

I shuddered. "Great. So that means that the ones that do come after us are going to be really strong."

❧

T HE FIRST THING I saw when I entered my apartment was Chami lying on the couch. He was ghastly white, his face paler even than the white pillow he rested upon. Upon seeing me, he tried to rise.

"Don't be foolish and try to get up," I said, pushing him back down.

"Any more foolish than attacking a demon?" Chami returned.

"That was foolish indeed. Did you know what they could do?"

Chami gave a short nod. "Still had to try. Haven't figured out a way to kill those bastards yet."

"Cut off their heads." I shivered as I remembered those awful eyes, aware and knowing in Kadeen's severed head. The memory was going to haunt my dreams for a long time to come.

"I'll try that instead of going for the heart next time. Should have told me sooner," Chami grumbled.

"I didn't know sooner."

"Is that what happened to the big guy who grabbed you?"

"Yeah."

Grim satisfaction colored Chami's blue eyes. "Good. One demon down. I wonder how many more to go?"

"Hopefully no more. What happened to Kadeen should serve as sufficient warning to the others."

He must have seen something in my eyes. "More to it than just cutting off the head, huh?"

"I don't want to talk about it," I said quietly.

Chami was instantly contrite.

"How are you feeling?" I asked.

"Drained," Chami said, straight-faced.

"Yuck! That's a terrible joke." I slapped him on the shoulder.

Chami shrugged and grinned wickedly. "It happens to be true. But I'm much better already. We are a hardy lot."

I smiled, very thankful for that fact. "You talk like a human, more than the others," I said and grimaced as I heard myself. I was beginning to speak like them.

"Comes from watching too much television."

Chami's easy grin flitted away, leaving a quiet, wary seriousness in its place as I put my hand gently over the mangled, puffy flesh of his neck. It made me wonder: Was the assassin like me, touched so rarely by others, with care, with gentleness?

His wound had already begun to knit together. A scab had formed and the bruises were green-yellow. Two weeks of healing in several hours. Amazing.

"Your ouchie looks just like mine," I murmured.

My palm tingled over Chami's neck, easing his pain, and his eyes widened.

"Your ouchie. Is that what I smell? It feels much better now," Chami observed with wonder as I lifted my hand away.

"Good. Rest now."

"Yes, my Queen." He said it lightly, but the lightness did not touch his serious eyes. He meant those words. I was truly his Queen.

"Where's Amber?" I asked.

"In your bedroom. It was the only bed in this place. I hope you don't mind."

"Of course not."

I entered my bedroom and closed the door behind me. Golden amber eyes gleamed at me from the bed where Amber lay with the sheet drawn up to the waist, leaving his chest bare.

Amber had been split open, leaving that strong, fragile heart so vulnerable—another image that would frequent my nightmares. But that miraculous healing ability we possessed had already knitted back enough viscera so that his heart no longer was exposed. However, the repair had not reached the bones quite yet. The white jagged edges lay cracked, exposed, the separate pieces of his broken ribs moving disjointedly with each slow breath that lifted his chest.

"Oh, Amber," I breathed, tears welling up. I could not even begin to imagine the pain he must be in.

"Can't lift my arms without moving my ribs," Amber whispered, his deep voice strained. "Touch me, please."

I knelt beside him, cupped that dear harsh face in my hands and brushed the hair tenderly back from his damp forehead.

"You're real," Amber breathed at my touch and closed his eyes. I kissed the warm tears from his lashes. "I apologize for failing you," he said.

I jerked back. "Don't be ridiculous."

"You were under my protection."

"He was a *demon*," I said, my voice edging with temper. "It was crazy of you to even try to fight him."

"It was my duty to keep you safe. I failed you," Amber insisted.

Hot tears splashed down my face. I angrily swiped them away. "Stubborn fool. Then I failed you, too. You belong to me," I proclaimed arrogantly. "It's my duty to keep you safe."

"Shhh. Don't cry."

"Then don't make me angry by saying stupid things. We're alive! We're still alive. That's all that matters."

A smile twisted Amber's lips. "Yes, milady."

"Milady," I chided at his distancing formal address, a smile wobbling on my lips. "Now you're trying to really make me mad. Oh, Amber." I brushed my lips against him, felt the stern lines of his mouth soften and move against mine. We'd never really kissed before, I realized. Just chaste pecks. I coaxed his mouth to open, delved within, tasted his sweetness for the very first time, and let the sexual heat between us slowly build.

"No," Amber said, turning his head away.

Ignoring him, I pulled the sheet down from his lap, crooning with approval at what had risen to greet me. I stroked his erection once with a tight possessive stroke.

"Why not?" I asked softly. "Am I hurting you?"

"You are slaying me," he gritted, his amber eyes mere molten slits. "It is not my wish for you to come to me like this, when I am injured, to heal me. I made a promise to myself that the next occasion you came to me would be because you desired me."

Yes, monsters all of us, I thought. And so horribly fragile.

"Next time," I said tenderly.

"Shall there be a next time?"

"Yes," I whispered, and awareness of what I just promised was reflected in both of our eyes—it was a promise that I would try what they had suggested, being with them both.

My lashes swept down beneath his heated gaze. It was easier to kiss Amber's bunched abdomen, run a string of kisses down the crisp hair that arrowed down the center of his belly. Rub my soft cheek against his rigid staff and relish the texture of the buttery velvet skin that covered hard stone within. I felt him shudder.

One quick jerk to loosen the belt and my borrowed pants pooled around my feet.

Amber stopped me as I moved back toward him. "Your shirt," he demanded.

Hesitating briefly, I unbuttoned my shirt and let it fall away. I felt his gaze touch upon the marks on my left breast, touch upon my wrists and ankles.

"Remove the necktie," Amber commanded softly.

I loosened the cloth, my eyes downcast. His angry hiss of breath made me flinch even though I knew it wasn't directed at me. Having Amber see Kadeen's brutal marks upon me made me feel vulnerable, unclean, a victim's guilt. Stupid though I knew the feeling to be, I could not shake it. I felt Amber struggle to contain his anger and stood there in naked uncertainty.

"Did Halcyon send the demon to his final death?" Amber asked roughly.

"Yes."

Amber absorbed that for a long moment, let it calm him, and gentled his gravelly voice as much as he could. "Do you still want me?"

I nodded.

"Then take me. I am yours."

And I knew as he spoke that he remembered how I had healed myself as well as him the last time. Crawling hesitantly onto the bed and between his thighs, I lay a hand upon a muscled leg, and bent down to take him into my mouth.

"Can you take me within you?" he asked, stopping me.

"Yes," I answered in a small voice.

"Do you wish to?"

"Oh, yes," I breathed.

My answer made Amber smile.

"Will it hurt you?" I asked.

"It will hurt me more if you do not."

My answering smile caressed him as I carefully straddled him. His sex was huge and hard. I loved the feel of him in my hand: big, warm, and pulsing. I squeezed him tightly and his eyes fluttered shut. I dipped down onto him, letting him enter me slightly before lifting back up after wetting the tip of him. His thick neck grew taut.

"Next time I shall be on top," Amber muttered through gritted teeth, his eyes narrow gold slits.

I laughed. "I don't know about that. We might have to wrestle for it. I'm beginning to like this position."

Amber's growl turned into a groan as I lowered back down. Leaning back, I rubbed his wonderful thick rod against my wet outer lips, moving up and down gently against him. I spread the moisture around the rest of him and slowly pushed down onto his stiff member. There was just enough lubrication to allow him to enter me, increment by increment. Just enough so that I could feel every single sensation as he stretched me, feel every delicious rub of his ridged tip as it bumped and pushed its way with excruciating, killing slowness into my tight greedy flesh. I swallowed him up, inch by glorious inch, and he filled me so blissfully full so that only then did I realize how empty I had been.

I sighed with the satisfaction of a difficult job well done when he was finally buried fully within me.

"Come here," Amber rumbled.

I braced my arms, bent down over him, and felt his hardened staff resist then bend within me as I angled my body over him.

"Closer," he said.

I lowered myself down until my lips were a breath away from

his jaw. Amber turned his head and licked Halcyon's neat puncture marks, laving away the Demon Prince's scent and replacing it with his own. My inner muscles clenched around Amber in involuntary response to his tongue's rough caress. He twitched within me, stretching my posterior vaginal wall and I gasped and bit back a moan. I felt his teeth clamp upon my neck. Felt Amber bite down hard enough for it to hurt, but not enough to break skin. Felt him suck hard, laving the spot with the rough texture of his tongue, leaving his own mark there over Halcyon's. My body pulsed and spasmed, screaming within, glowing, even as my scream of pleasure strangled in my throat as I desperately tried to be quiet.

I felt Amber's mouth move in a demonic smile against my neck as he tortured me as thoroughly as I had tortured him, without even lifting his arms.

The power built and our incandescence lit the room. So close. So close to the edge now. Supporting my weight completely on my left hand, I wrapped my other hand around his bulging bicep, needing something to grip on to.

Amber moved to the other side of my neck, licked gently along the swollen, tender flesh and made me whimper as he breathed over the open wound. Made me gasp and quiver as he touched his tongue just there and then pushed slowly, oh so slowly, down into my raw flesh. Not moving. Just there. Exquisite pain. Exquisite pleasure.

One gentle push deeper with his tongue, filling me, stretching wounded flesh and I convulsed, exploded within, my inner muscles clenching and contracting about him, gripping his huge, thick sex. My body tried its inner best to milk him dry as I held still, frozen above him in immobility, unable to move for fear of hurting him.

Amber groaned as if I were killing him as he climaxed without even a single stroke. His stillness within me allowed me to feel and absorb every spurt and shuddering jet of his pleasure.

I lifted my head. Looking at the astonishing wholeness of Amber's flesh put a whole new meaning to good sex. His ribs had knit back together. His muscles and sinews were untorn. His skin was once again velvet smoothness. A bloody miracle.

"I must apologize," he said suddenly, stiltedly. "I was too forward."

"I don't mind, Amber," I said, pushing back my hair. "I like it that you were a little bossy. It means that you feel comfortable enough with me to be yourself. Is that what you're really like?" I asked teasingly. "Arrogant and domineering?"

"I do not know."

The utter sincerity of his words punched me like a fist, destroying me. My lashes swept down to shield my emotions from him. Dear sweet Jesus. Over a hundred and five years of life and he did not know what he was really like.

"Thank you for healing me," Amber said, gifting me with another of his rare sweet smiles. "Now we can go find your brother."

Twenty-two

Pelham Manor was a quietly affluent residential neighbor-hood perched at the edge of Westchester County. Birds chirped cheerfully, welcoming the day as we disembarked from the limo several blocks away. Lawns were neatly manicured and the thick hedges planted long ago.

An odd mix of feelings assailed me at the thought of my brother, Thaddeus, growing up here—hope that he had been happy and loved, along with a twisting pain at the possibility that he may not need me or welcome my intrusion into his life. They might have moved, I had told myself repeatedly. But still I'd had to come and see for myself in case they hadn't.

The house I sought was a stately Tudor with a dark tiled roof and large windows set in a cul-de-sac in front of a large wooded lot. There didn't seem to be any danger in this quiet, peaceful neighborhood. No foreign scent or sign of intrusion.

We moved into the trees and I opened my senses. There were

three heartbeats within the dwelling. Two beating human-fast, one slower. My heart gave a painful thump. The sounds from within the house came clearly to my ear.

A woman's voice calling upstairs, "Thaddeus, I made you a turkey-salad wrap."

A boy's answering groan. "Aw, Mom, can't I buy lunch at school?"

"No, dear. They use white bread and too much greasy meat. Plus, it's not organic."

Feet galloped downstairs. A muttered, "I hate organic stuff."

"It's good for you."

"Morning, Dad."

A man's lower voice. "Ready to go, son?"

"Yeah." The sound of a quick kiss planted.

His mother's "Good luck on your math test."

The cocky reply. "Piece of cake."

The garage door rose and a black Mercedes sedan pulled out onto the road, driven by an older, bespectacled man with gray, thinning hair. He looked kind and intellectual. A boy with the slighter, rangier build of youth sat in the passenger's seat beside him. His pure black hair glistened as the sunlight streaking through the trees fell upon it.

With no warning, the boy turned his head to where I stood back among the trees. His gaze seemed to look right upon me. I had one too-brief moment to see his dark eyes, tilted up at the ends exotically like mine, before he disappeared around a corner and from my sight.

A long silence ensued.

"He seems happy," I whispered finally. I'd been so sure that he'd needed me. But he didn't. He had a home and a loving family. He was safe. There were no signs of intruders. My presence would only disrupt the tranquility of his life.

I swallowed the lumpy conclusion down my painfully tight throat. "Come on. Let's get back to the others," I whispered.

Maybe someday I would introduce myself to him, I told myself. Someday when he was older.

⟡

AQUILA HAD GOTTEN a suite with connecting rooms at the Pierre. It must have been the Presidential suite or something. The rooms were huge, bigger than my entire apartment. I turned on the television to the local news channel the next day as was my habit, half listening to the low volume, screening for any unusual events that might help pinpoint Sandoor's whereabouts while half listening to Chami instructing his raptly attentive three warrior novices—Jamie, Tersa, and Rosemary.

Chami was discoursing like a university professor on the proper way of holding a dagger when a newscaster's mention of a familiar name snagged my attention. A truck whose driver had fallen asleep had drifted across the road and struck an oncoming car, killing the two front passengers. A third passenger had miraculously survived and was listed in stable condition at Westchester County Medical Center. The driver escaped with minor injuries.

Just another motor vehicle tragedy on the Hutchinson River Parkway. Nothing unusual but for the names of the dead victims: Henry and Pauline Schiffer. Thaddeus's adopted parents. A brief commentary followed on the hazards of cross-country truck driving and tight deadlines that frequently did not allow drivers adequate time for sleep. Accidents and death-rate statistics were listed.

I made no sound, but the sudden pounding of my heart alerted the men to my distress.

"What is it?" Gryphon asked.

"Thaddeus's parents. I think they're dead." Numbly, I picked up the phone and dialed the Pelham Manor telephone number seared into my memory.

Five rings. And then ten. No answer.

I hung up, called Information, got the medical center's phone number, and listened to the usual hospital recording that said, "Thank you for calling Westchester County Medical Center. If this is a medical emergency, please press four now. If you are calling from a touch-tone phone . . ."

I pressed the appropriate numbers to reach Patient Room Information and waited impatiently for a live person to finally come on the line.

"I need to know the room number for Thaddeus Schiffer, please." I spelled out the last name.

A moment later I hung up the phone and looked at Gryphon with stricken eyes. "He's there," I whispered. "His parents are dead."

TWENTY-THREE

THE DRIVE TO the hospital took an interminable thirty-five minutes during which time Gryphon, Amber, and Chami left me to my brooding silence.

In the grand atrium of the busy medical center, a plump woman in her forties told us with a professional, regretful smile that sorry, only two guests were allowed up at a time to see a patient. Her gaze lingered on Gryphon's striking loveliness for a moment, and the apology became more sincere, but the presence of the other two receptionists beside her prohibited her from bending the rules.

Amber was left behind in the lobby, his formidable face wreathed in a ferocious scowl. Chami simply turned a corner, vanished, and followed us up, a blending blur.

Once we were on the floor, it wasn't even necessary to look at the room numbers. I just listened for the slow heartbeat and followed it down a corridor to the last room. Taking a deep breath, I knocked on the open door and entered, Gryphon and Chami behind me.

He looked so young and fragile. The other bed was unoccu-
pied, neatly made up. Scrapes and bruises marked Thaddeus's face
and arms. A brand-new, creamy white fiberglass cast encased his
right arm.

"Yes?" his flat voice demanded.

How did one introduce oneself? "My name is Mona Lisa. I just
found out about your accident and came here to see you."

"I don't know you," Thaddeus said, his face and voice devoid of
emotion. "Did you know my parents?" he asked more softly.

"No. I . . ." Reaching beneath my shirt, I drew out my silver
cross. "Does this mean anything to you?"

Recognition sparked in his eyes briefly before he blanked them.
"Who are you?"

I turned my cross over. "The back has my name and something
else on the bottom."

"Monère," Thaddeus said without expression. So he'd been
able to see it, too.

"Does that mean anything to you?" I asked.

Dark, intelligent eyes swept over me in careful assessment, then
moved on to study the two men behind me. "No."

"This cross was the only thing that identified me when I was left
on the steps of Our Lady of Lourdes Orphanage as a baby. Did
your parents tell you that you were adopted?" I asked quietly.

"Who are you?" There was a new hard edge to his voice, a wary
boy thrown early into manhood, so heartbreakingly different from
the carefree kid I'd glimpsed just the day before.

"I'm your sister."

Thaddeus didn't challenge or deny the statement. Just complete
and utter silence. There was the faintest trembling in his left hand
before he curled it into a tight fist.

"We have the same mother and I believe the same father. Our

eyes . . . they had to have come from him." Because they hadn't
come from our mother.

Thaddeus said nothing.

"Did your adopted parents have any brothers, sisters, parents?"
I asked.

Thaddeus shook his head. "No, they were only children. No living parents or grandparents. Only distant relations."

"Anyone you can go to? That you want to live with?"

"No," said Thaddeus, slowly. "I was going to ask a neighbor to
become my legal guardian for the two years that I needed one. Live
in my own apartment. Continue in school."

It wasn't a bad plan. He was old enough to drive and to get a job
if he needed to. It would be safer than living with me. But, oh how
I wanted him with me.

The intensity of that desire shook my voice. "I would like, very
much, for you to come and live with me. But if you did, it would
disrupt your entire life." I immediately castigated myself over my
bad choice of words. As if his life wasn't entirely disrupted already.
"I'm moving to New Orleans to take up a position there. And there
are a lot of other complicated things besides that," I finished lamely.

Something flickered in Thaddeus's dark eyes, then was gone. I
wondered at such control in one so young. And wondered why he
would need it.

"Who are they?" Thaddeus asked, his gaze flicking to Chami
and Gryphon.

How to answer? Guard. Lover. "They are special friends who
live with me . . . along with six others." I paused, helpless, unsure
of what else to say. "Do you still wish to know more?"

"You were there the other day. Outside my house," Thaddeus
said suddenly.

"Why . . . yes."

At my admission, hot emotion darkened his eyes . . . triumph or relief, perhaps. I felt a brief flare of power so quickly reined in that I would have thought I'd imagined it but for the fact that Chami and Gryphon instantly moved forward to my side.

"He is like you," Gryphon said in a low voice. "More."

Another brief spurt of energy emanated from Thaddeus.

My brother had an amazing ability to shield or suppress his power, I realized, that cracked only when he felt strong emotions.

"Release your control, Thaddeus," I said quietly. "Let me feel you."

"I don't know what you're talking about."

I searched those eyes so like mine and wondered if he spoke true. Did Thaddeus really not know what he did? Did his power scare him so much that he was in denial? Or was it an unconscious suppression?

"Are there things different about you from other people?" I asked gently. "Can you hear things, see things others can't? Jump farther, run faster? See better at night? Are you stronger than others?"

"How did you know?" Thaddeus whispered shakily.

"Because I'm the same way, as are Gryphon and Chami here."

Thaddeus expelled a trembling breath. "I thought I was going crazy these past several months. That maybe insanity ran in my genes. I'd always had an active imagination."

"No, it's very real," I assured him. "Insanity doesn't run in our blood,"—at least I hoped it didn't—"but other things do. From the time I could remember, I was a little quicker, faster, stronger than others. Just slightly enough for it to pass as advanced physical development when I was young. But the abilities grew and blossomed beyond the point where they could be considered normal when I hit puberty at thirteen. I reached puberty later than other girls."

Thaddeus didn't say anything, just listened to me with hard attention.

"I always knew I was different, but never *why* until I met others like me a couple of weeks ago. Since then, my whole world has changed into one that is much more dangerous and deadly. But I have never been happier." I hesitated. "Do you want to know, really know, what you are?"

"What, not who," Thaddeus observed dispassionately. "Why were you outside my house?"

"I'd just discovered where you lived. I wanted to see if you were well."

"Why did you leave without making yourself known to me?"

"You were well, happy, loved. There was no need to disrupt your life."

"I was loved but not well. Not mentally," Thaddeus said. "And yes, I would like to know."

And so I told him. About the Monère, about Full Bloods and Mixed Bloods.

"You can shift into animal form?" Thaddeus asked, natural skepticism warring with a desire to believe.

I smiled. "Only some of us. I do not possess that ability, though Gryphon does."

Locking his eyes on Gryphon, Thaddeus demanded, "Show me."

"It would be easier to allow Chami to demonstrate his gift," I said, turning to the slender man beside me. "If you don't mind, Chami."

Chami grinned, bringing a wolfish cast to his sharp features. "Not at all, milady," he said and disappeared.

"Holy shit!" Thaddeus exclaimed, his face pale.

Chami reappeared and bowed with a flourish like an actor on stage.

"Thank you, Chameleo," I said, my lips twitching.

Thaddeus came to an abrupt decision. "Get me out of here."

"How long did the doctors want to keep you?" I asked cautiously.

"There's nothing wrong with me but for a broken arm and a mild concussion. They're only keeping me overnight because there was no one to observe me at home for twenty-four hours. They're getting a social worker involved tomorrow," Thaddeus said quietly.

That decided it. It would be much easier keeping him out of the system in the first place rather than trying to extricate him out of it later.

"You may have to sign out against medical advice," I warned.

"No," Thaddeus corrected. "As my sister and closest of kin, you will. You're over twenty-one, right?"

"I am twenty-one."

"Good enough," Thaddeus declared and depressed the call button to summon a nurse.

"Would you like to come live with me in New Orleans?" I asked.

"Come with me to my home," Thaddeus invited. "Let me spend the next few days with you and your other 'special friends' before I decide."

"All of them?" I asked.

Thaddeus nodded. "Yes. I'd like to meet them."

"All right," I agreed, liking his caution, wanting the opportunity to know this intelligent young man better.

"It's the full moon tomorrow," Gryphon reminded me quietly.

"Yes, I know. Even more reason," I said, remembering the thick woods behind Thaddeus's house.

A young nurse entered the room. "Did you need anything?" she inquired.

"Yes," I replied, taking charge. "I'm Thaddeus's sister. I'd like to sign him out of the hospital and take him home now."

"Oh. I didn't know he had a sister." Her forehead furrowed together in a frown. "I'll have to call Dr. Smith and let him know."

After her departure, I told Thaddeus, "I'll be right back. I need to call the others."

"No need," Thaddeus said. Reaching over into his bedside drawer, he handed me a cell phone.

He had to show me how to use it. I'd never had one. Why should I? There'd been no one for me to call before.

Aquila answered on the second ring and I explained the situation to him. "Pack up everything and check out of the hotel. We'll be staying with my brother." I gave him Thaddeus's address and telephone number, and after a brief aside to Thaddeus, his cell phone number as well.

"How old are the others?" Thaddeus asked curiously after I handed the cell phone back to him.

"Aquila and Tomas are much older than you and I. But Jamie is nineteen and his sister, Tersa, is twenty-four. They're Mixed Bloods like us, but more like humans. We're three-quarters Monère, only a quarter human. You'll meet them and their mother, Rosemary, later."

A gray-haired doctor entered the room, brusque and abrupt. "I've got to get back to an admission in the ER," he said to me. "What's this about you claiming to be my patient's sister? He told me quite plainly this morning that he had no other family."

The doctor eyed Gryphon and Chami with frank suspicion and didn't look too kindly upon me, either, despite my most winsome smile.

"I'm his half sister. We share the same father. Different mothers. That's why he didn't think to call me until later," I told him, concentrating fiercely on appearing trustworthy to the bristling doctor.

"So he hardly knows you," Dr. Smith said, shaking his head. "Sorry. I'm not going to let a near-stranger waltz out with my patient even if you are who you claim you are. You can deal with the social worker tomorrow."

I was in front of him before he could turn to go, capturing him with my eyes. "You see no reason why Thaddeus cannot leave under my care," I murmured as my power strummed the air.

"I see no reason why Thaddeus cannot leave under your care," Dr. Smith repeated obediently.

"I am an experienced nurse and can monitor him just as well at home," I said.

The doctor parroted, "You're an experienced nurse and can monitor him just as well at home."

My voice was a low, hypnotic whisper. "You feel happy and reassured that your young patient has family who will take care of him, and will go sign the orders immediately for his discharge." I released him.

Dr. Smith blinked and smiled at us. "I'll go and take care of the orders right now. The nurse will give you the rest of the instructions and sign you out. Make sure you follow up in one week with an orthopedist to ensure that the arm is healing well. Good luck, young man." He strode from the room.

I couldn't look at Thaddeus. Could do nothing but let the silence thicken in that sterile room.

"Wow," Thaddeus said. "Will I be able to do that someday?"

I looked up into his excited eyes. There was no fear, no horror. My smile of relief was dazzling. "Maybe."

Twenty minutes later the five of us piled into the limo, Thaddeus sitting in the front passenger seat so his cast-encased arm wouldn't be jostled, the rest of us in the back .

"Cool ride," Thaddeus said.

"We're borrowing it for the moment," I said.

"You grow stronger," Gryphon murmured in an undertone too low for Thaddeus to hear.

"What do you mean?" I breathed back.

"You are not fatigued."

And I realized with sudden shock that he was right. There was none of that drained feeling, none of the tired shakiness that usually plagued me afterward. The expenditure of energy had cost me nothing. And I wondered just what that meant. I *was* growing stronger. But why? What had caused it? For that matter, I wasn't sure exactly if I liked it. Some people might crave power, but I'd never been one of them.

That dark force inside me stirred and stretched and blinked at me with bright gleaming eyes. *Soon,* it promised before it went back to its patient slumber.

No, I thought with a dry mouth. I didn't crave power. I feared it.

❧

THADDEUS RETURNED TO morose somberness when we entered the house he had grown up in. It was even more beautiful inside than out, with large windows, raised ceilings, and thin oriental rugs thrown over a parquet floor. The burnished mahogany wood of the staircase was echoed by matching mahogany molding trimming the upper walls. There was a cozy lived-in clutter to the house—a bowl of change by the side table alongside unopened mail, a blue quilted jacket hanging over the end of the banister.

"I thought I'd feel better at home," Thaddeus said. "But home is people, not just a place. Christ, I can't believe they're gone." He surreptitiously wiped his face with his fingers.

"Come on," Thaddeus said, his voice rough as he climbed the stairs. "I'll show you the guest rooms."

The sound of a car pulling into the driveway drew us back downstairs.

"Go ahead and help carry our luggage in," I said to Amber and Gryphon, shooing them out the door.

"Aren't you scared of him?" Thaddeus asked me quietly, once we were alone. I knew to whom he referred. Upon first meeting the towering Amber, Thaddeus had flickered briefly with power. He had quickly doused it, but the taste of it had been enough to widen Amber's eyes with surprise.

"Amber?" I replied. "He's a gentle teddy bear."

A dark brow arched up in a gesture so like mine that it stole my breath.

"With you, maybe," Thaddeus said dryly. "Not with others, I bet."

Jamie, Tersa, and Rosemary trudged in loaded down with bags. Tomas and Aquila entered behind them, carrying trunks of luggage followed by Amber and Gryphon who hauled in even more stuff so that it filled the entry hall.

I made the introductions and watched Thaddeus juggle the sleeping arrangements around in his head before suggesting, "Tersa and Rosemary can sleep with me in the guest room. The other men can bed down in the library, if that's okay with you, Thaddeus." The library called up images of nineteenth-century elegance, with large, commodious wing chairs and dark-toned wood paneling. Chairs and side tables invited one to linger and read. But more importantly, the library had a closing door and thick curtains. Left unspoken was the tacit agreement to leave his parents' bedroom untouched.

Thaddeus nodded jerkily in assent and moved to help the others settle in.

Stopping me with a light touch, Tomas said in his soft drawl, "Milady, I thought I should tell you, I felt another Monère's presence for a brief moment when we left the hotel. I kept my senses open coming here but didn't feel it again."

A cold prickle of unease raised the tiny hairs of my forearm. I glanced at Gryphon and Aquila and saw that they had heard. They drew near.

"Could it have been one of Mona Sera's men?" I asked Gryphon.

"Perhaps," Gryphon said slowly. "We are in her territory."

I looked at Aquila. "Could it be Sandoor?"

Aquila stroked his neat Vandyke beard thoughtfully. "He has never moved far from the Minnesota forests of Koochiching territory. But he's never had reason to before."

"It's a long way from Minnesota to New York," I observed.

"True," Aquila said. "But it is an easy enough matter to take money from humans and acquire a car. We took his Queen from him. So now he must find another, preferably a young Queen more easily controlled. You are not only the youngest but also the newest Queen."

"But not so easily controlled," I said darkly. "Would he be foolish enough to try for me?"

"He is desperate," Aquila replied. "But as you say, New York is a far distance from Minnesota. He may have chosen to go north into Canada and Tomas may indeed have just sensed one of Mona Sera's men. Still, I would suggest that everyone, you especially, milady, take adequate precautions and be on close guard."

I nodded in agreement and smiled wryly at Amber and Gryphon's carefully blank looks. "Warn the others. We'll follow whatever security measures you, Lord Amber, and Lord Gryphon deem necessary," I told Aquila. "It would be foolish of me to be careless when I have only just found my brother."

"Thank the dear Mother for that," Amber muttered.

I pretended not to hear that and left the men to their planning.

Catching a familiar delicious aroma, I let my nose lead the way to the bright kitchen. It was decorated in the casual ambience of country, with pale frame-and-panel cabinetry, wainscoting, and plank flooring. Thaddeus and Jamie were just biting into gooey slices of pizza. I snagged a plate, slipped a hot slice onto it, and took a bite.

"Umm. It's good," I mumbled.

"Not bad for something organic and frozen. Mom made me eat this stuff instead of the fresh kind," Thaddeus said quietly.

"She loved you very much," I observed.

"Yeah."

We chewed in quiet reflection for a bit.

"I'm going to have to make arrangements for them tomorrow," Thaddeus said. "The funeral and burial."

"I'll help you," I offered.

His lips spasmed. "Thank you," he said roughly.

Thaddeus turned to Jamie. "Have you lived among the Monère all your life?" He listened with interest as Jamie detailed his life growing up at High Court.

"You never went to school?" Thaddeus asked with disbelief.

The information shocked me as well.

"No. Tersa and I were tutored by a Learned One in the basics until we were sixteen. Reading, writing, math," Jamie said. "The rest I gleaned from books and television. We were the only ones who had one. A television, that is. Had to get a satellite dish installed to get any reception up there."

"So you've never been to a city before?" I said.

"Never been anywhere," Jamie said with a grimace. "Manhattan was amazing. Those huge buildings that scraped the sky. And all those people, everywhere you turned. I never really knew how many of them there were," he exclaimed with bug-eyed amaze-ment, making Thaddeus and I smile.

"Would you like to go to school, Jamie," I asked.

"I don't know," he said thoughtfully. "Tersa would, I know. But I'm not sure about myself."

"I'll talk to her about it then. What grade are you in, Thaddeus?"

"I'll graduate from high school this year," my brother answered.

"Skipped a couple of grades, did you?" I said, lifting a brow.

Thaddeus's lips twisted sardonically. It cast his features into sharp prominence, giving me a brief glimpse of the handsome man he would become. "My body developed slowly. Not my mind."

"So you'll be starting college soon. Any idea which one you wish to attend?" I asked.

"I've been accepted into both Harvard and Yale," he said qui-etly. "Mom and Dad were so proud."

"That's an amazing opportunity," I forced myself to say. "If you wish to go, I'll pay for your tuition. You could come to New Or-leans on vacations and during the summer."

"That's generous of you, but Mom and Dad already put enough away in my education fund to cover everything. I haven't decided yet where I'll go. We'll see."

That night, if some of us heard a few sniffles, a few half-muffled sobs, we didn't comment on it.

Thaddeus was up at noon the next day, his quiet movements downstairs drawing me from my own bed. I silently dressed in the jeans and T-shirt I had reverted back to, and slipped out of the room, leaving Tersa and Rosemary still fast asleep.

Thaddeus's eyes were grim and reddened and the skin around them puffy, but his voice was steady as he called and made arrange-ments to have his parents' bodies transported to a local funeral home. He arranged to meet with the funeral director in an hour to discuss funeral and burial arrangements, contacted the family attorney, and scheduled an appointment with him several hours later. There were numerous other details to take care of and he handled them all with a confidence and maturity far beyond his years. He gathered information on how to obtain copies of the death certificates that he would need from the hospital, typed up a moving account of his parents' lives and accomplishments, and faxed it to the funeral director who in turn would pass it to the local newspaper to use in the obituary notice.

Remembering my promise, I awoke Amber and Gryphon and let them know Thaddeus and I were going out. Amber accompanied us while Gryphon remained behind with the others.

We swung by the medical center to pick up the copies of the death certificates first, then went on to the funeral home. Thaddeus chose the most expensive coffins and plots, and decided upon a closed-coffin arrangement. The memorial service and burial were to be held the day after tomorrow. When the solemn-faced funeral director discreetly inquired about payment, Thaddeus pulled out a credit card and paid for everything in full.

"You didn't really need me," I murmured back in the car.

"It helped having you there, as well as the big guy. One look at him and nobody's going to try and take advantage of me just because I'm a kid."

Amber stoically ignored Thaddeus's comment.

The visit to the lawyer's office was just as efficiently handled. Mr. Compton, an attorney who specialized in estate planning, was a short, portly older gentleman, his lined, wise face one you instantly trusted. He had a copy of the Schiffer's will. To no one's surprise, it left everything to Thaddeus.

Thaddeus read and signed the various papers the lawyer put before him.

"A wise man, your father," Mr. Compton said, his fingers laced precisely on top of the will he had just read. "He had his affairs nicely in order. The house and car are paid off and your parents both had current life insurance policies and healthy retirement portfolios, all of which name you sole beneficiary. I'll just need several copies of the death certificates before I can get started on the paperwork allowing you access to these funds and submit the claims to the life and car insurance companies."

Mr. Compton expressed no surprise when Thaddeus quietly handed him the copies of his parents' death certificates.

"Efficient like your father," the lawyer said gruffly. "The government will take a sizable chunk out of your inheritance with the death tax, but not nearly the amount it would have taken, which would have been half, had your father not had the foresight to plan things. He came to me, you know, when he first adopted you. You made him—both of them—very happy."

Tears welled up in Thaddeus's eyes and only by sheer dint of will did not overflow. "Thank you, sir."

"You have access to a joint checking account in you and your father's name, do you not?" Mr. Compton asked.

"Yes."

"Let me know if you need more," Mr. Compton said. "It'll take several months for probate to clear."

"That's very kind of you, Mr. Compton, but I have more than enough to meet my needs for now."

"Thaddeus."

"Yes, sir?"

"Your father was a friend as well as a client," the lawyer said with kind sincerity. "If you need anything, call me."

The moon was round and full, hanging like a pale globe in the sky as the ebbing day flowed to the west. The others were already up and about when we returned, the men dressed and fully armed.

"Holy Christ!" Thaddeus exclaimed as Amber returned from the library with his own very long sword dangling at his side. "Is that a sword?"

"It's a Great Sword."

I wasn't sure if Thaddeus was more surprised by the weapon or by the fact that Amber had finally spoken to him.

"Can I get one of those?" Thaddeus asked.

Amber grunted noncommittally, heading for the kitchen.

"Was that a yes?" Thaddeus asked me.

"I think it was a maybe," I said, hiding my grin.

Aquila and Amber slipped quietly outside the back door.

"They're going to patrol the neighborhood and secure a good area for Basking tonight," Gryphon said, answering my silent query.

"Will you and Amber Bask, now that you no longer need to?" I asked.

"We no longer need to, but we would like to," Gryphon replied softly. "It is a joyous feeling when the light enters you, is it not?"

"Yes," I answered. But inwardly, frustration and worry seethed within me at the inopportune timing. It was as if even the very elements were conspiring to show Thaddeus how different we were, how foreign, how other. Even the moon.

How would Thaddeus react to the Basking? With wonder or fear? Would he feel left out? For that matter, how did Tersa and Jamie feel watching others experience what they would never know? Thaddeus might, one day, if his power grew, if he no longer suppressed it.

There was so much I hadn't told my brother. Our mother, for one thing. Wisely, he hadn't asked, perhaps sensing that if there had been anything good to tell, I would have told him already. I also hadn't mentioned the demon dead to him. There were enough frightening wonders Thaddeus had already witnessed in this short period of time.

"Can we? Can we, Mona Lisa?" Jamie asked, pulling me from my reverie. Thaddeus and Tersa were beside him, their eager, young faces all turned to me.

"What? I wasn't paying attention," I said.

"Chami agreed to instruct Thaddeus and the rest of us in the proper handling of a dagger if we had your consent," Tersa informed me. She spoke so rarely, much less asked anything, that I hated to deny her.

I looked to Thaddeus. "I'd hate to scar up the floor or damage anything in the house."

Thaddeus waved the objection away. "We'll practice in the living room. It's carpeted. And we'll be careful."

He looked so eager. "Very well . . ."

They whooped.

". . . if you all promise to be very careful."

"Don't worry, little mother," Chami said, leaning like a slender shadow against the doorframe. "I'll take good care of them."

"I'll watch to ensure you do," I replied.

"Good. Maybe you'll learn something as well," Chami tossed cheekily over his shoulder.

I snarled and trailed after the excited kids.

"It's not just cut and slash, but an art," Chami lectured, as serious as any professor of academia once we were all assembled before him. Rosemary had been persuaded to join us as well, without too much protest. Tomas and Gryphon sprawled lazily on the sofa beside me, silent observers.

"You will be going up against warriors who have had basic

knife training, years of experience behind them, and greater strength. The only way you can hope to defeat them is by being better. You must go beyond basic techniques and become masters of the blade," Chami told his enthralled students. "Fortunately, you have a rare master artist up to the task, and at your disposal."

Chami ignored my impolite snort and began with the proper way of holding a dagger. It was review for the others but new and necessary information for Thaddeus. Rosemary, Tersa, and Jamie had their knives in hand. I bent down and took out my dagger, sliding it from its sheath where it had been concealed with handle downward for easy grasping, along the outside of my boot. I caught a look of surprise on Thaddeus's face. I shrugged as I passed him the blade to use. I went nowhere unarmed.

"Holding your dagger properly is one of the most essential fundamentals," Chami admonished. "For an underhand strike you should grasp the hilt with your forefinger just slightly below the guard, squeezing firmly with your fingers, with the thumb across the forefinger overlapping onto the middle finger. Wrist firm, but not tense. If you hold it correctly, it will feel as if the blade is an extension of your hand."

Chami demonstrated then had the others try.

"Don't hold it too tightly," Chami instructed Tersa. "Much better," he said as she corrected her grip. "Too tightly and you lessen your flexibility and actually reduce your strength, but it must be tight enough so that your opponent cannot easily knock it out of your hand."

Chami demonstrated the reverse grip for a downward strike. "Eventually, you'll be able to switch grips quickly," he said, flipping the knife in the air and catching it easily in a different grasp. He grinned and winked at the boys. "But don't try that just yet."

When Chami was finally satisfied that they all knew how to hold their weapons correctly, they were ready to move to the next step. After some creative rummaging, we ended up securing two pillows in front of a wooden sled Thaddeus had dug out of the garage. The sled's metal rungs were padded with towels and propped securely against the massive stone hearth of the fireplace. The stones would be less likely than the walls to show signs of damage.

"Are you certain you are willing to sacrifice these pillows?" Chami asked Thaddeus with mock solemnness, marker in hand.

"It's for a good cause," Thaddeus replied blandly. His added aside, "Besides, *I* won't be using them," made Jamie snicker and Tersa actually giggle.

At the go-ahead, Chami drew the outline of a man's chest, ribs, stomach, and neck on the pillow.

"Where would you strike, Rosemary?"

"Over the heart?" she answered uncertainly.

"Here?" Chami asked, pointing to the center of the chest.

Rosemary nodded.

"A good supposition but not correct. Can anyone tell me why not?"

"Too many bones," Thaddeus said. "The sternum's right there and then there are the ribs."

"Ah, very good, young master Thaddeus."

Thaddeus flushed with pleasure at Chami's praise.

Chami drew the outline of the sternum onto the pillow. "The sternum and ribs, the body's bony armor around its most crucial organs, the heart and lungs. But the lungs are not our primary target. Only striking the heart will possibly kill one of us, and only with a silver blade," he explained to Thaddeus. "Those who have the strength to break through the ribs to the heart should strike the left side where the major mass of the heart lies. Where would you suggest striking, Thaddeus, for those of us with lesser strength?"

"Just below the sternum. Upward into the heart," was Thaddeus's thoughtful reply.

"Correct," Chami said, pleased. He drew the outline of the heart over the sternum and marked the spot to enter. "Down here, where it is soft and unprotected, angled up forty-five degrees into the heart, just so." He demonstrated with the marker. "Then a quick sweep inside to the left and then right so that if you miss the heart, at least you'll sever the great vessels connected just below. That will put your opponent out of commission enough for you to either escape or finish the kill."

Chami made them find the spot just below the sternal notch, first on themselves, then on a partner, pairing the two women together and Thaddeus with Jamie.

Jamie made a horrible gurgling sound and bent over as Thaddeus stabbed him with a finger. Rosemary exchanged a smiling look with her daughter that plainly said, *Boys will be boys*.

"Having established that proper knife work is an art," Chami continued, "for practical purposes, we shall begin with the basic slash and stab. Slashing with your leading unarmed hand at your opponent's eyes, followed immediately by stabbing with the knife hand into his left side or, if you are able, up beneath the sternum. Angle your body. Feet shoulder-length apart, and knees bent like so, holding your knife close to your chest protectively so that it is hard to kick or grab." He demonstrated the stance.

"Never lead with your knife hand and leave an open target out there for your enemy. That stupidity you will only see on TV where we want the bad guy—who always happens to be threatening the good guy with a knife, of course—to lose. No, the only time we extend the knife is when we are using it; otherwise it is held back protectively against your lower chest.

"The target for the open leading hand is your opponent's eyes.

But it is not important that you actually strike the eyes—though that would be ideal—so much as you impair your opponent's vision in any way. Such as by throwing dirt into his eyes, a towel, or just thrusting your fingers toward the eyes and causing them to close in reflex. Practice going in hard, with full force. Lead hand strike. Knife hand thrust. Like so."

Chami pounced into the pillow mannequin, fingers stabbing the eyes and thrusting the other hand with savage force into the left chest, again and again.

They watched the impressive, lethal display with wide eyes, all sense of play sobered by the deadly reality of what they were learning.

"Stab, remove. Stab, remove, for as many times as you can. Keep striking until your opponent is down. Then finish the kill by removing the heart or, far more easier, the head."

Not exactly a pretty bedtime story, I thought, deliberately suppressing my guilt, but we lived now in a scary, deadly world.

Amber and Aquila returned from their outside reconnaissance and settled down in the other sofa to watch with the rest of us as Chami took the others through their paces.

"Harder," Chami told Rosemary. "Think of it like a frozen steak you have to stab through," he told the cook, and had her repeat the thrust-strike move until he was satisfied with the force of her lead and follow-up blows.

Stuffing popped out from the stabbed pillows and was quickly repaired with masking tape, over and over again. If it was play, it was deadly, earnest play.

When they were all comfortable with the maneuver, Chami had them sit and rest while he continued lecturing. "That was the face-to-face approach. A more ideal approach is from the back, which would be much better for you ladies. For us all, actually. It is easier to kill someone when you do not have to look into their eyes. Rear take-outs are taught all the time to soldiers.

"The optimal entrance into the spinal cord is through the base of the skull. With a rear attack, you place your free hand down hard over your opponent's mouth or chin and pull down as you thrust the knife through to the front of the neck. Do not worry about him trying to bite you. Believe me, when your blade is slicing through him, biting you will be the last thing he thinks of."

Chami turned to me. "Milady, if you will help me demonstrate."

I went reluctantly forward to play his intended victim, not a task I would have volunteered for. Facing away from him, I waited for his move. Chami struck with a quickness and strength that was quite frightening, in truth. His hand was suddenly there over my mouth and yanking me back as he thrust two fingers, simulating a knife, into the base of my skull. Sheesh, I'd have had no chance.

Having demonstrated what he wanted, Chami had them pair up once more and practice the move first on themselves, using their fingers as he had done. Then, turning over the pillows and drawing a new rear target, he had them try it with real knives, taking great pains to ensure that they did not stab their own hands.

More stuffing flew out.

"He's good with them," Gryphon murmured to me.

"That's because he's a child himself," I said, sotto voce.

"I heard that," Chami said. "No appreciation."

"You appreciate yourself enough for all of us," I retorted.

"You wound me, my Queen."

I snorted. "After that demonstration? Not likely."

Chami finally called a halt to the practice. "Enough for today."

"That was cool," Thaddeus said, handing me back my knife in the correct manner, blade pointing away from me.

"Come on, Jamie," Thaddeus said, the two of them totally at

ease with each other now. "Let's go surf the Internet. I want to
check out how much a dagger like that costs and where I can get
one."

"You're hooked up to the Internet? Awesome!" Jamie exclaimed,
trailing up the stairs after Thaddeus like an eager puppy.

Gryphon and Tomas left to make their rounds outside as Tersa
and Rosemary went into the kitchen, chatting about what they had
learned. Above it all, I felt the fullness of the moon calling, beckoning us. We would be answering its summons soon.

Chami plopped himself down beside me. "Your turn."

"Mine?"

"Try calling your knives to your hand," Chami said softly.

I stood up reluctantly, knowing he was right. Many of the things
I had done had been in the heat of battle. Some, like channeling the
energy through my hand and searing Miles's flesh, I doubted I could
reproduce. Unless I was fighting, power and the use of power made
me uncomfortable. Still, I needed to know if I could call my knife to
me reliably, as I had called Mona Louisa's blade when she had tried
to stab Gryphon.

I concentrated. The silver dagger came easily to hand. Nothing
happened, though, with my non-silver dagger.

"How do you call the silver dagger?" Chami asked.

"I think of silver. How it tastes, smells, feels in my hand."

"Do the same with your other dagger."

I brought the blade close to my nose, inhaled the faint metallic
smell, stuck my tongue out and licked the blade, concentrated on
the weight of the dagger, how it felt in my grasp. I resheathed it
along the outside of my boot, and knelt down with my hand a foot
away and concentrated.

It came to my call.

"Nice," Chami said. "Try it standing up."

A more concentrated effort but still it came. I felt the force of it as it left my boot.

Amber, who had remained with us, watching, handed me his forty-inch Great Sword. With my strength, the weight was not a problem so much as getting used to the feel and balance of the larger weapon. The smell was unique and the taste different from other metals—old, with the smell of ancient battle and spilt blood, as if it had absorbed some of its prey's pain and power.

I laid the sword on the glass coffee table, stepped back, and called it. It flew to my hand like a deadly giant-winged bird, hilt first.

"Give me your silver dagger," Amber said and walked to stand with the distance of the room between us, about thirty feet. "Call it to you."

A pulse of power and it flew to my hand, straight and true.

"Wow," Jamie said from the stairs where he and Thaddeus watched with fascination. The small surges of power had probably drawn them down.

"I've never seen anyone do that before," Jamie said.

"That's because no one else can," Chami said dryly. "Try my knife." He tossed his silver stiletto to Amber, who snatched it from the air.

With a burst of concentration, I called it to me. Silver blades seemed to be no problem. I tossed it back to Chami and he snatched it with an easy flick of his wrist, sheathing it.

"Not too bad," Chami said.

"Not bad? That was amazing!" Thaddeus exclaimed.

"You must familiarize yourself with all of our knives, milady," Chami said, "so that you can call any of them to you should the need arise."

"It's a good suggestion, Chami, but some other night," I said quietly and sank down onto the beige sectional sofa.

Chami acquiesced to my wishes with a nod, seeming to sense my discomfort at being the core of attention, and drew the boys' interest from me with an impressive display of twirling stiletto play.

If Jamie and Thaddeus felt the edgy restlessness, the eager anticipation the rest of us felt as the witching hour of the full moon brushed nearer, they showed no signs of it.

When it was almost midnight, Chami asked, "Would you like me to speak to your brother about tonight?"

"Please," I said gratefully.

Chami explained Basking to Thaddeus in his simple didactic manner, much the same way he had discussed dagger-fighting techniques.

"Any questions?" I asked Thaddeus after he had digested the information.

"No. I'd like to see it."

That was good. We needn't spare anyone then to guard Thaddeus, Jamie and Tersa. They could be there with us, close enough to protect during the ceremony.

TWENTY-FOUR

WE STEPPED OUTSIDE and the night greeted us, caressing us with cool fingers of airy wind. The refreshing scent of pungent pine filled our nostrils as we went deeper into the wooded lot until we reached a little clearing freshly made. A few trees had been uprooted and some brush cleared, just enough for our little group to stand together under the round pale glory of our mother moon. Thaddeus, Jamie, and Tersa stood a little apart and to the left of us.

The others looked to me. It was time.

The one other time I'd done this, I had sort of stumbled into it and it had just happened. Now my official debut performance was to occur before my newly found brother, whose secure world had just been ripped apart by the death of his parents, and then turned upside-down once more by my entrance. Then there were the men I'd taken responsibility for, whose very lives depended on me. Shortened lives, if I couldn't draw down the moon's renewing little flutters of light. Plain, steadfast Tomas whose smile lighted his whole face. Neat, proper Aquila who would not have minded dying after a last honorable act if the Council had so decreed. Sly, wicked, oh-so-deadly Chami who teased and pushed, but was sensitive enough to deflect attention from me when it discomforted me. No pressure. Sure.

They should have offered a course: Fundamentals of Basking 101. Maybe I'd suggest it to the Council next time. Right.

I took a deep, cleansing breath, then another, opening myself to the night, unfurling my senses, reaching out further and further until it hit against something foreign yet familiar. Something that was other like us, but did not belong. Then it was too late.

They pounced. Not on me. Not on my men. But on the one sure thing to stop me, to stop us all: Thaddeus.

Sandoor held the sharp edge of his sword against Thaddeus's fragile neck as another man shoved Tersa and Jamie toward us, centering us all. There were only five men beside Sandoor. I wondered what had happened to the other two.

"Well," Sandoor purred in a deep rumble, "we meet again."

"What do you want?" I demanded.

"What do you think, little Queen? To Bask, to begin with. Do not let us interrupt your little tête-à-tête. Pretend we're not even here." He pressed the sword's edge so that it indented Thaddeus's skin, his voice a clear warning and command. "Continue."

Anger flared along with my power and I felt something deep and wild stir within me, my beast wanting out, snarling that I caged it still.

I lifted my eyes and arms to the blessed moon and opened myself to the drawing power that filled the night, welcomed it, asked it to come down and fill us. And it did.

Soft, gentle rays of moonlight fell upon me from that smiling white lunar face, sprinkling down benevolent butterflies of light that caressed my being with whisper-light wings before vanishing within me like little darts of joy.

I saw the men's rapturous faces as the shower of light began to spread to those closest to me, filling them with glowing renewal—Amber, Gryphon, Chami. I saw the shining wonder and awe in Thaddeus's enraptured eyes. Saw him lift his face and arms up to the sky. Felt that flare of energy like mine yet different. Male. Masculine. Powerful and throbbing. Wonderment and embracing love.

The moon recognized and answered him.

Another shaft of light fell upon Thaddeus, illuminating that ecstatic upturned face with an exultant glow of adoration. Fluttering light bathed him, entered him. And spread to Sandoor and his men, encompassing them all in the glorious celebration of renewing life.

A long time passed—six, maybe seven seconds, after that last flicker of light was absorbed into us.

"Sweet Night!" Sandoor exclaimed, gazing down at the boy he held in his hands with awe. And I knew then what was in his mind. He was going to take only Thaddeus. And I knew I would *never* let Sandoor have him.

I walked slowly toward him. "You came for me, Sandoor, did you not?"

"Stop right there!" Sandoor commanded.

I laughed and paid him no heed, swaying a few steps closer. "Or you'll what? Slit Thaddeus's throat? Your male miracle of light? I think not."

Sandoor smiled, his eyes so like Amber's. The difference between them lay within their hearts, their souls. Sandoor lowered his sword so that it pressed against Thaddeus's shoulder and called my bluff. "Slit his throat, no. But I would not mind carving him up a little. Do you wish to hear your brother squeal like a pig, little girl?"

I halted.

Sandoor smiled. "That's more like it. Have your men put down their weapons."

I smiled back. "And leave them defenseless to your armed men? Even you should know better." I laughed unpleasantly. "Or perhaps you don't. Maybe you just don't have the ability to rise to the level your own son has risen to, no matter how many Queens you fuck or how many times you Bask."

I saw Sandoor's eyes fall on the medallion chain around Amber's neck and widen in surprise.

"And not just your son, but my other lover, Gryphon." I drew Sandoor's eyes back to me by stroking a finger from my lips down. Down to the shadowed valley between my breasts. I watched Sandoor's eyes follow the tantalizing trail. My head tilted thoughtfully. "Or maybe you've just been fucking the wrong Queens. Poor Sandoor. Bumbling around for over a decade, scraping by with a meager existence in the forest. Night after night of free access to a Queen and still nothing to show for all your thrusting efforts. How it must grate you to see your own son recognized and honored as a Lord by the Council, knowing that you will never be."

Sandoor shook with fury. "Cease your foul prattling, bitch!"

My lips curled coldly. "Now is that any way to talk to someone you want to light up for you? Not good courtship technique, darling."

"Balzaar!" Sandoor snapped.

Solid, heavily built Balzaar stepped forward, chains held in his hands. Cold unease slid through me when I saw that they were not silver but the dark metal alloy of what had bound me down in Hell.

"Demon chains," Sandoor said with chilling satisfaction. "Not so much prattling now, eh? Turn around and put both arms behind you."

When I hesitated, Sandoor said slyly, "You *do* want to come with us, don't you? When I take your brother?"

Abruptly I turned around and surrendered my hands. The cold, harsh manacles clamped tightly around my wrists and about my ankles. Balzaar swung me around and stripped me of all my weapons.

I looked up into Balzaar's black beady eyes. "Don't worry," I whispered. "I'll get them back soon."

Balzaar yanked the chain. His face remained impassive as I fell to the ground. He tightened the chain, winding it between my wrist shackles, drawing my legs back, bent at the knees so that my toes almost touched my hands, immobilizing me completely.

Balzaar set his dagger to my throat.

"Throw down your weapons," Sandoor commanded.

"Do not!" I told my men, my voice ringing loudly.

For once they obeyed me.

"You will not kill her," Amber said.

Sandoor laughed with twisted pride at his opponent, his son. "You are correct. She may still be of some use to me in the future. But not now. Not when I hold our entire people's future in my hands. He is all that matters for the moment. A nice deep slice into the side, Balzaar."

I cried out as hot pain knifed through me as Balzaar sank his blade into my right flank. I heard a rustle of movement.

"Uh, uh, uh! One step more and we shall have to cut her again," Sandoor warned. "Very good, boys. I'll leave your injured Queen to your tender care while we depart. Do not try to follow us or we will slice the boy as we did his sister. A cut for each one who comes after us."

Sandoor began to back away, flanked by his men, pulling Thaddeus with him. My eyes locked on my brother's pale, frightened face. His eyes met mine and clung.

"No!" I cried, thrashing. But the demon chains held me as securely here, in the darkness above, as it had held me in the darkness below.

I stopped fighting. Everything. Stopped fighting that dark power, my beast that prowled restlessly within me, that had waited so long to awaken, to be freed. I stopped fighting it and embraced it, opening my body, my heart, my soul to that frightening, scary part of me, welcoming it, whispering for it to come out. *Come out and play. Come out now, I need you.*

My beast rippled out from within me with a shock of power that snapped the demon chains. It overwhelmed me with rippling sinews and roiling muscles, possessed me and covered me with a thick wash of protective fur, filled me with a roaring cry that pierced the night and struck terror into the hearts of all who heard it. I snarled with a sound that no human throat could ever make. A sound that quickly swelled into one long, loud, continuous angry scream utterly anomalous and inhuman. A wailing shriek such as might have arisen out of Hell.

I rolled upright on all fours. Muscles bunched and coiled, I sprang at my target—the man who held the littler one. I soared through the air, covered twenty-five feet with bounding ease and hit my prey and brought him to the ground.

Something sharp sliced into me and the pain enraged me. Snarling, I struck the cutting thing away, slicing open flesh with my long black claws. I smelled the hot sweet tang of blood and licked the limb I had torn open. Loud screams and the batting and flailing of another limb annoyed me. I snapped it with one easy bite of my jaw, felt my teeth sink with satisfying deepness into tender meat, felt the warm rush of blood fill my mouth and slide down my throat, and felt the hungering need to gulp down the hot flesh.

Others fought and battled around me, but as long as they did not bother me or threaten to take away my prey, I was content to leave them alone to their fighting. The creature, my food, was still struggling to my annoyance, that thing that would soon fill my stomach, and the loud screeching noises it made hurt my sensitive ears. One tearing bite into the little bones of its neck and its throat was ripped away. The screeching stopped. It still lived, breathed, but barely struggled now. I settled down, my body pinning my helpless quarry, and prepared to feast.

But the other little one, the cub, stopped me, calling out to me. "Mona Lisa! Mona Lisa!"

The voice was familiar, was supposed to mean something to me, but I could not make the connection. I couldn't understand it. I snarled at the little animal, warning it to back away from my food.

"Mona Lisa. Please don't. It's Thaddeus, your brother. I need you!"

His words penetrated me. *Thaddeus . . . Thaddeus . . . brother . . .*

I shuddered, closed my eyes, and concentrated. Fought against the ravenous beastly hunger that just wanted to rip and feed, and tried to understand.

Brother . . . brother . . . brother . . .

I looked into the cub's eyes. Shook my head.

"Mona Lisa . . . Please!"

The word. The name. Something connected within me.

With a rush of energy I forced myself to change. My skin prickled, shivered. Fur flowed, receded, disappeared. Bones stretched and changed, and it no longer felt natural to be on all fours.

I stood up and found blood covering my naked skin, blood that even now called to me. I fought not to lick and savor it like hot, sticky taffy.

I watched from a surreal distance as Amber covered me with his raincoat and buttoned it as I stood swaying over Sandoor. I noted with curious detachment that Gryphon stood next to Amber. That Rosemary clutched Tersa and Jamie protectively back against the trees. That empty clothes lay fallen on the ground next to piles of ash scattered about the clearing. Only Tomas still battled an opponent, big-headed Greeves. They were surrounded by Chami and Aquila, preventing any escape. Only Tomas was injured, a slicing gash along his left ribs, the reason why he was taking so long to finish off his adversary.

Tomas lunged suddenly, a piercing thrust of his sword through Greeves's stomach. Withdraw, lift, downward strike, and the head was severed from the body. I watched with a curious disconnection as light shimmered as it was released from the body, as the empty remaining husk disintegrated into ashes, as the clothes fell to the earth when nothing was left to support them.

A gurgle, a raspy indrawing of breath drew my attention back to what lay at my feet. Sandoor. Already his bleeding was slowing, the miraculous regenerative ability quickly closing in the previously gaping wounds. He was far from dead. He was healing, and I knew I could not let him live. He would be a threat to Thaddeus as long as he drew breath.

With a thought, I called Amber's sword to my hand. It sang from its sheath and flew to my grip. One clean downward strike and Sandoor stopped healing. Stopped ceasing to be.

Light scattered free, out of the opened body. I watched Sandoor disintegrate until only ashes and empty clothing lay upon the ground where his body had been.

I lifted my gaze to Amber, to the face that bore so striking a resemblance to the man I had just executed. "I'm sorry."

Amber's eyes were shadowless, blameless. "I am grateful it was not me," he said.

Suddenly weakened, I fell to my knees, onto my hands, feeling odd. The blade slipped from my hand with a sense of foreignness, as if I was not meant to hold such objects in my grasp. As if I was meant instead to feel the cushioning earth springing beneath my paws.

The call of blood lifted my head.

"Christ! Her eyes," I heard Thaddeus say, though the words held no meaning for me. Nothing had meaning but the deep, rich burgundy of blood against pale flesh. It drew me. Beckoned to me. I crawled to it and pulled myself up a lovely living body that bled. My tongue unfurled and licked that rich wine of life.

That living body moved, disturbing my enjoyment and I growled.

"Do not move, Tomas," Amber warned. "She's sliding back toward her beast."

"You want me to let her fucking eat me?" Tomas asked shakily.

I heard the creature's heart speed up, and tasted an emotion almost as mouth-watering as blood. Fear. A delicious spice to flavor the meat.

"Tiger's teeth are even sharper than human teeth. If you run, you'll trigger her chase reflex," Amber said evenly, carefully calm. "You do *not* want her to change back into her beast."

My fingers clenched my prey's lower back and full buttocks. I was surprised when claws did not pierce the soft tissue. I buried my face against the open wound along his ribs, lapped at the sweet bleeding flesh until I laved away all the blood, and felt the creature shake as I dug in with my tongue and nipped delicately at the tender meat.

A new, fresher scent drew my attention and lifted my face.

A line of blood on a pale limb waved tantalizingly in front of me in silent offering. I released my hold on Tomas, fell to the ground on all fours and grasped the proffered limb, lapping up the blood.

"That's right, darling," Gryphon crooned, "look at me."

The sound lifted my gaze to Gryphon's face. A surge of power prickled and lifted the fine hair along my entire body. My lips pulled back in a silent snarl that faded as I beheld the beautiful, sensual creature before me, irresistibly lovely with his rich dark fall of hair so dramatically black against white tender skin. A cloud of cinnamon-musk pheromones enveloped me, turning my hunger to a different direction. I looked at that full, red mouth, and I suddenly knew that lovely body could satisfy me in a different, more pleasing manner. I climbed up Gryphon's body until I could lick and eat from that succulent candy-apple mouth. He tasted like honey and I purred with delight. Purred even louder as his hands stroked along my neck, delivering spine-melting bliss to sensitive pleasure points.

A loud, jarring wailing and flashing of lights broke my attention.

"Oh, no, darling. Look at me," Gryphon murmured.

Another burst of cinnamon sweetness enveloped me, making me purr and rub against him. I wanted to rub my naked body all over his and wrap that delicious scent around me and roll on top of him like catnip. My arms twined about his neck and my legs wrapped around him, holding him captive. He began to carry me away, supporting me with one arm, the other continuing to stroke those exquisite sensitive spots along my neck.

"Amber, hide the clothes and weapons," Gryphon murmured as he kissed me in the responsive hollow behind my ear, causing me to writhe against him. "Then rid us of the policemen. Leave us in private."

We entered a dwelling. A quick ascent up a flight of stairs and then I was being lowered onto a large, soft, elevated surface. Gryphon freed us of our clothes and I was finally able to rub my naked skin against the velvety bareness of his as I had so desperately craved. It was wonderful. And then it wasn't enough.

Hands stroked down my body.

Yes, yes. That was what I needed. To be touched there, rubbed harder here, pinched over there. I gasped, arched, lifted myself into his hands and spread my legs in silent demand as everywhere he touched built a terrible blissful ache in the center of me. I whimpered as he kissed his way down me, snarled when he lingered too long over my belly's hollow indentation, and clasped his head tightly when he finally reached that destination where the sultry need caused my body to weep honeyed tears. He lapped delicately, making me gasp and cry out, arching up against the torturing light pressure of his clever tongue.

"Yes, open wider, darling."

And when I did, he rewarded me by driving into me with that versatile oral organ, spearing me with delight, making my body shudder and all the muscles in my body clench tight. Wild sounds escaped my throat as my head tossed and turned. And still it wasn't enough. I snarled with frustrated rage, wanting something more, and he gave it to me.

Two fingers slipped into me with ease, filling me, stopping the ache for a moment. But it returned all too quickly when those fingers stayed quiescent within me, unmoving. I rocked my pelvis violently against him, and he let me ride his fingers until the wildness eased so that I was able to slow my motion down to a more languid rhythm and enjoy it longer.

He rewarded me by slipping a third finger in me, stretching me even more and kissing my curly thatch, his dark shining eyes gauging me for discomfort or pleasure. I purred, the rumble deep in my throat as I rode the even fuller sensation for a long, blissful moment. Quick, hard thrusts of my hips at first, then slower, deeper, more savoring surges as I quickly caught on to his game. He gave a hot, pleased smile and rewarded me for my unhurried gentler rhythm by pushing a fourth finger in. He had to work it in slowly as I panted and growled and whimpered and widened my legs even more.

We both lay breathing hard for several seconds as he watched me closely, as I adjusted to and relished the torturingly acute pleasure of having my outer tissues stretched thin almost into pain. I flexed my hips, just barely, and groaned, relaxed, panted, and flexed again, allowing my tissues to slowly soften, relax, expand, until my inner juices dripped down his hand, easing the way. Achingly slow, I impaled myself upon him, my head thrashing as I enveloped him by torturing blissful increments until he was buried inside me up to the halting juncture of his thumb.

"More," I grated harshly, panting, whimpering in agonized pleasure, wanting his whole hand, thumb and all, buried within me.

"Next time," he breathed and licked the swollen nub that he had plumped to such fullness and sensitivity so that I jerked at the hot wash of sensation that was almost too pleasurable, causing his hand to move within me. His mouth surrounded my erect clitoris and sucked hard as he pulled out then pushed in with careful rough force until almost his entire hand was within me.

I screamed and exploded, my entire body convulsing in hot waves of ecstasy that washed over me, overwhelmed me, and cleansed me.

Gryphon's gentle stroking hands slowly brought me back to myself. And I didn't know if I had passed out or fallen asleep or how much time had elapsed.

He peered cautiously into my eyes when my lids fluttered open. "Your eyes are normal," he said with relief.

"What were they before?" I rasped.

"Orange-yellow."

"What happened?" I asked.

"You came into your other form."

"What was it?"

"A Bengal tiger."

I remembered the orange, black, and white striped fur along my legs, remembered that terrible hunger and need to gulp down hot bloody flesh. I buried my face against my knees and rocked myself in fear, in comfort.

"Sweet Jesus," I shuddered. "I didn't know myself. Another mind . . . that *creature* was controlling me. I just wanted to sink my teeth in and tear flesh. I was going to eat Sandoor."

My stomach lurched and I struggled wildly to rise from the bed. Understanding my urgency, Gryphon swept me into the bathroom where I retched and heaved over the toilet. Then supported me as I shakily rinsed out my mouth.

"I need to shower."

Without a word, Gryphon carried us into the stall and turned on the water. He washed me twice, scrubbing me all over, then propped me weakly against the wall as he quickly washed himself.

He toweled me off and squeezed my hair with another towel until most of the wetness had left it, then carried me back to bed and held me in his arms.

"I hate it," I murmured against his neck.

"It is hardest at first but it becomes better. You shall gradually be able to control your beast, to remain in control if you so choose. It was harder this first time as well because you changed back too soon, before your bloodlust had been satisfied."

"You distracted me, turned my bloodlust . . ."

". . . Into sexual desire, yes." Gryphon stroked my back comfortingly. "I substituted one appetite for another."

"What you did . . . that's your real power, isn't it? Not just the compulsion or being able to shift form."

Gryphon's hand paused for a split second, then continued its soothing caress. "Yes, that is my greatest power," he admitted quietly.

"Why did you never use it before?"

I felt his lips twist wryly against my forehead. "When you first laid eyes upon me you fairly spat with rage when you thought that I dared try to manipulate the attraction between us."

"Is that why you hid that part of yourself? I did not know you then as I do now."

"It was not my desire to become your whore or to have you see me as such."

I pushed back so I could look into his face. "You are my love, my mate," I declared in a low, passionate voice.

Gryphon drew me back down as if he could not bear my scrutiny after making his painful confession. "You loved me, even when I was too weak to bind you to me in that manner, even had I so wished to. Your love, given freely to me like that, is a most precious gift, Mona Lisa."

"You used your power to help me."

"Anything you need or desire that is mine to give is yours— flesh, blood, or sex. Although I prefer the latter." He smiled. "Which is why I savored you from below."

"You mean I could have eaten you?" I exclaimed in horror.

He shrugged eloquently. "One hunger may turn quickly and easily into the other."

I traced a sharp nail down over his nipple, making him shudder. "I don't want to eat you now," I said, running light kisses down his lovely, smooth chest. "Or maybe I do."

Gryphon rolled over me, locking my hands to my side. "Allow me," he whispered. "Allow me to show you my love."

And I did, lying there in sweet surrender, giving him what he needed as he began to love me with gentle kisses and reverent strokes: my soft sighs, my gentle moans. He kissed down my arms, placed a delicate caress to my surprisingly sensitive inner wrists. I savored the indescribable feeling of his breath wafting across my shivering belly, the silk of his hair falling across my knees, his soft lips pressing against my susceptible instep. I abandoned myself to him, to my senses, let him do with me as he willed.

He mated with me and made love to me with such exquisite tenderness and heart-rending beauty that tears filled my eyes and overflowed when our quiet gasps of release shimmered the room with light and gentle pleasure.

"I didn't know it could be like that," I whispered.

"Neither did I," was Gryphon's soft reply. "Neither did I."

TWENTY-FIVE

NOON LIGHT PRESSED against the drawn curtains and the rest of the household still slumbered when I awoke, all but one. I dressed and slipped quietly downstairs. My brother looked up calmly from his breakfast cereal when I entered the kitchen.

"Do you want some?" Thaddeus asked.

Surprisingly, I did. He poured me a bowl of Frosted Flakes and the sugary sweetness satisfied a craving I hadn't known I'd had.

"Tastes grrreat!" I said, imitating Tony the Tiger.

A grin flashed across his face then disappeared. "How are you feeling?"

I set the spoon down carefully. "I'm okay now. How about you?"

Thaddeus shrugged. "Shocked. Awed. Okay now, too, I guess. I don't know." He fiddled with his spoon. "I did that eye thing with the police."

"Eye thing? You mean compulsion?"

He nodded. "Aquila came with me to talk to the policemen who'd driven up. A neighbor had called in a complaint about the loud noises coming from the woods. They didn't buy my explanation about wild cats mating and wanted to have a look themselves."

I forced myself not to react to that unfortunately accurate comment about wild cats mating; he had uttered it entirely without guile.

"So I tried to do that thing you did to Dr. Smith. Amazingly, it worked, and they went away." He seemed undecided whether to be pleased about it or not.

"It's a gift not all of us have. Among us, only Gryphon, I, and now you possess it."

Thaddeus smiled, deciding to be pleased. "Really? It knocked me out afterward, literally. I think I conked into sleep right after they left."

I sent up a prayer of thanks for that merciful fact and felt much more at ease with him. "You must have questions."

He looked at me with somber eyes. "Basking . . . when those little bits of light entered me . . . it was the most incredible feeling. Indescribable."

"I know," I said softly. "As if that was what we were meant to be."

"Yes," he whispered. "Lunar creatures of light."

"Did the others explain how unusual it was for you to be able to do that?"

"Not really. No time. But I caught some of what you and that Sandoor guy said. He was going to take me because I could draw it down like you did, wasn't he?"

"Yes. Before you, only Queens were able to Bask and allow others to share in the Basking. No males. Ever."

"Ever?" His young voice jumped an octave and cracked.

"You're very unique."

"A unique target, you mean. For other men like the one you just killed."

I flinched at the last word. *Killed.* Couldn't help myself. It was the first life I'd ever taken. But there was no regret. I'd done what I had needed to do to keep us safe. I just wasn't entirely easy with that fact yet.

"Yes," I made myself say. "You'll also be a target to most of the Queens who rule by that power. They would be most displeased to see an ability they have long considered uniquely theirs spreading to the male gender."

"What do we do?" he asked.

"We keep it a secret."

Thaddeus took that in, digested it slowly.

"You can still try to lead a normal life," I said softly. If he wished it, I would do everything within my power to make it so.

"I don't think that's possible now, even if I wanted to," Thaddeus said with surprising wisdom. "And I don't want to. I want to learn more about us, about what I am. And I want to stay with you. It feels right being with you and the others." He grinned. "It's certainly much more interesting."

My lips twisted into a feeble smile. "Well, let's pray it will be less so from now on. It's all new to me, too. I'd like to be able to catch my breath, rest a little, adjust."

"That's right. It *is* new for you also, isn't it?" he said wonderingly. "We can adjust together."

I reached out and squeezed his hand. Felt him squeeze back. "I'd like that."

EPILOGUE

I CALLED LORD Thorane to inform him of what had become of Sandoor and five of his men and found out that the other two rogues had been killed in an encounter in Indiana.

When I heatedly mentioned that it would have been nice to have been notified of this earlier, Lord Thorane invited me to bring up the matter before the Council when next it met. The inefficiency and infrequency of communication among the territories had long been a complaint of his, as well, he said blandly, and took the opportunity to remind me once more of the next session's date.

We buried Thaddeus's parents in a small, quiet ceremony. I stood beside my brother as his parents' coffins were lowered into their graves and made a silent promise to them. *You did a good job raising him. He's a wonderful young man. I'll do my best in your stead. I'll do my best to keep him alive.*

Thaddeus arranged for Mr. Compton, first his parents' and now his attorney, to have the house listed and sold. He packed his belongings, selected a few precious mementos of his parents, and traveled with us back to the island of Manhattan where I closed down my apartment.

A new private jet picked us up at LaGuardia Airport. It came along with the territory, I was informed. A lot of other things would come with the new territory, I suspected, both good and bad, and perhaps a few unpleasant surprises left behind by Mona Louisa, the bitch Queen I'd kicked out of there. I hoped she hated her new territory and prayed that she stayed far, far away from me. Not because I was afraid of her, but because I was afraid I'd kill her the next time I saw her.

Lastly, I prayed for wisdom and the power to protect all who depended on me now. Yes, power. It was not just me anymore. I could no longer afford to hide from my beast, that dark power that I had kept muted and leashed all my life. It was a living, growing force now that prowled restlessly within me, eager once more to be loosened. More powerful and difficult to control, perhaps, because of how long I had suppressed it. I had embraced the wild beast within me once to save my brother and would do so again to keep him safe. To keep us all safe.

Dear God, I prayed, pressing my palm over the gold gilt cover of the Book of Holdings, the scepter of my Queendom. *Please help me be able to control my beast.* And to control that other even more frightening part of myself that was emerging, that part that enjoyed another's pain, exulted in it. That was my most ardent prayer of all. *Please, don't let me become like my mother. Let me become myself, a new breed of Monère Queen.*

ABOUT THE AUTHOR

A family practice physician and Vassar graduate, Sunny was finally pushed into picking up her pen by the success of the rest of her family. Much to her amazement, she found that, by golly, she actually *could* write a book. And that it was much more fun than being a doctor. As an author, Sunny has appeared on *Geraldo at Large* and CNBC. When she is not busy reading and writing, Sunny is editing her husband's books, *New York Times* bestselling author Da Chen, and being a happy stage mom for her two young children who have appeared as extras on *Saturday Night Live, Sesame Street,* a Fuji commercial, and Adam Sandler's upcoming movie, *Empty City.*

Mona Lisa's story continues in January's *Over the Moon* anthology, and *Mona Lisa Blossoming* in February '07. For excerpts, please visit www.sunnyauthor.com.